Life, Liberty and the Pursuit of Murder

LIFE, LIBERTY AND THE PURSUIT OF MURDER

A REVOLUTIONARY WAR MYSTERY

KAREN SWEE

BRIDGE WORKS PUBLISHING

Bridgehampton, New York

Published by Bridge Works Publishing Company, Bridgehampton, New York, an imprint of The Rowman & Littlefield Publishing Group, Inc.

Distributed in the United States by National Book Network, Lanham, Maryland. For descriptions of this and other Bridge Works books, visit the National Book Network website at www.nbnbooks.com.

FIRST EDITION

The characters and events in this book are fictitious. Any similarity to actual persons, living or dead, is coincidental and not intended by the author.

Library of Congress Cataloging-in-Publication Data

Swee, Karen, 1945–
    Life, liberty, and the pursuit of murder : a Revolutionary War mystery / Karen Swee.
      p. cm.
      ISBN 1-882593-78-2 (alk. paper) — ISBN 1-882593-81-2 (pbk. : alk. paper)
United States—History—Revolution, 1775–1783—Fiction. I. Title.

PS3619.W44 L54 2003   2003017772
813'.6—dc22

10 9 8 7 6 5 4 3 2 1

♾™ The paper used in this publication meets the minimum requirements of American National Standard for Information Sciences—Permanence of Paper for Printed Library Materials, ANSI/NISO Z39.48–1992.
Manufactured in the United States of America.

For David E. Swee

This book would never have been created without
your belief in me, your support, and your tireless editing.

LIFE, LIBERTY AND THE PURSUIT OF MURDER

"We hold these truths to be self-evident, that all men are created equal, that they are endowed by their Creator with certain unalienable Rights, that among these are Life, Liberty and the pursuit of Happiness."

—The Declaration of Independence in Congress, July 4, 1776

ONE

Death often arrives unannounced, even in the midst of war. On the 26th day of February, 1777, I stood in the doorway of Chandler's Mercantile, having just placed a large order of goods for the tavern kitchen. I took a moment that sunny morning to enjoy the view down the Raritan River. A graceful line of sloops, flying the British Union Jack, headed toward Raritan Landing a mile upriver. With a boom, a cannonball hurtled into the water a few feet ahead of the lead ship. A thirty-two pounder I assessed, knowledge I would never have possessed just a few months earlier. That was before the War for Independence from England arrived at our doorsteps, before New Brunswick, New Jersey, was an occupied town, and before Raritan Tavern, where I was tavernmistress, overflowed with young British officers clamoring for food and lodging. A sailor in the lead sloop, standing in the bow sounding the fathoms, was drenched when the first cannonball hit the water. He continued measuring the depth of the shallow river, in spite of frequent, anxious glances at the

Jersey for the preceding six months. During his flight westward, General Washington, tired but unbowed, had been a most welcome guest at Raritan Tavern one night in December. The next morning he continued toward Pennsylvania where he ensconced himself, his army, and all the available boats on the far side of the Delaware River, visible but unreachable by the British. General William Howe, the British commander, left a small force of Hessian mercenaries in Trenton, on the Jersey side of the Delaware, to keep an eye on what he assumed was the defeated rebel army. Hieing back to New Brunswick, he established his army's winter cantonment, a day's ride from either New York or Philadelphia, and alongside the Raritan River for salutary water transport. Much to the surprise of the British, the Americans attacked Trenton on Christmas night, 1776, and Princeton on the first of January, successfully routing the best army in the world and sending the remnants scurrying to the safety of New Brunswick.

Sixteen thousand troops, English, Scots, and Hessians, were now wintering in the area about New Brunswick. They outnumbered our town's population by ten to one and it took massive stores to feed so many. While some of the food was foraged from the countryside, much of it was brought from England to the ports of New York and Amboy and then transferred to shallow hulled sloops that could reach New Brunswick, upriver.

Raritan Tavern was fortunate that the owner, my uncle, Samuel Holt, had a prospering farm which supplied a large part of our needs. Because our cook was considered the best in the area, word had spread that Samuel's farm was not to be raided, thereby ensuring that British officers would continue to enjoy our fine table. While provisioning was always a concern to me, our stew would be hearty tonight. I assuaged my guilt from treating the enemy so well because it allowed me to maintain control of the tavern and, on occasion, to obtain tidbits of information valuable to the American patriots.

The skirmish I witnessed was brief, though deadly. Five sloops were sinking and three sailors seemed to be killed, with many injured, and likely to die of their wounds. Cannonballs and falling masts wreak havoc on the human body.

Bidding Mr. Chandler farewell for the second time, I walked up Albany Street, passing knots of people watching the death throes of the ships. A cluster of foot soldiers from the Black Watch regiment had long since stopped firing their rifles, the distance to the patriot battery on the east side of the Raritan River being prohibitive. Three young officers waved men to row out to the sinking ships to rescue sailors and cargo. Further up the cobbled street, a clump of older officers muttered softly among themselves, every face knotted in anger. Nearby, a flock of young maids from the Indian Queen Tavern whispered and giggled to themselves, their eyes on the young soldiers rather than the sinking sloops. Dr. Henry Dillon stood in front of his office and winked solemnly as I passed by, his patriotic enthusiasm circumspect.

Raritan Tavern was three blocks west of the river, at the corner of Albany and Nielsen Streets. Standing in the middle of the intersecting streets was my daughter Elizabeth, or Beth as she preferred to be called. She rushed over to me, face flushed with excitement, her blue eyes alight. Her light brown hair, several shades lighter than mine, was gathered with a ribbon at the nape of her neck and hung down her back, her mobcap precariously perched on the top of her head. She was bouncing up and down, but I knew not if it was from the customary enthusiasm of a fifteen-year-old or from the cold, as she had thrown only a knit shawl over her blue calico dress. Beth was accompanied by my steward, John.

"Oh, Mother," Beth said. "What did you see? John wouldn't let me go any farther down the street, and I can hardly see anything from here. How many ships are there? Is anyone hurt? Was the Mercantile damaged? What did Mr. Chandler do?"

Putting my arm around my daughter, I noticed again how she had grown, reaching almost my height of five feet and three inches. "Come, let's go inside. You're shivering and the excitement is over."

"But Mother, I saw almost nothing. I was too far away because . . ."

"Because John was keeping you from harm, and has my thanks for doing so."

Leading them to the side gate, I promised to tell all I had seen and heard as soon as we were in the warming kitchen. Once I passed through the tall wood gate, a sense of calm draped itself about me. I felt sheltered, however briefly, from the tumult and ragged emotions of the town. Relishing the peace, I paused, while Beth and John hurried inside to warm themselves.

From where I stood in the cobbled yard, the rear of the tavern was to my right, with the kitchen, bakery and laundry to my left. The second floor of this work building provided rooms for some of the female servants while the male servants lived above the adjacent stables and carriage house. Directly in front of me was the ballroom wing of the tavern, Uncle Samuel's dream made manifest. All together, Raritan Tavern took up a quarter of the block, a sizable and prosperous establishment.

Opening the back door of the tavern, I entered the warming kitchen, where food was kept hot before serving. The constant threat of fire dictated that the cooking kitchen and bakery be separated from the tavern proper. The warming kitchen also served as the family center of our establishment. Matty, Raritan Tavern's esteemed cook and my friend, held out a steaming mug of coffee in her black hand.

"Just made this pot fresh, Mistress. I knowed you'd want a cup when you got back from Mr. Chandler's. Didn't expect you'd have to dodge cannonballs to get it."

I sipped the flavorful brew, enjoying the presence of my family, absent only Samuel, my infamous uncle. Matty and John, their soft East Indies accents revealing their island births, had been part of my family since their freedom had been purchased by a group of Princeton Quakers when I was a child. After working for my parents, they had chosen to accompany me when I married Jared Lawrence. Eight years had passed since they followed Beth and me to Raritan Tavern after my husband and two-year-old son, Matthew, had died of a fever. Uncle Samuel had broken his leg and needed help running the tavern. Or so I was told. More likely it was a conspiracy between Uncle Samuel and his brother, my father, to distract me from the morass of grief into which I was sunk. A year or so later, aided by the loving and pestering of Beth, Matty, and John I had regained my sense of equanimity. Samuel named me tavernmistress and retired to his farm to make revolutionary mischief.

Matty and John had been my constant support. They picked me up when I stumbled, making me laugh when I thought to cry, and loved me without reservation. I had estimated that should I live to a hundred, I would never be able to repay them, and that was before December when the British arrived. For the past eleven weeks, since the occupying British army settled in to wait out the winter, every house, church and building in New Brunswick had been used to billet as many soldiers as was physically possible. Many patriot families left town fearing more for their own safety than for whatever ravages would be wreaked upon their abandoned homes. But, hearing stories of the spiteful and unwarranted destruction of property as the British army withdrew from other colonial towns, I decided to conceal my patriotic sentiments in an effort to protect my uncle's enormous investment in Raritan Tavern. Matty and John agreed to remain with me, as did most of my servants.

My ruminating ended when Matty spoke. "Amos asked me to give this to you," she said, handing me a new puzzle.

Amos Warren, the town blacksmith, was diabolically clever at creating these wrought iron games to torture the guests at the tavern. I felt a certain responsibility to solve each puzzle before handing on such addicting entertainment. Over the years, I had become proficient at finding their solutions and was eager to work on Amos's newest challenge.

"What does he call this one?" I asked.

"Traveler's Bane," Matty said. "I thinks that's a mighty unlucky choice of names to be used in a tavern. I told Amos he should find a better name for it, but he said it were always called that."

I was already absorbed in the complicated, vaguely spiral-shaped puzzle, trying to remove the ring, and missed John's question.

"Mistress Abigail, is this attack going to hurt our supplies?" he repeated.

"Mr. Chandler didn't seem concerned, as none of the ships were his," I said. "We still have ample vegetables in the root cellar at Uncle Samuel's farm and in the ice-house here. We could use more meat, but for now we have enough. I'm not worrying yet."

I retrieved the coffeepot from the fire, refilled our cups, and sat contentedly sipping the nectar of the patriot gods.

"I'm right glad we has enough coffee," Matty said. "Having to ration it would be like the end of the Lord's good world."

"If those ships was all army supplies, them redcoats gonna be on short rations," John said. "Wonder how soon they'll go out foraging again?"

"I don't know, but certainly too soon for our beleaguered neighbors," I said. "It's no wonder the farmers around here are furious; the British have taken most of what was stored for the winter. Even some spring seed."

"How's a family gonna survive without seed to plant?" Matty asked.

"Or without their milk cow what was butchered, or their plowing horse what was taken?" John added. "Only good coming out of this is that a lot of loyal families is right angry at that king of theirs. The redcoats is pushing them into the patriots' open arms."

I left John and Matty and headed up the back stairs to check on the cleaning of the rooms on the second floor. Raritan Tavern had four large sleeping rooms, each of which could accommodate eight men. At the end of the hall there were four individual rooms for guests who were willing to pay for their privacy. Most women travelers stayed in the homes of friends or family, or else with New Brunswick widows who made their livelihood by opening their houses. On the rare occasions we did have a woman guest, she was always with her maid, and they were given a private room. Since December, when the British commanded the billeting of soldiers in all homes and buildings in New Brunswick, our four dormitories and the ballroom had been filled with officers of lower rank than those who could commandeer a room in a house, and of higher rank than those who lived, wet and very cold, in tents. We were granted the use of our private rooms for civilian or army travelers. I was grateful for the unexpected income, and thought it a fortuitous opportunity to spy on the King's travelers.

Ruth, the youngest of the housemaids, met me in the hall, mop and wooden bucket in hand.

"Mistress Abigail," she said. "I've finished all but the front room. They don't answer my knock. I know they arrived late last night, but they can't still be asleep, can they?"

"I doubt it. Let me try to rouse them." I grimaced, suspicious that these guests had left without settling their account. For all that the times were hard and uncertain, I rarely had trouble collecting monies owed the tavern, except for the British, of course. Our clientele were generally prosperous and honest, so unlike some of the other taverns in New Brunswick, I didn't regularly ask for payment in advance. This time it may have been a mistake. I had assumed that Mr. and Mrs. Lee would stay the day, as they had arrived so late the previous night.

I knocked quietly on the stout oak door. No response. I knocked more loudly. Still no response. Finally I pounded

on the door, irritated with people who leave without paying a fair night's rent, and even more irritated with myself
for not being sufficiently prescient to have collected the
money in advance.

The door opened when I depressed the latch. The
room was dark, the curtains still being drawn over the windows. The fireplace gave forth neither light nor heat. And
the room stank, the heavings of a drunk mingling with an
indefinable smell that reminded me of a slaughterhouse.
Strange. Striding toward the window to open the curtains,
I tripped. I righted myself by grasping onto the bedstead,
and with some preternatural awareness knew I had fallen
over a corpse. My heart pounded so violently I placed my
hand on my chest to protect it from imminent explosion.
After a seeming eternity, I reached the window, flung
open the curtains and when I had raised the sash to its
highest level, found I could breathe again. Light-headed,
the blood drumming in my ears, my vision narrowing to a
small circle, I sank down under the windowsill. I focused
on breathing, deep breath, exhale, deep breath, exhale.
Gradually, the world regained its usual shape. The roaring
in my head was replaced by a guttural, wordless cry of distress; the animal instinct to mourn the passing of one of
its kind. I was the one making the sound.

A moment later, Ruth screamed. Her mop and bucket
fell to the hallway floor, dirty water sloshing over the clean
floorboards.

I rose but was stopped in midstride by the man's body
sprawled in front of me. My thoughts arrived slowly and
quite distinctly. I knew he was dead because of the profound stillness that surrounded him. Of course, there was
also the sword that rose upright from where it impaled his

chest, pinning him to the floor, like a skewer through a plump tomato.

I could not bend my mind around what I saw, but rather, assumed I was in the middle of a dreadful dream from which I would waken at any second. But no awakening ended this malignant scene, no sunlight roused me to a more peaceful morning. Even though I was forced to acknowledge I was awake, I still could not comprehend what a dead man, with a sword through his chest, was doing in my tavern. From a great distance, muffled, I heard someone running up the stairs.

"Oh, Lordy, help us," John said, as he entered the room.

With John's arrival, the pace of life approached normal.

Ruth cried softly, a little girl's cry, pitiful and afraid. I stepped over the corpse and walked to her putting my arm around her, protecting, consoling.

John bent over the body, though there could be no question the man was well and truly dead. After a moment he rose. "I think we'd best get Dr. Dillon to declare him."

"We'll need Constable Grey, also," I said, discovering I sounded quite normal.

John nodded. I would have preferred that he had offered an alternative, even an improbable one, like burying the body in the stable or burning down the tavern. With no alternatives forthcoming, I sent him to escort Ruth to the kitchen and to find the doctor and the constable. I would stay with the body until he returned. I would have preferred to be anywhere else on earth at that moment.

When John closed the door on his way out, a shiver ran down my back with such intensity I felt cold to my very marrow. I found myself taken aback at my reaction to this death, for it was not as though I had never seen a corpse. Death was not an experience removed from our lives any more than was birth, both happening at home as was natural. I had washed and shrouded the bodies of my husband and little son myself to prepare them for burial, my final loving duty. And yet here I sat on the ladder-back chair next to the fireplace acting like a shocked child, staring at the man's body, his cravat untied, his white shirt pulled out of his black pants, and one of his stockings sagging so it showed his calf. Whatever character his face had displayed in life was missing in death, leaving only grey flesh and dilated eyes staring dryly at the ceiling. His mouth sagged as if he would comment on this final indignity to his person. Most unsympathetically, I found him odious, a middle-aged man with stringy, grey hair and a paunch like a hillock at his exposed waist.

Perhaps what had so disquieted me was the unexpectedness of finding a body in a room at Raritan Tavern. Since I was constantly mindful we were in the midst of a war, I would have expected to find a corpse at a military hospital or on a battlefield, not one in my own house. I knew the murdered man was but a guest, yet I felt personally violated, timorous and brittle.

Gradually my feelings of shock diminished, my hands regained their warmth. As I waited interminably for John to return, curiosity crept in, the curiosity that had been known to overpower my common sense on more than one occasion. Who was this man? Why was he murdered? And why in my tavern? Just as I heard John and the constable come down the hall, in a moment of crystalline clarity, I wondered aloud, "And where was the dead man's wife?"

TWO

There was a brief knocking and John opened the door followed by Constable Josiah Grey, a square-faced, blue-eyed man in his mid-thirties, whose broad shoulders and height of six feet easily intimidated many men and brought second glances from many women. When I first moved to New Brunswick, the attention he paid me was deliciously flattering, but I was inconsolable from the deaths of my husband and son. Despite the continued matchmaking of my family and friends, I was content with my life as a femme sole, a woman alone, as the lawyers would call me, making my own living and accountable to no man. Josiah and I developed a platonic friendship, strengthened by our common beliefs, including the desire to remain in New Brunswick although it was now occupied by the British. Josiah Grey was a patriot in disguise who thought he could best serve the cause of independence by remaining to tend to the peace and safety of the community.

"G'day, Mistress Abigail," he said, moving to stand over the dead man. "I see you have a small problem this morning."

How like Josiah, I thought, his understatement bringing comfort as did his very presence.

But, my relief at the constable's arrival was short-lived, for striding in behind him was a tall, thin, British officer, resplendent in his red uniform and brightly polished, knee-high, black leather boots. A handsome but most disagreeable man, I had found him.

"Do you know Captain Edward Phillips?" Constable Grey asked. "He was in my office when John arrived with your summons."

"Captain Phillips," I said.

"Mistress Abigail, murdering one's guests is frowned on in English taverns. Is this another of your quaint colonial customs?" He hovered over the body, his smirk sardonic.

Clenching my fists behind my back, I responded as civilly as possible, "It's never happened here before. Perhaps it is a custom your officers brought with you."

The constable interrupted, "Who was this man?"

"He signed the book George Fenton Lee of Philadelphia and wife."

Captain Phillips inhaled sharply, then unsuccessfully tried to cover the sound with a cough.

"Did you know this man, Captain?" the constable asked.

"No, of course not. Never heard of him." Phillips coughed again. He would never succeed as an actor.

"Did you say 'and wife', Mistress Abigail?" Constable Grey asked.

"Yes, he was accompanied by his wife."

"Where is she?"

"I would like to know that, too," I said. "She has apparently fled, leaving me with a dead man and an unpaid bill."

"Your highest concern is the money, no doubt, even in the presence of the corpse," Phillips said.

"I wouldn't be as concerned about payment if your officers would pay their bills promptly," I shot back.

Constable Grey held up his hand to stop the bickering. "Did either you or John see them arrive?"

"Come in by horse, both of them, late yesterday and them horses was lathered up like they'd been rode real hard," John said. "The horses was gone this morning."

"What time was that, John?"

"Whit, one of the stable boys, said they was gone before he got up, and he gets up early, before sunrise."

"Did you hear anything during the night?" I asked. John and Matty's room was located adjacent to the carriage house and stable.

"Nothing. But I'm a real sound sleeper."

"And you say they both came on horseback?" Josiah Grey asked.

"Yes," I replied, "which I thought was strange, Constable. The clothes Mrs. Lee wore were more appropriate to a carriage ride than travel on horseback. She had on an elegant midnight-blue velvet cloak and her skirt was more elaborate than I would have thought comfortable as a riding garment."

Phillips stared at the corpse for several minutes, then shook his head irritably, as though he had ordered it to speak and it had refused. He began searching the room, pawing through each drawer of the highboy and into the pockets of the cloak draped on the wall pegs. He picked up the weathered leather valise from the chair on which it rested and dumped out its contents: men's shirts, a shaving kit, several pairs of men's stockings, a night shirt and cap, complete with tassel. He shook out each piece before placing the items back in the case.

"What was Mrs. Lee's appearance?" he asked, continuing to rummage around the room. "Or didn't you notice anything beyond the velvet, and . . . what have we here?" From under the bed he pulled a wine-colored wool skirt and an underskirt of linen, heavily embroidered with wine silk. The exquisite stitchery was torn in several places and the whole garment was deeply soiled with mud.

"Do you recognize this bit of frippery, Mistress?" the captain asked, shoving the clothing into my arms.

"Yes, Captain. That's the skirt and petticoat Mrs. Lee was wearing when she arrived last night. I remember the embroidery quite clearly."

"But the description of the embroidery won't help us find her, will it, Mistress Abigail? To do that we need a description of the woman. If you would be so good, tell us what you observed of her beside the clothes, or did the novelty of observing such elegance blind you to anything else?"

I will not let him rile me, I told myself firmly. "She stood behind her husband most of the time, so I saw little of her. She was about my height, five feet and three inches or so. She had auburn hair and her eyes were a dark color with smudges under them as though she were very tired or maybe ill. She never spoke to me, only to her husband, and that was in a hoarse whisper."

"Would you say she was the same age as her husband?" Constable Grey asked.

I looked at the pasty face of the corpse with its staring eyes and open mouth, and struggled to recall the man's appearance from the previous evening in the candlelit hall. "I think she was younger. I would guess Lee to have been in his fifties and Mrs. Lee, perhaps, in her forties. She seemed very tired and that can make someone look

older. Oh, and she had a strange way of walking, very upright, as though she could not bend at the waist."

"I remember that too," John said. "Ain't the usual way a
person walks. And she about cried out when he helped
her off her horse. Something was ailing her."

"Anything else you remember?" the constable asked.

"Not at the moment," I said. "My overall impression was
that she was weary, in fact, exhausted. I can't imagine how
she arose and left so early this morning."

"You could probably manage to get away early if you'd
murdered your husband," Captain Phillips said.

"How do you know she killed him?"

"Seems obvious to me."

"Well, it's not to me." I knew this was unfounded, but I
was unable to resist disagreeing with whatever the man said.

Phillips shrugged, my opinion of no importance to
him. "Constable, I think you have here the unfortunate
result of a marital quarrel, perhaps some form of insanity,
but a domestic situation that doesn't fall under my
purview. I assume you'll send out men to retrieve her. She
can't have gotten far being so fatigued, and a woman to
begin with." He smiled at me disdainfully. "It is my responsibility to see to the safety of the officers who live
here, so you will inform me as soon as you have her in jail.
At that time I will question her to ascertain this event in
no way affects my men."

"I am not yet prepared to draw the same conclusion,
Captain. I will inform you when I have completed my investigation," Constable Grey said. He turned to address
me, ignoring the captain's protest. "Mistress Abigail, is the
body exactly as you found it?"

"Yes. I did naught but open the curtains and the window before I sent John for you."

The constable stood near the body, careful lest he touch any part of it with his shoe. A frown drew his bushy eyebrows together. He motioned Phillips, John, and me closer that we might have a better view. "Have you seen this sword before?"

I looked carefully, noticing the length to be a bit shorter than a yard, with a simple, graceful hilt and an embossed handgrip. It was obviously an officer's sword, complete with family crest, though whose I did not know. John and I shook our heads simultaneously. "Beautiful work," John muttered. I assumed he meant the sword, not the method of murder.

"This looks to be a British sword, with this type of metal handgrip," Constable Grey said, addressing the captain. "Do you know who owns it?"

Phillips bent down, peering closely at the crest. "Have to look at it from a better angle." Viewing was difficult as the sword remained embedded in Lee's chest and in the floorboard. None of us ventured to pull it free. "I hope you're not thinking that because it's a British sword, the murderer would of necessity be British. Mrs. Lee must have found it lying about and used it to murder her husband, hoping to deflect suspicion from herself."

"Do you often leave your sword lying about where someone might take it?" I asked.

"Of course not. Only a woman would misunderstand how important a sword is to the man who carries it."

"Then how would this sword come to be separated from its officer?"

Phillips's hand clutched the sword at his waist so tightly his knuckles were white. We were saved from any outburst by the arrival of Dr. Henry Dillon, a hearty, broad-shouldered man in his late fifties. His white hair was tied in a queue and he wore silver-rimmed, oval eyeglasses that were continually sliding down his nose. His cheeks were pink from the exertion of his walk in the cool winter air. "Came as fast as I could finish with my last patient." He moved to join the circle the four of us had made about the body, "What happened here?" We related the little we knew. Captain Phillips, convinced the murderer was the missing wife, became rapidly bored with the proceedings, and took his leave, demanding again that the constable inform him as soon as Mrs. Lee was returned to New Brunswick.

"Strange," I said, when he had left. "He says it's a marital dispute but can't wait to question her. And he never offered troops to help you find her, Constable."

"He knows better than to send his troops," Dr. Dillon said. "Our militia would have them picked off within an hour of their riding out. No, it's safer for him to wait here and let Josiah find her."

"I wonder why he wants to question her? I don't believe that story about his concern for his men."

"Don't sound right to me neither," added John.

"Just one thing among many that isn't quite right about this murder," I said. Three sets of eyes looked at me. "Where is the blood?"

Dr. Dillon smiled at me. "You observed that? Very good."

"What blood you talking about?" John asked.

"Actually, it's the lack of blood that caught my attention," I said. John ran his fingers through his kinky, graying hair, still looking puzzled. "If this sword had been thrust through Lee's heart while he was alive, there would have been blood splattered all over."

"And there's none," Josiah Grey said.

Dr. Dillon knelt next to the body, separating the skin where the blade had entered the chest. "Just a little bit from where it actually pierced the heart. You can see for yourselves." We looked and there was but a small pooling of blackened blood against the sword.

"So you saying he were already dead, his heart stopped, and then he were stabbed? Why would anyone put a sword through a dead man? Don't make no sense to me," John said.

"Certainly is strange," I said.

"Doctor, how do you think he died, if not from the sword? I don't see any other marks on him," the constable said.

Dr. Dillon examined the body, first looking at the eyes, then feeling about the waist as far back as he could reach with the sword still in place. "His eyes are dilated and there is a slight dampness to his clothes where he has lain on them. I'll have to take a look at some of his organs before I can tell what actually killed him. That'll take a day or so. And I'll want the contents of the chamberpot, Mistress."

While the three men readied the body to move to the doctor's office, I looked around the room. A coat hung on the wall, its pockets empty. Except for the fineness of the cloth and the simplicity of its cut, which bespoke an expensive garment, there was naught revealed of its wearer. Similarly, the muddy boots were of soft, pliable leather, but whispered no secrets. I looked through the valise, as Captain Phillips had previously, and found nothing to raise my interest. The ashes in the cold fireplace were only ashes. There was no sign of a struggle, and if the ghost of the murdered man still haunted the room, I did not feel his presence.

I missed the moment they removed the sword, unpinning the corpse from the floor and then wrapping it in a sheet from the bed.

"John, did Mr. Lee have saddlebags when he arrived?" I asked. "I can't find anything that would hold his money or papers."

"He had saddlebags. I took them off the horse after he dismounted and offered to carry them, but he wouldn't have none of my help," John said. "Don't see no sign of them now."

John and the constable carried the wrapped body out of the room, the doctor taking his medical case and a jug containing the contents of the chamberpot. The body would be examined at the doctor's office and then stored in the icehouse until someone could be found to claim it.

I saw to the cleaning of the room with Miriam Ilon, our most capable maid. A woman in her mid-twenties, her perpetually unsmiling countenance made her appear at least ten years older. She professed being unmoved by the presence of death, although I thought her dour face was whiter than usual. I discovered two unusual items during our work. The first, hidden behind the lantern on the mantel, was a tavern glass with wine that smelled like no wine I ever served. With my finger, I put a minuscule drop on my tongue and found it was strongly acidic. I poured the wine into a stoppered bottle Miriam brought from the kitchen and wrapped the glass in a cloth to give to Dr. Dillon. My second discovery had been caught in the counterpane on the bed, a lovely silver earring, with insets that glittered. At first I thought they were diamonds, though more likely they were cut glass. I put the earring in my pocket for safekeeping.

Miriam took Mrs. Lee's skirt and petticoat to be brushed and the bed linen to be washed. I sent Ruth to Dr. Dillon's with the glass and the bottle of its contents I had found on the mantel. I wrote a note asking him if it could be poison. I would hold the remainder of the deceased's possessions to be given to the claimant of the body. The gouge in the floor where the sword had been pulled out needed to be sanded to remove the splinters before the room could be let again. I left the window open to air the room and was closing the door when I recalled Captain Phillips's statement that this was clearly a marital dispute. Odd, I thought. If that was so, what had he been searching for in the drawers and under the bed?

THREE

I had not anticipated the public's voracious appetite for scandal manifest as soon as Raritan Tavern opened its doors for supper at five o'clock. All fifty-two billeted British officers were in attendance, seated in groups of four or six, with one group of ten where they had pulled tables together. In the adjoining room were a number of New Brunswick professional men and merchants who dined here regularly, though more often for midday dinner than for supper. A goodly number of others presented themselves for food and for the latest fact and fancy surrounding the murder of Mr. George Fenton Lee. We filled the tables in the two dining rooms and the taproom. I thought we might need to convert the game room to meal service, but the three rooms proved sufficient.

Mr. Chandler from the Mercantile entered with his wife, Amariah, so titillated by the day's events that she seated herself in the men's dining room, forsaking her usual place in the quieter side room reserved for ladies and their escorts. Mr. Chandler, having surrendered years before to his wife's craving for the latest gossip, sat meekly beside her. Fanny, our seventeen-year-old waitress, her blond hair peeking prettily from under her mobcap, was immediately subjected to a barrage of questions. As I watched, Mrs. Chandler's eyes widened, her hand flying to her mouth in reaction to Fanny's enthusiastic replies.

Grace Plough, the head waitress, and, like me, a woman in her mid-thirties, leaned toward me, "That'll be spread all over the countryside before tomorrow."

"Probably," I said, "although who knows what fiction Fanny is spinning."

"She certainly is good at her tales."

"Not half as good as Mrs. Chandler is at spreading them."

Grace laughed, her hearty chuckle enticing a smile from me, as I moved from the doorway. I picked up the teapot and began to refill the British officers' cups.

"Getting tired of hearing all these British accents, are you, Mistress?" teased one of the redcoated young men.

"Good thing he wasn't a soldier or I'd be afraid to sleep at night," said another, pretending to shudder.

"Afraid Matty'll come after you with her carving knife?" called another from across the room.

"So, who was he, Mistress Abigail?" asked Lieutenant Alan Reade, whose tea I had just poured.

"He gave his name as George Fenton Lee. Did you ever hear of him?" Heads shook in synchrony. I forced the image of Mr. Lee's dead, staring eyes from my mind and turned to the next table, where I repeated my question. I asked every officer in the room but no one admitted to knowing the deceased. At the serving table, I exchanged the teapot for one with coffee and moved to the next room reiterating my query at each table.

In a small windowed alcove, barely large enough to hold a table for two, Mr. Bradford Jamison, a traveling supplier of printers' goods, finished his apple cobbler. I knew Mr. Jamison to be in his late thirties, though his curly brown hair and the deviltry that flashed in his brown eyes gave him a younger aspect. Watching me approach his table, he frowned, his mouth turning down at the corners.

"Mr. Jamison," I said, "whatever can be amiss? Do you not like the apple cobbler?"

"The apple cobbler's delicious as always and that's the problem with coming here, Mistress. Always makes me realize how unpalatable most tavern food is." He leaned toward me as though to confide a great secret, "I think I should give up my job and settle down in New Brunswick. Then Matty could cook for me forever. On the other hand, if I were to marry you, would she come along when we moved to Boston?"

I laughed. "I don't think John would be too happy about that. More coffee?"

He nodded. "Mrs. Rachel Morton sends her regards and asked that I tell you she will come as soon as she can free herself. She was in the middle of gluing bindings when she heard of the murder and Mr. Morton had to persuade her to finish before she came to console you. Actually, he threatened he would never print another book if she ruined today's work. She decided to finish the gluing, saying you were completely capable of dealing with any crisis without her interference. Her words, not mine."

Rachel's husband, Nathaniel Morton, had printed the local newspaper, *The New Brunswick Gazette*, until the arrival of the British forced the patriot-oriented paper to cease publication. These days Nathaniel printed broadsides for important community events like the new shipment of goods received at Chandler's Mercantile. Once their three sons had grown, Rachel had become increasingly involved in the business although she preferred the more artistic and laborious production of pamphlets and of the occasional book. She was my best friend.

I worried about the secret press she operated sporadically in the basement of a farmhouse outside New Brunswick. She believed patriot ideas and their perspective on the war needed to be read as well as the official British views. If she were caught, she could be hanged for treason, and yet she worried about the tavern full of British soldiers I managed.

"I just arrived this morning, so I am not well informed about your sudden notoriety. What was this murder Mrs. Morton referred to?"

I related the day's events to Mr. Jamison, who was sympathetic although not surprised, saying all manner of strange occurrences happened in the midst of a war.

"And you say his name is George Fenton Lee?" Jamison asked.

"That's the name he gave last night, though who knows the truth of it," I said. "The constable will have to find out who he was."

"I know a man by that name from Philadelphia, a wealthy merchant with whom I have had some dealings."

"Would you be able to identify him?"

"If it is the same man." He paused. "I hear he was stabbed to death?"

Something in the way he spoke, maybe the flatness of his voice, maybe the way he looked away from my eyes, maybe the fact that few people knew about the sword, made me wonder at his question. "Mr. Jamison, may I ask as to your interest in the matter?"

He smiled disarmingly, "I'm not sure I have any interest beyond curiosity over this man you want me to identify." He looked about the room, "I doubt anyone else in this tavern has more of an interest, and yet they seem to be talking about nothing else. Human nature, I guess."

"Constable Grey would surely appreciate your help in identifying the body. I will accompany you to Dr. Dillon's after you finish your coffee. John can ask the constable to join us there."

Supper ended without my discovering any additional information about the deceased. When I saw Mr. Jamison rise, I hastened to the warming kitchen to fetch my cloak. The faint clink of dishes came from the pantry as the scullery maid shelved the clean pewter plates. The waitresses, Grace and Fanny, were scraping dirty dishes in preparation for washing.

". . . said he must have been a spy and the British killed him," said Fanny.

"I think they usually hang spies," responded Grace.

"Well, perhaps he had information that was so important they couldn't let him get away with it."

"They would have put him under arrest then."

"What if they was afraid that he would murder someone first?" Fanny said, her eyes widening with youthful exuberance.

"Is that what the soldiers you served were saying?" I asked.

"Oh, no, Mistress. They thought his wife probably killed him because he wouldn't buy her a new gown. They were saying she stabbed him so she could steal his purse."

Grace chuckled at Fanny's naiveté and that of the young soldiers. "If every wife who wanted a new dress killed her husband to get one, the world would be devoid of men in a hurry."

"Then what do you think happened, Grace?" asked Fanny, enthusiastic to add another theory to her ever-growing collection.

"I don't really know, and I'm glad it's not up to me to find out. It's a terrible responsibility for the constable."

Grace and I both knew that Constable Josiah Grey was under great pressure to resolve this murder in a way that would not inflame the patriots or the loyalists, to say nothing of the sixteen thousand British troops, who could wreak havoc if they disliked Grey's solution. I didn't want to consider how easily the redcoats could take Raritan Tavern from my control, justified by their need to billet their soldiers in safety. I just refused to think on it. I grabbed my navy wool cloak from the peg near the door and joined Mr. Jamison.

"Do you travel frequently?" I asked, as we walked the short distance to Dr. Dillon's office.

"Yes. I supply goods for printers throughout the northern colonies—ink, paper, letter molds, even the actual presses. I make regular rounds of both my customers and purveyors, mostly between Philadelphia and Boston, where I live, and I have journeyed as far as Baltimore."

"Do you find it interesting work?"

"Yes. Printers are fascinating men," he looked at me, "and women, of course, as with Mistress Morton. Thoughtful, persuasive, and certainly opinionated. I find much to admire in their craft."

"Though you don't want to practice it yourself?"

"I did for many years in Cambridge, and enjoyed it greatly, but I find the traveling even more to my liking. This way I have access to the most recent books and I can feed my admittedly voracious appetite for reading."

"How long have you done business with the Mortons?"

"They have been my customers for some years. They were the people who referred me to Raritan Tavern, informing me of the excellence of your cook."

I remained unsure of Mr. Jamison. His gallant manner and winsome smile failed to convince me he was telling the truth. No, I thought, it was not that he was lying but rather that he was withholding something.

I saw Constable Grey knocking at the doctor's door. Like many professional men in New Brunswick, Dr. Dillon had his office in the two-story brick building where he lived.

Dr. Dillon opened the door and escorted us to a back room, where the body was lying covered on a worktable. Bringing a lantern for additional light, as the room's shutters were closed, the doctor drew away the linen sheet.

I observed that Dr. Dillon had closed the eyes of the deceased and had tied a black band about the head to keep the jaw closed. Mr. Lee's garments had been neatly arranged, and his belly no longer protruded as it had when he had lain on the bedroom floor. But despite these superficial adjustments, the waxy grey skin and lifelessness of the body turned my stomach.

Mr. Jamison edged close to the table, leaning over slightly to view the face. He immediately drew back, his eyes hooded and his voice low. "Yes, that's George Fenton Lee," he said. "I have known him for some years, though not well, and am positive it is he. Poor man, to have died so far from his home in Philadelphia."

Leaving the doctor to his tests, Mr. Jamison, Constable Grey, and I moved back to the receiving room. "Was Mr. Lee a printer?" I asked.

"Oh, no, nothing so humble. George Fenton Lee is, I mean was, a wealthy shipowner. He traded extensively between England and the colonies, sometimes including the Caribbean."

"Has he continued shipping during the war? Or has the British blockade in Boston and New York been a problem?" asked the constable, his blue eyes keen with interest.

"Mr. Lee's main concern was profit, not politics. I doubt his trading was much affected by this conflict. He could have avoided the blockade by going to Philadelphia or to other harbors. He could have ignored the American colonies altogether. The route from England to the islands is profitable, whether or not the ships stop here."

"Was he a slaver, then?" I asked.

"No, Mistress Abigail, that is one rumor I have never heard about him, although, in years past, he did a substantial business in procuring indentured servants."

"From among the poor of England?"

"More likely from those regions around the Baltic." Jamison ran the fingers of his right hand around the edge of his tricorn, seemingly bored with the discussion.

"For that to be a profitable business, as you say, it would have meant the transport of many people. It's one way to get servants," I said, "to have your pick from those your husband brings. Surely, Mrs. Lee never had problems getting servants."

"I doubt finding servants for the Lee mansion had been of recent concern to her," Jamison said. "Mrs. Lee has been dead for several years."

The constable responded to my startled glance with a slight shake of his head. Frustrated with this admonition, I walked to the window hoping to control both my expression and the unwanted tapping of my right foot.

"Do you have any idea why Mr. Lee was here last night?" asked the constable.

"About his business, I would guess," responded Mr. Jamison. I heard the slight pause before he responded and turned to find him looking off into the distance.

The constable continued, "Might you know where he was coming from?"

"No."

"Or going to?"

"Again, no. I'm sorry I can be of no further assistance to you, Constable," he said.

"You have been of great assistance to us by identifying the body, Mr. Jamison. How long will you be staying in New Brunswick?"

"I will be at Raritan Tavern for at least another day," Jamison said, nodding in my direction. "My business with Mr. Morton is not yet concluded. Then I must proceed on my way to Philadelphia."

"If I could impose on you further to write a statement concerning the identity of Mr. Lee and deliver it to me before you leave on your journey, I would be most indebted," Constable Grey said.

"Of course." Bowing slightly, Jamison took his leave of us, his tricorn firmly on his head.

After the solid oak door to the street was heard to close, I turned to Josiah. "I think he knows more than he's telling us."

"I had the same thought. He was forthcoming about the identity of Mr. Lee until I asked if he knew why Lee was here."

I nodded. "I am most curious about his statement that Mrs. George Fenton Lee was deceased. If that is correct, who was the woman who spent the night in my tavern?"

Constable Grey shrugged. "I had best go tell Captain Phillips that we have identified the body. Perhaps that will help him recall if he knew the man."

We let ourselves out through the street door, the constable escorting me to the tavern. I said little, mulling over
the day's occurrences. My inability to immediately disen-
tangle the entire mystery was an irritation. I had always
prided myself on the rapidity with which I could solve
Amos Warren's wrought iron puzzles, those marvelous
bits of mischief made by our blacksmith. Perhaps a bit of
patience and I could make the pieces of this mystery, like-
wise, fall into place. When I knew what had transpired in
my tavern, I thought, it would lessen my unease, make the
horror of the day recede and finally become as no more
than a bad dream. I was so preoccupied, I failed to notice
the paving stone sticking up from the road before I
tripped on it. Josiah Grey grabbed my arm and helped me
right myself. As I paused to thank him, I noticed the several bonfires on the other side of the Raritan River, the
patriot side, from whence had come the cannonballs that
had sunk the sloops this morning. I pulled up the hood of
my cloak, the chill wind or icy premonition sending shivers down my neck. I was disquieted. It's not every day we
have a murder at Raritan Tavern.

FOUR

New Brunswick was a city occupied by an invading army, or so those of us who considered ourselves patriots believed. I called the British billeted at Raritan Tavern "guests," and indeed, they were a group of charming young men whose company I easily tolerated if not enjoyed. Nevertheless, quartering officers in time of war presented great difficulties for me. The first of these was guarding my tongue, a virtue I never perfected, as my family and friends will attest. But knowing one's life depends on what one says, or doesn't say, I had become more circumspect these past two months.

I believed the British to be oppressors, a conviction I kept deeply hidden in the hope I could keep the tavern and its wealth in my Uncle Samuel's name. It was my home and livelihood, and I resolved it would remain so. If I could learn to lower my eyes and defer to all who wore buff breeches and red coats, I should appear a perfectly agreeable lady, sought by many an Englishman to wife.

This seemed unlikely, and thus I was all the more determined to keep the tavern. I realized the decision to remain in New Brunswick was criticized by several of my patriotic friends who chose to flee, seeking the safety of the Somerset hills. Whether our friendships would recommence on their return from exile after the British left, hopefully in the spring when winter quarters would be abandoned, remained to be seen.

A second problem was the need to finance the workings of the tavern. Paying my suppliers and my staff had proved impossible with the irregular and insufficient monies doled out by the British paymaster for the food and lodging we provided his troops. After hours of pacing up and down the wide boards of my second floor suite, I had decided to give over my lovely rooms to paying guests. My daughter and I moved to the attic, to a low-ceilinged room under the eaves. Beth shared my bed for two nights then, politely but firmly, said she was moving to an adjoining windowless closet, barely sufficient for a bed, chair and narrow dresser, but which would allow her a reprieve from my tossing and turning. At fifteen, Beth was on the cusp of womanhood, old enough to involve herself in a world of ever-expanding horizons, but young enough that she retained the wide-eyed enthusiasm of one who had not yet come up against the mean, ugly, disappointing side of life. Having her own miniscule room allowed her to plot and dream of a glorious future.

My aerie now mine alone, I brought up a short-posted mahogany bedstead and outfitted it with my featherbed, lace-edged linen, and a rose matelassé counterpane. Despite the lack of bed hangings, it was as warm and comfortable as my tall-posted bed and canopy, which would not fit under the slope of the roof. A small mahogany dresser with brass fittings I had used since childhood, with its multitude of small nicks and scratches, sat neatly on the window wall.

Three of the walls were plastered white and had been marred in places where boxes and trunks had been carelessly stored, but I knew there was neither the time nor money to repaint the room, so I ignored the marks. The fourth wall, the short wall under the eaves, was paneled in rough pine. Pegs had been attached to the boards from which I now hung those garments that would not fit in the wardrobe. A washstand by the door, a trunk serving as a nightstand next to my bed, my maple rocker sitting on a Persian carpet with a candle for reading placed on a trunk next to it, and I was content. I wondered if the male travelers who slept in my former rooms appreciated the rose painted walls with their delicate border of ivy and blue forget-me-nots, which an itinerant artist had painted scarce three months before we were occupied.

Having been used for storage, the room had a lock on the door to the hall. While a lock on a bedroom door is unusual, I discovered that locking my door when I was not in the room bolstered my sense of security. I thought of myself as a trusting person, but the idea of a bored soldier curiously looking about my room caused me discomfort. When I moved to the attic, I always locked the door except when I was in my room, and, of course, at night in case Beth had need of me.

Thursday morning, the day after I had found the corpse of George Fenton Lee in my tavern, and following a night of nightmares and restless sleep, I soaped my hands and face with much splashing of water from the basin onto the floor, trying to awaken sufficiently to meet whatever the day would bring. I brushed out and pinned my brown hair, and dressed in a simple gown of green wool, cut squarely and flatteringly across my chest. I added a white lace neck scarf and a small lacy cap on my hair, two lappet streamers hanging down my back. I began to descend to the first floor to obtain a desperately needed cup of coffee that would help raise my eyelids above half-mast, when I heard whispers and giggles coming through the open door to Beth's room.

"You could have stayed with me if you were frightened." I recognized the voice as that of Lucy Hopper, the vivacious daughter of a New Brunswick lawyer, and Beth's friend.

"I piled everything I own up in front of my door. No one had a chance of getting in without making so great a noise that the whole house would have woken and every soldier on the second floor would have come, bayonet in hand, to rescue me," said Beth, her fifteen-year-old voice sounding theatrically wistful. "Alas, nothing happened, so I did not need rescuing."

"And you did not get to swoon dramatically into the arms of the most handsome young officer who had arrived at your door."

"I was not hoping for the most handsome."

"No. Well, who then?"

"Lieutenant Reade," Beth said. "I think I would prefer Lieutenant Reade, the soldier with the light brown hair and freckles. I find him quite out of the ordinary and not nearly as conceited as most of the English."

"Ah," sighed Lucy. "And after he rescued you, he would fall madly in love with you and decide that his sympathies truly lie with our side. He would abandon the army, leaving forever some poor tea-drinking lass back home in England."

Entering the room, I found the two giggling girls sitting on Beth's bed, shawls pulled around their shoulders, shoes in a heap on the floor, their feet tucked under the comforter.

"I am not sure I can imagine you waiting patiently for someone to rescue you. You've never waited patiently for anything in your life," I said. "You could plan to have a bayonet under your pillow and not need a soldier to rescue you. You didn't need a soldier to tell you to move your dresser in front of your door."

"I know, Mother," said my daughter, "but it's not nearly so romantic that way."

Lucy looked intently at Beth. "We need to find a bayonet so you can defend your honor. Maybe that young man with the freckles would lend you one."

"I fancy I'd rather have a cutlass," said Beth. "I saw a British naval officer with one. It was long and thin, with a brass handle that shone bright as a mirror. Quite magnificent."

"And deadly," added Lucy.

"Well, I do have substantial honor to defend."

"Do we know anyone who has a cutlass?" asked Lucy. "I don't think my father has one, he was never a sailor. Maybe we could borrow . . ."

I closed the door, leaving Beth and Lucy to their plotting. I regretted I had not asked Beth if she wanted to sleep in my room the night before, forgetting that she might be frightened by the day's events. It was difficult for me to avoid trampling on her growing independence and yet remain appropriately her protector. Our current living situation only compounded my concern.

Descending the back stairs to the warming kitchen, I found Matty dishing up bowls of hot cereal for John and

Amos Warren, the blacksmith. "Now you take some of this here bread and get out of my way, Amos, I has too much to do right now for you to be taking up good room at this table. You just use that table over by the window and don't forget to take a big hunk of cheese to go with that bread."

"I'm going to get fat on all you feed me," mumbled Mr. Warren, as he munched his first piece of bread.

"If your wife can't manage that, good as she cooks, I doubt I'd be able to either. You works too hard, Amos Warren, you ain't got a bit of flab anywhere on you."

"Now how you know about his 'anywhere'?" teased John.

Matty raised the ladle over her head in mock attack, splatters of oatmeal falling on the table.

"We best move, Amos, before we injured by flying oats." John moved to the side table as Amos filled his massive hand with freshly sliced bread.

"Morning, all," I said. "It's a pleasure to see you, Mr. Warren."

"Have you solved the Traveler's Bane puzzle yet, Mistress Abigail?"

"Not yet," I said. "But I'm working on it."

"Do you want me to give you a hint?"

"Of course not. I'll solve it myself, thank you very much, Mr. Warren." To even admit that a clue would be helpful was anathema to the unspoken rules of our contest. It would be the equivalent of defeat. So far, I have always figured out our blacksmith's puzzles, though it sometimes has taken me a few weeks.

"I'm not sure we should be encouraging him about these puzzles. I think we got ourselves a real puzzle to worry on," Matty said. "Don't know why I support this puzzle-making mischief by feeding him whenever he shows up."

"And how could I ever pass up an offer of a meal from you? You know when a man's starving just by looking at him."

"We're always concerned that you're about to become a wraith," I said, as I slowly ran my eyes over Amos Warren's six-foot, heavily muscled body.

Matty ladled more cereal into Mr. Warren's dish. "Now what's this news you wanted to tell Mistress Abigail about?"

"Jacob Schmidt was on his way home yesterday when he found a horse wandering on the road from Princeton, no rider, nobody around, just standing looking for some grass to nibble. Schmidt didn't recognize the beast, so he asked me if I knew who the stallion belonged to." Mr. Warren smiled broadly at me, daring me to figure out where he was leading.

"And, what did you say?"

"Well, I had never seen that horse before. So I asked around a bit." Mr. Warren munched on another piece of bread. As crumbs fell on his graying beard, he pretended to ignore my intense gaze. "I finally got around to speaking with John. Seems it was here Tuesday night in your stable."

"Here?" Turning to John, I asked, "Do you know this horse?"

"I do. Don't see them like that often. It were the Arabian that Mr. Lee rode in on, a real beauty, pure black with white socks. I could buy me a farm with what that horse would bring in sale."

"Where is it now?" I demanded.

Laconically, Mr. Warren replied, "In your stable. Mind if I leave it there? John thought you might have room to store the saddlebags, um, 'til the constable could look at them, that is."

I was out the door the moment Amos finished his sentence. Halfway across the courtyard, I realized I had forgotten my cloak, returned to the kitchen to fetch it, and still preceded Mr. Warren and John through the stable doors.

I was an experienced rider, having been taught at an early age by my father. Though I occasionally enjoyed the exhilaration of a fast ride, the wind whipping my hair loose and my cares adrift, I didn't consider myself a horse lover and felt quite content to have John supervising the stables while I minded the two-legged customers. Nevertheless, it took but one glance about the barn to determine which steed Mr. Warren had brought. The animal's coat shone even under the layer of road dust; his large, wide-set eyes returned my look with disdainful superiority. His gaze alone proclaimed his worth more accurately than any bill of sale. Not an easy animal to control, I thought, but thrilling to ride.

"His saddle and blanket are there," said Amos Warren, pointing to a neat pile on one of the tack tables set against the wall.

John, Mr. Warren, and I crowded around the table with its amassed goods. For a moment, I thought the light from the open doorway was blocked by someone, but when I turned to see who was there, the door was empty. I was jumping at shadows, I told myself, and turned my attention eagerly to what lay before me. My fingers savored the exquisite softness of the tawny leather saddle. Near the saddle horn were the initials GFL branded in decorative script. Too ostentatious for my taste, but undoubtedly the saddle of George Fenton Lee. The horse blanket was thick, black wool with a red band around the edge, the GFL initials embroidered in the corner. Each piece of tack had similar characteristics: the finest quality materials, workmanship, and all initialed. Mr. Lee had expensive tastes and wanted his ownership clearly marked.

Mr. Warren dragged the saddlebags from under the table where he had placed them out of sight. While not wanting to dirty the contents by dumping them out in the stable, I could not resist a quick perusal. The first bag contained a loaded pistol, a sharply honed dagger with a cherry wood grip, a wooden-cased pocket compass, a leather cartridge box, and a well-worn parchment map of New Jersey. Nothing unusual for a man traveling in the midst of a war. Opening the second side, I saw a book and a small leather-wrapped package placed at the top. My hands were on these to push them aside and so be able to investigate what lay beneath, when the raucous squeak of the main stable door announced an uninvited arrival.

His crimson uniform ablaze with light from the open door, Captain Edward Phillips strode across the hay-strewn floor.

"So, you have found the horse that belonged to the murdered man. And why, pray tell, have you not informed me of this? Did I not make it sufficiently clear that you were to notify me should you chance upon any relevant news? Had I not been informed by one of my men of the horse being led down the street, how long would you have waited to notify me?"

"I believe you asked the constable to inform you when Mrs. Lee was in his custody," I said. "I fail to recall you mentioned anything about your interest in his horse, without Mrs. Lee on its back."

"I now believe it to be in His Majesty's interest to look into all aspects of this murder." Looking down his patrician nose he said, "I am surprised to find your continuing interest in this foul business, Mistress Abigail. It appears a most unseemly endeavor for a woman."

"A murder occurring in my tavern is most unseemly also, Captain."

He ignored me. "I have come to remove the victim's horse and belongings," Phillips said to Mr. Warren, John having disappeared while the captain and I argued. He moved to the stall, placing a possessive hand firmly on the stallion's hindquarters. The animal slowly turned his elegant head to look at Phillips. He flicked his tail as though to chase a fly and when that failed to remove the unwanted hand, placed a hind foot firmly onto the captain's boot. Yelping, more with insult than injury, the officer hastened from the stall. "I will have one of my men come for him. I will just take the saddlebags with me for safekeeping." He reached out to take the leather bags from my grasp.

"They are quite safe here, Captain, until the constable comes for them." I gathered the saddlebags protectively into my arms, but they were ungainly and began slipping from my grasp. Phillips moved forward as I managed to hoist them securely over my shoulder.

"Here, let me have those," demanded the captain.

"Thank you, no. They are quite light," a statement demonstrably untrue, as they immediately began to slip off my shoulder and fall to the floor.

Phillips grabbed for them, but a fraction too late. The blacksmith had retrieved them and easily slung them over his massive shoulder. "Let me take these inside for you, Mistress Abigail."

"No, I will take them." The captain placed himself directly in front of Mr. Warren, a brave, if foolhardy, action considering the smith's height and breadth.

"No, Sir. I think not," Constable Grey said, striding into the stable. "They are a part of my investigation. You are welcome to come with me while I examine the contents, but they will remain in my hands until you can demonstrate that this is a military matter." Taking the saddlebags from Mr. Warren, he turned toward John who had reappeared behind him in the shadows. "If you would continue to stable the horse, I will notify you when the next-of-kin have been informed and I receive instructions about his disposition."

I was grateful I would not see the stallion ridden about New Brunswick on the morrow with a certain redcoated officer on his back.

John stroked the horse's neck affectionately. His touch was not rebuffed.

The constable and Captain Phillips left the stable, Josiah with the saddlebags. The smith headed home to his wife. John returned to the kitchen to eat more of Matty's breakfast. I followed him, but did not remove my cloak to hang on the kitchen peg as was my custom, keeping it clutched about me as I went up the back stairs.

Hurrying to my room, I unlocked the door and re-locked it behind me, appreciating anew that the former storage room allowed me such enviable privacy. Whipping off my cloak, which fell onto the carpet in a swirl of navy wool, I raised my skirt to untie the ribbons that held my pocket about my waist. When I had chosen to wear the blue pocket this morning, I had not realized I would be stuffing the little cotton sack well beyond its capacity. The book I had removed from Lee's saddlebags under the confusion of Captain Phillips's arrival, barely fit through the skirt opening at my hip and into the pocket. Worse, the leather envelope I had also taken bulged out of the pocket, making an unexplainable bump under my skirt that I had feared would be detected. Had my thievery been discovered, I would have been escorted to a British jail. With no one pounding at my door, I assumed I was safe. I had taken the items to prevent them from being filched by Phillips, who was unlikely to share any information with the constable and certainly not with me. Once they were under my skirt in my pocket, I could hardly return them to Constable Grey when he left with Phillips at his side. No, I thought, they were safe in my possession until I could hand them unobserved to the constable.

I had known where I would hide them as soon as I had placed them in my pocket. The back wall of my room, the wall that fit under the eaves of the house, had a small door concealed in the pine paneling. It gave access to the area under the roof where the eaves descended to meet the floor below. This was storage space, too low for even a short woman to walk upright at its highest side. It was cluttered with barrels and boxes and trunks from years past, all covered with thick dust. Spiderwebs hung from the roof, gossamer tendrils giving the area a fantastical appearance. The space behind my room continued past Beth's closet of a room, which also had an opening into this area, and on down the entire length of the roof. A perfect hiding place where I had already stored the pistol Uncle Samuel had insisted I keep, against my protestations.

From inside the eave space, I could hear Beth's footsteps come down the hall and pass her room. I removed my keys and handkerchief from my pocket, hung the pocket over a nail that protruded from a convenient stud and closed the nearly invisible door, just as Beth knocked on the door.

"Mother," she called out. "Mistress Morton is in the warming kitchen to see you. She says not to hurry as she is drinking the coffee Matty gave her."

"Thank you, Beth. Please tell her I'll be right there."

I tied a white linen pocket about my waist and placed the keys and handkerchief in them, adjusted my skirt, and checked quickly in the mirror to make sure no cobwebs or dust betrayed me. As I left the room, which I locked carefully behind me, I determined that I would look through the book and also see what the envelope contained before I gave them to the constable. My curiosity demanded that I do so.

FIVE

I hurried down the back stairs to the warming kitchen. Seated in the sunlight at the table, sipping coffee, was my dearest friend, Rachel Morton. Seeing me descend, she strode across the room to embrace me, her long legs setting dark skirts aflutter.

"Oh, Abigail, I am so dismayed I could not come to you earlier. We finished binding the book well past midnight and Nathaniel said traipsing about at that hour was irresponsible and that you would undoubtedly be long abed. Forgive my tardiness and tell me truthfully how you are coping."

"Well, I'm . . ." I took a moment, trying to find expression for how I did feel.

"Disquieted," Rachel said, finishing my sentence as she was apt to do when I paused too long. "And rightly so, with all you've endured. Come, have some of this delicious coffee Matty brewed and tell me what has transpired."

We sat at the table while I related all that had happened since yesterday's baleful discovery. I had known Rachel for the eight years I had lived in New Brunswick. She was tall for a woman, big-boned and lanky, her grace coming from her glorious spirit rather than from physical movement. She and her husband, Nathanial, were printers. Born in New York City, she had learned the art of printing at her father's side, that being the way he kept his eye on her after her mother's death. Rachel had always delighted in the world of publishing, from the ink stains on her fingers to the ideas bantered about with her father and two older brothers in the back room of their New York City office. Eventually, she fell in love with her father's journeyman, Nathaniel. They had married and moved to New Brunswick to establish their own press and Rachel's adjacent stationery shop.

"Thank you for coming and cosseting me," I said, my spirit lightened by the absolute attention of someone who demanded nothing but to share my dilemma. What blessed fortune to find a friend with whom to share life's dark and frightening moments.

"My one aim in life is to be a good cosseter." Rachel poured herself coffee from the pot keeping warm near the fire, then resettled on the bench, her black skirts and apron falling as they would. She perpetually wore black, the only color she said that could survive her work without showing smudges. As it was, a pattern of black fingerprints adorned her white mobcap, permanent testimony that she had once tucked back a loose strand of dark hair.

"What are your sentiments at this moment, Abigail?"

"I've never had someone murdered in my tavern before. Dead bodies I may have seen, but none with a sword rising up from its chest. Thank God, Beth wasn't there. And Rachel, I am uncertain how I feel: afraid, numb, confused. It's all a jumble."

"It is a philosophic question: how should one properly feel about a murder in one's establishment?" The seriousness of her tone was negated by the whimsy in her warm brown eyes. "I shall consult *Poor Richard's Almanac* when I return to the shop. Surely he has something to say about the appropriate attitude to be adopted by tavernkeepers on the occasion of a murder."

"Dr. Franklin has something to say on every known subject, and a few unknown," I said. "Have you heard how his mission in Paris is progressing?" Rachel was a vehement patriot and willing to confide to me, at least, all the latest information, gossip, rumors, and political intrigue that were within her purview. I had expected Rachel and Nathaniel to leave New Brunswick with the arrival of the British. That they remained and assumed a façade of neutrality I knew was but a mask to cover Nathaniel sending information about the British forces to his patriot associates. I constantly worried that the British would become wise to the charade and arrest not only Nathaniel, but by association, my friend.

Rachel looked about, reassuring herself we were not being overheard. "There is little news yet, though I have great hopes for his success with the French. With their help we will get these bloody British off our property, but you have heard me on this topic a few thousand times at least. Tell me rather what is happening about your murder."

I grimaced. "Must you style it 'my murder'? I would not claim so intimate a participation. I wish it had never happened, although I confess I find myself thinking in those same terms. Perhaps it is my anxiety that the matter be resolved before Raritan Tavern is dubbed 'Journey's End Tavern' and I begin to see ghostly apparitions."

"Does Constable Grey have any ideas about what could have happened?"

"I know of but one lead. Bradford Jamison, one of our guests, identified the body as a George Fenton Lee of Philadelphia. Have you ever heard of him?"

"Who? Jamison or Lee?"

"Lee," I said, catching the puzzled expression on her face. She was silent for a moment, then seemed to collect her wandering thoughts.

"Not that I recall, Abigail, though I will certainly ask Nathaniel when I get home. He has a prodigious memory for anything he's ever set in type, and most of what he's heard."

"A valuable talent for our favorite printer." My comment about her husband failed to elicit the expected smile. "What are you thinking?"

"I was wondering about Bradford Jamison."

"He said he knew you."

"Of course he knows me; we buy our printing supplies from him."

"You look puzzled. Are you surprised he could identify Lee?"

"Not really. Jamison travels from Boston to New York to Philadelphia regularly. He must know people in all those cities. Lee wasn't a printer, was he? I think I know most of the printers in Philadelphia."

"Mr. Jamison said Lee was a merchant; actually, I think he said a shipowner. You still seem perplexed, Rachel."

Rachel bit her upper lip between her teeth and stared out the window for so long I thought she had lost track of my question. Finally she said, "Bradford Jamison has other work besides selling printers' supplies. He carries messages from one patriot correspondence committee to another. He covers many of the northern colonies."

"I wondered why he stopped being a printer. This occupation provides him with a perfect reason to travel the countryside," I said. "However, he might have chosen to sell something else, printers being known as particularly rabid patriots."

"I know one or two of us who are just patriotic, not rabid. As a group we are rather vocal about our beliefs, aren't we?"

"A rhetorical question, if I ever heard one, Rachel. I wonder if there is some connection between Jamison's presence here and Lee's death, or merely a coincidence?" I rose and moved to warm my hands at the fire. After a moment, I turned toward my friend and asked, "Do you think Mr. Jamison could have strong enough beliefs about independence that he would take a life to further that cause?"

Rachel stared at the cup she held in her ink-stained fingers, then looking me in the eye, said, "I think he would give his own life, if need be, to further that cause."

"What if Jamison himself were threatened?"

"You mean if someone was trying to kill him?"

"Or turn him over to the British?"

"I don't know, Abigail. I don't know how I would react if someone accused me of treason and threatened to take me for a little visit to their headquarters. How can I possibly imagine another's reaction? I am a simple printer, Jamison is . . . well, he is . . . ." Rachel put her fingers to her lips, stopping herself from saying more.

"I am your friend, Rachel, even if there are matters you are not free to share with me. You know that."

"I think it might be better if I talk to Jamison myself. I'm sure there is a good explanation for my confusion." The momentary hesitancy Rachel had displayed was replaced by her normal bustling as she dressed for the cold, her cloak and leather gloves ubiquitous black. "Now, you will be all right? You won't fret and hurry-scurry about, will you?" she asked as she gave me a parting hug, promising to look in on me on the morrow.

After she left, I realized I had not mentioned the book and packet of letters I had secreted in the attic storage.

The arrival of Matty and one of the young kitchen maids, with cast-iron pots from the kitchen, announced the dinner hour of one o'clock. Placed over the coals in the warming kitchen hearth, the redolent fish chowder would keep warm through dinner. Checking the order of the house, I found Grace, responsible as always, in the first dining room setting out flatware of fine steel. Nearby, young Fanny flirted with an officer until Grace beckoned for her assistance in distributing baskets of corn bread. The fireplace radiated warmth and welcome, beckoning hospitality with nary a hint of a ghostly presence.

Dinner that day was uneventful, the number of diners only slightly higher than normal, as the morbid curiosity of the New Brunswickers had already lessened a day after the murder. Mrs. Chandler returned to the same table as the day before and solicitously inquired after Fanny's health, wondering how well the young waitress had slept in a now infamous house. Fanny, of course, obliged with details of her restless night, complete with ghostly embellishments about every sound she had imagined. That Fanny's room was, in fact, located in the kitchen building and not in the tavern proper, did nothing to curtail her telling. For a second day Mrs. Chandler left the tavern replete with a host of wondrous rumors she could spread through town. I was certain that she would dine with us again on the morrow.

Acting as hostess during dinner was work I enjoyed. I conversed with my guests, exchanging the latest news and gossip for replenishment of ale, wine, coffee or tea. Grace and the waitresses did the heavy work while I made the clientele feel welcome, their tariff appreciated. That day, however, I was distracted and after catching myself about to pour coffee in British teacups for the second time, left the serving in Grace's capable hands.

By the time I had reached my room on the third floor, I realized my distraction was caused by a feeling of wariness about the items I had secreted in my room, perhaps the reason I had forgotten to mention the occurrence to Rachel. I am not a foolhardy woman and yet I was most disquieted that I had acted improvidently when I took the book and packet from George Fenton Lee's saddlebags. Locking the door, I was determined to see if I had thoughtlessly jumped into a kettle of boiling water. My blue pocket hung on the bent nail under the eave exactly where I had left it. As soon as my breathing had slowed and the fluttering in my stomach calmed, my curiosity staked its authority over my fear and I took up the book.

It was a small volume which fit neatly in my hand, and appeared much used. Its brown leather cover was scratched and softened, its pages well thumbed. The first section of the book revealed itself to be a ledger of names and dates going back nearly forty years. Next to each name was a series of letters and numbers. Then a second line was indented with a different name, an abbreviation, and a final number, for example:

14 Nov'ber, 1743, Fredek Jenci, m.s.ger.24.lab.52.
Daniel Ridgway, Phila. 420.

There were many entries with two such lines and then a space, then two more lines and another space. I could figure the pattern as far as the date followed by a name and that the second, indented line, was also a name. That pattern seemed consistent for numerous pages. What the abbreviations represented, I could not fathom. If I had a pen and paper, I could make a list of the notations and perhaps discover an overall pattern. That would have to wait until I could get the supplies from my office.

The remainder of the book was filled with dated entries, more recent now, that were clearly listings of ships and cargo with amounts tallied per shipload. The book was a ledger of accounts, possibly a personal journal due to its small size. I didn't know if anything herein related to Lee's death; certainly nothing caught my eye at first perusal.

There were footsteps on the stairs and I secreted the pocket, book, and leather packet back under the eaves before the knock came on my door.

"Yes, be right there," I called out.

Fanny stood at the door, breathing hard after running up from the first floor. "John asked if you would come out to the stable immediately. He says Captain Phillips is prying about with some of his men."

I arrived in the stables to find Phillips holding a lantern while three soldiers turned over straw with pitchforks. John stood to the side watching them.

"Captain Phillips," I said. "How thoughtful of you to have your men tend our stable. I can always use good servants, though I am not accustomed to having a British officer oversee the work."

"I have orders to search the stable. Neither I nor my men are here to change your straw." Phillips gave me a look of aristocratic distain.

"How unfortunate. They are doing such a thorough job. Would you care to tell me what you are looking for?"

"No, I would not."

"Then how can I help you look for it?"

"My watch," Phillips mumbled.

"Pardon?"

"My watch. I am trying to find my watch," he said, enunciating every word.

"A different watch from that attached to your watch fob?" I asked, indicating the obvious bulge on his waistcoat.

He glared at me. "You need not trouble yourself, Mistress. This search is none of your concern."

"Anything that happens at Raritan Tavern is of my concern, Captain."

"Then you had better return to supervise the after-dinner washing, and leave us to our duty."

"Oh, Captain," I said, "my servants have no need of my presence to do their work."

"Perhaps you can find a bit of embroidery to stitch on, or a petticoat to mend. Something, anything, to get you out of the cold." He bit down on his lips, prohibiting a spontaneous eruption.

"Why, Captain, your concern for my health is most appreciated." I smiled at two of his men who had stopped working to listen to the argument. Phillips snapped his fingers at them and they resumed their hay turning.

"Mistress Abigail, I am charmed by your presence, but I am under command to search the barn for something that was lost and I regret having to bid you a good day."

He bowed, making a leg, the sweep of his black tricorn ruffling the straw on the barn floor.

I was dismissed. For once, I listened to my common sense and left the stable before I got myself into very deep trouble. John would remain with the captain until the redcoats finished searching for their needle in the haystack. They wouldn't find what they were looking for, as those items were safely hidden in the eave space off my bedroom. What interested me more was how the captain knew that anything had been taken.

Six

A few hours later supper had almost ended. Beth yawned as she shelved clean dishes in the pantry off the warming kitchen. Matty had retired to the room she and John used behind the stable and carriage house. John would remain serving drinks until the tavern closed about midnight. He philosophized that the happiness of their lives was because her work began at sunup while he worked at night. With great seriousness, he said, "Never see each other, so course we still lovebirds." A few individuals of a literal bent believed him.

It being a cold, winter night, the windows were shuttered on the inside. Fires blazed in every room and all the candles and lamps were lit, enclosing us in a cocoon of warmth that just begged a man to spend an extra hour drinking our ale before he returned home through the dark or retreated to his room on the second floor.

In the game room, a group of young officers clustered about the billiard table, while two of their number removed their coats, took cues from the wall and chalked the leather tips amidst the jocular challenges from their compatriots. One man took the role of scorekeeper, setting to zero the hands of the wood scoreboards affixed to the wall. Many officers played billiards exclusively with their redcoated peers in as close an approximation to an evening in London as they could obtain, complete with ribald jokes and too much to drink. Though individually they were nice enough lads, they were far from home with too little to do. It was from this group that trouble would develop should they perceive the barest whisper of patriot sentiment.

Next door in the taproom, the men were of a more varied and tolerant nature. Tonight, for example, as I entered the room four colonial gentlemen of New Brunswick were sitting at a square, mahogany table dealing out cards for a game of five and forty, while at the next table two British officers relaxed, talking over the day and smoking tobacco in the white clay pipes they had rented from the tavern. John was inside the bar cage, mixing a bowl of rum punch to be shared by a group of local residents already engrossed in hazard, a game of dice. Less than two days after I had discovered the body of George Fenton Lee the tavern activity appeared precisely normal. How was it possible, I wondered, that these men could pursue their usual daily activities while I remained dismayed at the least thought of the murder?

Untouched by my discomfort, Mr. Chandler, from the mercantile, sat drinking a glass of port and reading the papers that had arrived by post. I had long since ceased to display old copies of *The New Brunswick Gazette* or any papers that had a patriotic proclivity. Affirm the cause of independence I did, fan the flames of disagreement and fighting inside Raritan Tavern I did not. And so far, though there was little collegiality between the British and the men of New Brunswick, there was civility.

I was about to head to the kitchen for the bread and sliced chicken that would constitute my supper when three young officers entered the taproom. With the obliviousness of youth, these three had let slip information on previous occasions that had proved of interest to Uncle Samuel. With all that had occurred at the tavern in the last two days, I thought this an auspicious time to eavesdrop.

Lieutenant Southerland was the tallest of the three and tended to wave his arms in big sweeping arcs when he talked. Lieutenant Downes was quieter, with wire spectacles and a scholarly mien. The last was Lieutenant Reade, whom Beth and her friend, Lucy, had been discussing earlier. With his light brown hair, boyish freckles, and charming manner, Lieutenant Reade seemed an object of every woman's affections, except that his uniform was red. And there were many who wouldn't care even about that. I grimaced, realizing my daughter Beth would be among them.

The three young men headed for the skittles table, signaling for drinks as they went. John measured out ale with a certified quart measure, allowing them their fair share. In our tavern, we never used a measure with a false bottom, so each man got what he paid for. Using a false bottom was not only illegal, but in my opinion, it created a disaffinity that was bad for business. Downes set the skittles pins aright, picked up the ball and walked to the end of the alley where he aimed and let roll. As fast as I was with the libations, they were several rolls into the game when I approached. I hoped I hadn't missed anything important.

"Good shot, Downes," said Southerland, as he took the tankard from me. Turning back to his friends he added, "Had Phillips after me today."

For once, I was thankful that soldiers never really saw those who waited on them. We might have had hair like Medusa for all the notice they took. Hopefully, this would work in my favor tonight.

"What did he want?" asked Downes, setting up the nine pins again.

"Wondered if I had seen anyone leave New Brunswick while I was on guard Tuesday night."

At this my ears perked up and I found there was a wick that needed trimming on the candle nearest the skittles table, and troublesome it proved, requiring that I concentrate on restoring the flame for some minutes before I could return to the bar.

"Asked me the same, he did," said Alan Reade. "Was quite insistent about it. Wanted to know especially about a woman. How he thought there would be some woman out on the roads during the hours that I had watch, I can't fathom. Only people I saw were other guards. Nobody else was fool enough to be abroad in that kind of cold. I told Phillips that and he wasn't too pleased."

"Captain's not pleased with much these days." Southerland paused before his roll of the ball. "I think he's bored, being stationed in the colonies. Misses the glamour of London."

"Misses the female adulation his uniform brings him in London is more like it. New Brunswick women just don't swoon over him the way he's accustomed to back home." Grinning, Reade added, "Now, they seem to like me just fine."

"Like you enough to be out in the middle of the night, freezing their little bums? Not even for you, Romeo," said Southerland.

"There was someone out, though not a woman. Some man rode past me about an hour or so before sunup," said Lieutenant Downes. "Had two horses and was setting a rather fast pace when I saw him, headed for the King's Highway toward Princeton. It's not all that unusual to have people on the road before daybreak so I didn't really think too much of it until Phillips started asking questions. Didn't seem very interested when I told him I'd seen a man."

Southerland stopped in the act of setting up the skittle pins to look at Alan Reade. "I wonder if it had some connection with the dressing down Phillips received from Colonel Belding. The colonel was furious. Came to the door of his office saying something about 'the woman is gone and Lee's dead,' his face red as it gets when he's seething. Told me to fetch a messenger and when I got back with the rider, Phillips was waiting, looking pale as a ghost, to escort him into Belding's office. Couldn't hear what they said unfortunately."

"And you think this could be over some woman? I thought the good colonel was the epitome of marital probity. Hard to see him chasing after some petticoat," said Downes.

"You never know. Look at General Howe and Mrs. Loring, his New York oyster basket. They say we could have defeated Washington once and for all if Howe had followed him into Pennsylvania, but our good general didn't cross the Delaware last December because he was too anxious to get back to his little sweetie."

"Watch what you say, Southerland," said Reade, glancing about. "Now that the general is back in New Brunswick, you never know who might hear you and take your statements as disloyal."

Chastened, Southerland turned his attention back to the game, and I moved away from the brightly burning candle I had tended so meticulously. Uncle Samuel probably knew more about Washington and Howe than these young men, and I doubted he would be interested in their comments about the notorious Mrs. Loring's effect on the war. My spying may not have aided Uncle Samuel, but it was provocative concerning the vanishing Mrs. Lee.

The evening wound down, the fire warming the room less and less as the cold of the night seeped through the walls and the shuttered windows. The games were gradually abandoned as the players moved closer to the fire with their white clay pipes and their last drinks of the evening. Constable Grey came, as was his nightly custom, and after I talked with him in the entryway, he joined the three redcoats for a friendly conversation. Included in the talk were a few surreptitious questions from Josiah Grey. After the patrons had left, he sat with me relaying what the young officers had said, most of which agreed with my conclusions.

"The description Downes gave of the two horses he saw heading for the King's Highway exactly match those ridden by Lee and his wife when they arrived Tuesday night," the constable said.

"One of which is again stabled here," I added.

"Indeed, Mistress Abigail. So, it would seem possible that Mrs. Lee left town very early Wednesday morning dressed as a man with the same two steeds she and Lee had ridden when they arrived. I find that very hard to conceive, although Downes did repeat he had seen a man leave, just as you said."

"And you can't imagine a woman wearing breeches?"

He shook his head.

"I have heard there was a time in France when men costumed themselves in women's dress, so why couldn't a woman wear trousers?" I watched his face closely.

He sputtered, nearly choking on the ale he had been drinking. "Be serious, Mistress."

"I am," I said. "I understand Mrs. Nathaniel Greene wears them and says they are very modest for riding."

John came to refill our glasses. I continued, "On the other hand, I got only a brief look at Mrs. Lee. What if she *were* a man?" The constable started to protest but I persisted, "A clean shaven young man. I saw very little of her, as she hid behind her husband most of the time."

Taking me seriously now, he asked, "Could her build have been that of a man?"

"She was not tall for a woman or excessively muscular, but it is not rare for a man to be small and slim. If I stop assuming she was a woman and think only about her shape, her voluminous cloak could have concealed either a woman or a small man. It's strange to think without the usual assumptions of convention."

"Truly," he said. "But it may be the only way we will ever solve this puzzle. And solve it we must, Mistress Abigail, before the British impose *their* solution upon us."

I nodded in heartfelt agreement, the fear of losing the tavern never far from my mind.

Soon after Constable Grey left, John began to close the bar. He lowered the wood spindle grates from the ceiling and locked them into place across the front and sides of the counter. While he finished washing the tankards and glasses, I sprinkled the remaining coals with sand from the fire bucket. The room in order, I lit my candle, carrying it in one hand and my skirts in the other and started up the steep back stairs. By the time I reached the second floor I realized that I was exhausted, the excitement, anxiety, and lack of sleep last night taking their toll with a vengeance. For a moment I doubted I could climb to the third floor, then laughed at myself for even thinking I had an option. Sleeping on the stairs was not an appealing thought.

As I neared the third floor, I was concentrating on retrieving the key from my pocket, navigating the last step, and watching the candle flicker in a sudden draft, when, out of the corner of my eye, I thought I saw a figure move away from my door and into the darkness beyond the flame's small glow of light.

"Hello," I said. "Who's there?"

There was no response.

I spoke a second time, sounding louder and harsher than I had intended. My heart was pounding in my chest as I walked the length of the hall, looking in on Beth, who was asleep peacefully in her bed. I continued on, staring down into the darkness and silence of the main staircase, looking into the two storerooms, and quietly opening the door to the bedroom at the end of the hall where the maids, Miriam and Ruth, slept. But naught was amiss and I decided my tired mind had played a trick on me. Closing my bedroom door behind me, I hung my dress on a peg, kicked off my shoes and unlaced my corset, which I dropped unceremoniously on the rocking chair. I pulled my night shift over my head, blew out the candle, and pulled the blankets up to my chin. The room was soporific with warmth from the chimney that passes through my room from the fireplaces on the first and second floors. For a trifling moment, on the threshold of full sleep, I thought I again heard footsteps outside my door, but being so exhausted, I decided it was only the ghost of George Fenton Lee come to haunt my dreams.

SEVEN

The previous night's cold had turned bitter by morning, a stiff wind sneaking through every crack and crevice into my room. I woke to find myself squirreled into a ball, blankets pulled over my head, permitting only the smallest possible breathing hole. Had my bladder not required urgent attention, I would have wafted back into my troubled dreams. The thought of leaving my snug nest was not felicitous. Wrapping a shawl about my shoulders, hopping on one foot and then the other as the icy floor nibbled hungrily at my warm feet, I hurried to the wash table under which the white glazed chamberpot stood. It was not in its usual place. I did soon find it, on its side, where it had rolled under my rocking chair. After relieving myself and giving thanks again for the inventor, who allowed us to remain indoors for our early morning necessities, I noticed that more was askew in my room than just the chamberpot. The door to my wardrobe was held ajar by the sleeve of a blue striped dress which I had not worn for several days. The book I had placed on my nightstand cum trunk was lying on the floor. The second drawer of my dresser was not closed properly on its left side, although long ago I had mastered the trick of its sticking spot. My heart began to pound when I realized an unwanted visitor had been in my room whilst I slept.

I had little of worth beyond two pieces of my grandmother's jewelry, which were of more sentimental than real value and which were still together in their brocade case in my drawer. My dresses and shoes were all in the wardrobe, though slightly rearranged. After a search of my small room, I could discover naught that was missing. Now thoroughly awake, I remembered the purloined items hidden under the eaves. Assuring myself that no one was about, I locked the hallway door, and with some trepidation opened the door to my hiding place. The book and bound leather packet remained hanging in my pocket exactly where I had left them. Relief washed over me for a fleeting moment. Yet I felt violated, not physically, as I had come to no harm, but mentally. The invincible perimeter of my privacy had been trespassed. I stood there in my shift and shawl, numb with cold, aware only of being vulnerable and alone. It was but a few moments until I regained my senses and began to feel angry. How dare someone intrude on me and make me feel disquieted in my own house?

I was so frightened and vexed, I failed to hear the footsteps in the hall and was jolted from my fuming by knocking at the door.

"Mistress Abigail, are you awake?" More knocking, and the handle of the door turned but the door held fast as I had locked it.

"I'm awake," I said. "Just a minute." I hastily, but silently returned the book to its hiding place under the eaves.

"Coming," I added, unlocking the door and opening it a crack, to find Miriam Ilon poised to knock again. She did not comment on the locked door.

"Master Samuel has arrived and is asking for you."

"Where is he?" I asked, peering over the maid's shoulder. I half expected my uncle to be directly behind her, for he cares nothing about propriety and would not have given a whit to find me in my shift.

"He is in the kitchen, Mistress, breaking his fast. Matty detained him, so you would have time to get presentable." Miriam smiled, sharing the womanly conspiracy to restrain my uncle. "Do you want help with your stays?"

"Please," I said. "Just let me change out of my night shift." I closed the door, changed into a day shift with a thin trimming of lace about the sleeve, and did a quick neatening of my room so there would be no trace of the intruder. That completed, I slipped my corset over my head and admitted Miriam.

"It's so much easier to have someone do this, isn't it?" Miriam asked, straightening the laces at my back before she would tighten them. She was very capable, but too withdrawn and sober to be a confidante.

I held the whaleboned corset in the front with one hand, smoothing the folds of the shift and adjusting the neckline with the other. "It certainly is. The neck never looks very good when I put on a corset myself. Lacing it in the front and then turning it around to tighten always pulls the shift out of kilter." I gasped as she pulled the laces tighter than I was accustomed to, and she automatically loosened them. Having nursed two babies, I needed more support than when I was younger, but my figure was still trim and, except for under my most elegant dresses, a moderately laced corset was sufficient.

"Maybe someday someone will invent a more comfortable undergarment," Miriam said. "One that doesn't have to be adjusted every time you put it on."

"One that a woman could put on by herself," I said. "Perhaps even one that would allow us to breathe."

"Now that is a truly revolutionary idea, Mistress."

We were standing in front of my mirror through this process and I noticed when Miriam looked up to speak she had dark circles under her eyes, as though she had not slept well for several nights.

"You look tired Miriam. Are you sickening?"

"I am well, Mistress. In truth, better than I have been for a very, very long while." She looked at me with such elation in her eyes I was taken aback.

"Oh?" I asked with raised eyebrows, hoping to elicit an explanation, but she only responded with a shrug. I tried to respect the privacy of my staff unless their work was in question. It was difficult to live in the insufficient quarters left to us by the British and then work side by side all day. Best to just ignore the comment, I decided.

"Thank you for your help," I said. "Please tell my uncle I'll be down immediately."

I dressed quickly, although with some thought to pleasing my favorite uncle. My rose wool dress with its tiny white flowers brought out the color in my cheeks. Adding a crisp white neckerchief with a ruffled edge and a white cap with embroidered green flowers, I hurried down the stairs into the kitchen. I had much to tell him.

My uncle was in his late 60s, and a head taller than me, probably 5' 9" or so. He appeared rather squarish, from the shape of his face to the broadness of his shoulders and chest. The top of his head was bald, though the sides were amply covered with shoulder-length, wiry gray hair. The only sign that he had once been a redhead were his eyebrows, which appeared as small, remarkably emotive bushes above each eye. His face was weather-beaten although he became an ageless scamp when he laughed and his blue eyes flashed.

Uncle Samuel athletically perched on a stool at the kitchen table, his arm around Beth's waist. She absentmindedly picked a long grey hair off his brown coat, running it through her fingers. Waving a biscuit in his unoccupied arm he reached the climax of his story. ". . . and with that, they took fright and ran off into the woods, and we never had another problem from them." Matty was standing across the table, laughing so hard she had set down the coffeepot to avoid spilling. John wiped a tear from his cheek and between guffaws managed to say "I wish we could sic them ghosts on the British."

"Yes, Uncle," Beth said. "That would get them out of New Brunswick in no time."

"I'll have to think on that, Beth. Unfortunately, I don't think they'd fall for the same smoke-and-mirror stuff that hoodwinked those ruffians."

After the death of his beloved wife, Rebekah, and the child she was birthing, Samuel had left Princeton to get as far away from his memories as possible. Working as a surveyor in the wilderness of Pennsylvania and Ohio, the occupation for which his Princeton education had prepared him, and then as a guide during the war with the French, Uncle Samuel had amassed an endless treasury of enthralling tales. That some of them were a bit far-fetched in no way affected our enjoyment at hearing them or Uncle Samuel's delight in telling them. Being Samuel had its privileges.

"My dear Abigail," he said. "I am so glad you decided to awaken and grace us with your lustrous presence, just in time for dinner." It was an old joke between us. When I had first come to live at his tavern we had suffered more than a few misunderstandings about our inherently different approaches to the morning. My uncle was by nature an early riser, treasuring the hours at dawn when he had the quiet world to himself. On the other hand, I pampered myself whenever possible by rising after breakfast was completed.

"I wondered if it would be necessary to roll you out of your blankets to awaken you. We all know that not even the town alarm will disturb your dreams."

"Oh, Uncle Samuel," I said, feigning disgust, though in truth, I had once slept through the clanging of the bell when a fire burned down two warehouses on Mueller's dock. My uncle, of course, had never ceased to tease me about it. Thinking to change the topic, I inquired after his health.

He waved his hand in the air, dismissing the question as irrelevant. "I heard gossip that you found a body a couple of days ago. Didn't I ever tell you that murder was bad for business? I had not thought it necessary to specify this when you took over as tavernmistress, Abigail, but Raritan Tavern could develop a terrible reputation should you allow this to continue. Would you permit your charming daughter to stay at a tavern where a guest had been slain and its ghost was haunting the very halls where she sought sweet slumber? I think not."

"No ghost," I said, knowing that last night's ghost had been a corporeal thief.

"Ah, then you have truly been shortchanged, for you have lost the tavern's reputation and not even gained a spirit whose presence would attract the custom of thrill seekers."

I appreciated my uncle's attempts to make light of the murder, although I could see the worry in his eyes and guessed this was the cause of his visit. For the moment I decided not to trouble him further by mentioning that someone had broken into my room or that I had taken the book and leather packet from the saddlebags of the dead man. I was sure I would have ample time to tell him when I had determined how they were related to the murder.

Sitting on a stool and sipping the coffee Matty handed me, I told most of what I knew about the murder, attempting to emulate Uncle Samuel's style of storytelling. Unfortunately, I'm not as accomplished, as was evident when John and Matty volunteered information. Even Beth remembered something I had forgotten.

"Has Phillips said anything about taking over the tavern?" Uncle Samuel asked.

"No, for the moment the captain seems content he doesn't have to manage it himself, and his men appear to have no complaints."

"I should hope not," Matty said.

"If he used this murder as a rationale to take over the tavern, he could easily fill the beds we keep open for travelers and get more of his soldiers out of those freezing tents," I said.

"Perhaps," said my uncle. "But he's been here two months and has not done so yet. I'm inclined to think he wants contact with the travelers who pass through New Brunswick and this gives him the perfect opportunity to meet them without a tavernkeeper's responsibilities."

"I think you're right. He and his officers can mingle with our guests, determine their loyalties, and pump them for information. Men can be amazingly forthcoming after a few pints."

We heard stomping on the back porch and the door opened, admitting Constable Grey and a blast of cold air. "G'morning," he said, nodding to the four of us. His cheeks were ruddy from the cold, his hair mussed when he took off his tricorn.

"G'day, Josiah," Uncle Samuel responded. "Come join us and enlighten us as to how your search for the murderer of George Fenton Lee progresses."

The constable pulled up a chair and reached for the hot coffee Matty was holding out. "Not much progress yet, Samuel. In an effort to discover any information possible, I sent four men out yesterday, one north toward Bound Brook, one south to Freehold, one west toward Kingston, and one east to Amboy. None of them are back yet. I'm hoping they'll find where Lee and his wife came from or what they were doing here."

"You think they may have come from someplace other than Philadelphia?" Samuel asked.

"At this point, I have no idea where they came from or for what purpose. I'm casting as wide a net as possible, to see what I can dredge up. I also need to send someone to Philadelphia to notify the authorities and Lee's family of his murder. There were papers in the saddlebags which confirm Lee's identity, but I'm hoping someone who knew him personally will come to claim the body. And I need someone who knows the area between here and Pennsylvania to determine if there is a trace of the elusive wife, assuming she was the person who took the two horses on the Princeton and Philadelphia road that morning."

"If it was a woman," I said. Josiah Grey glanced at me, although his look did not indicate if he accepted my theory any more than he had last night.

"Who are you going to send to Philadelphia?" Samuel asked.

"I'd like to go myself and ask a few questions of Lee's kin and business partners, but Captain Phillips is acting a strange duck about this murder, so I think I'd best remain here."

Uncle Samuel ran his fingers through his gray hair. "I know the countryside to Princeton and on to Philadelphia fairly well. As long as John and Matty can keep Abigail out of further mischief, and see she doesn't precipitate the ruin of Raritan Tavern in my absence, or turn up more corpses, there's no reason I couldn't go, if it would oblige you."

"I was hoping you'd offer. There is no man I would trust more. But don't you have any committee work?" the constable asked, referring to Uncle Samuel's patriot activities.

"Nothing that can't be handled without me for a few days. I take a personal affront to this murder, Josiah, it being committed in my tavern, and frightening my niece and her daughter so dreadfully. I would feel better if I were doing something to help find the villain."

"You certainly know diverse people in Philadelphia," I said. "Surely, some of them would have been acquainted with George Fenton Lee."

"I hope so, Abigail."

"How soon can you leave?" Josiah Grey asked.

"As soon as I go back to the farm, pack a few things and tell my manager, Benjamin, that I'm away. If I can get as

far as Princeton tonight, I could be in Philadelphia tomorrow, with time enough to take back roads and talk to
people I know along the way."

The constable nodded. "I'm in your debt, Samuel."
Looking at me he asked, "Have you quill, ink, and paper
I may use for the authorization Samuel will need to act in
my stead?"

"Of course. Beth will get them."

After gathering the items from my office and handing
them to the constable, Beth asked if Samuel would be
staying with her grandparents in Princeton.

"Wouldn't miss a chance to bother my brother. He
would never speak to me again if I didn't stop and tell him
tales of your mother finding a dead body."

I sighed, dreading how he would embroider the story
for my parents.

"Don't worry, Mother," Beth whispered. "Uncle Samuel
won't frighten them. His stories are never as scary as he
thinks they are."

My uncle laughed.

"Gingerbread," Matty said, hustling off to the pantry.
She returned immediately with the prized dessert and a
cloth in which to wrap it. "You'll be so kind to take this to
Mistress Holt, won't you, Master Samuel, in one piece,
and not nibbled at? I know it's one of her favorites and
this here's fresh baked."

Despite her warning, Uncle Samuel tried to break off
a piece of the brown spicy cake before Matty could finish
wrapping it. She slapped his hand, but promised to send
a piece with the lunch she would pack for him. Soon all
was organized and the constable, bundled against the
cold, took his leave. We bid Uncle Samuel Godspeed,
although he was out the door in such a hurry, I doubt he

heard us. I experienced a fleeting bit of jealousy that he would soon be surrounded by the affection and warmth of my parents' home and wished I could accompany him. Instead, I must face another day with the cloud of murder hanging over Raritan Tavern. But enough, I told myself. Uncle Samuel was traveling to seek out answers to the very problem that was troubling me and I had work to accomplish that would not get done if I stood around mooning.

As we approached the dinner hour at one o'clock, the beef roast, mashed potatoes, carrots and beans had been prepared and were ready to be served from the fire in the warming kitchen. Beth was placing fresh baked bread on cutting boards, while one of the kitchen maids stirred the gravy in the three-legged pan set amidst the coals. Fanny, our young and talkative waitress, scooped butter from the large crock into serving dishes and carried them into the dining rooms.

Everything was in good order and I was removing my apron to play hostess when Grace came in from the dining room.

"Mistress, Captain Phillips is requesting you attend him," she said.

"I'll wager he was a bit more insistent than you're stating."

Grace grinned. "You'd win that wager easily. I think the words he used were 'demand' and 'this instant'. I told him this was a busy time for you but he would not be deterred."

"That sounds more like the man I know." I motioned to the door, "Once more unto the breach, dear friends, once more."

"Why is it Mistress, that I find out everything concerning this tavern secondhand?"

Phillips shouted before the door had swung closed behind me. The expression of incomprehension on my face further incensed the supercilious captain.

"Your uncle, Madam. I am referring to your uncle. I understand he is on his way to Philadelphia." Phillips placed one hand on his sword handle, the other on his hip and continued to shout, "Why was my approval not obtained before he left?"

"Constable Grey sent Uncle Samuel with his authorization, Captain."

"His authorization! And did he think to consult with me first? I should say not. The man doesn't realize his limitations. I have specific questions I would have wanted your uncle to pursue. Now his efforts will be in vain for lack of the proper tack to follow."

"My uncle was sent to find someone to claim Mr. Lee's body. You can ask that person all your questions, Captain, as soon as he arrives."

"And what if Mr. Holt is unable to discover someone who knew the deceased? Then what will he do, Mistress? He will not have the least idea how to proceed. And it will be the constable's responsibility for not having instructed him properly, which Grey could not possibly have done."

"And why is that, Captain? Because this is not London? And anyone who lives anywhere else couldn't have sufficient wits to ask a few intelligent questions?" It was now my turn to put my hands on my hips, angry and unwilling to hold my tongue at the insufferable condescension Phillips exuded every time he spoke.

"You take offense, Mistress, where none is intended. Surely, even you must realize how limited experience is in the colonies compared with life in London. I daresay there are as many murders in a day in London as you would have in years in this hamlet. It would not concern me except that my officers are living here."

I knew I was on dangerous ground and had to control my temper immediately before Phillips took complete offense and threw me out onto the street. "I am certain Uncle Samuel will find someone in Philadelphia who will be able to claim the deceased, maybe even find out the reason he was killed. Unless the doctor was wrong and Mr. Lee was killed by whoever ran him through with that sword. Did you find out who the sword belongs to?"

He gave me a look that implied "What business is it of yours?" but he answered, "Yes, one of my lieutenants was able to identify the crest from my description. I have spoken to the owner and he has given me his word he was asleep through the entire night and neither knew of Lee nor killed him. I have complete faith in this man's statement. The murderer is someone else and until he is caught my men are not safe."

"As far as I know, Captain, Mr. Lee was a merchant, not a soldier, so the reasons for his death could not be military. As you have identified the soldier whose weapon was used to pin the corpse to the floor, and have found him to be innocent, it would seem to me that your men are quite safe."

"You colonists have a strange way of making soldiers out of the least likely men. One day a man is in uniform and the next he is taking in his fall crops. It is sometimes confusing to us English military men, who among you is and is not a soldier." Phillips sounded disgusted at my lack of understanding regarding military professionalism.

Hoping to avoid further confrontation now that the dining rooms were filling, I said, "Captain, I will notify you, as soon as I hear from my uncle. It will take some days, but I am certain he will find the reasons for this man's death."

Of course, I had no such certainty. I only wanted the captain to leave. It was not clear to me why Phillips had confronted me about Uncle Samuel's mission to Philadelphia, beyond the fact that he seemed to seek me out whenever he wanted to vent his spleen. Surely, it would have been more appropriate for him to have spoken with the constable, as he was the person who had sent off Uncle Samuel. That is, unless Phillips thought *I* had information he wanted. I did have George Fenton Lee's book and leather packet in my possession, although from what I had seen I thought it likely that Phillips would be disappointed in Mr. Lee's account book. On the other hand, I was more determined than ever to investigate the contents of the leather packet.

EIGHT

The conversation with Captain Phillips spurred me to examine more closely Lee's account book and to peruse the leather packet. What did those items contain that were of such import to the British? Anxious though I was to return to my room and the stolen materials stashed beneath the eaves, I thought it best to proceed with my customary duties. My actions should not appear unusual in any respect.

Dinner proceeded in its established manner, and I thought it remarkable how impossibly long minutes can become when one wishes to be elsewhere. Once the dining rooms had emptied and the cleaning was well in hand, I headed out to the laundry, hoping to find washed napkins and tablecloths. Our linen supply was sorely depleted by the increased number of patrons who had come to speculate about the murder.

As I approached the laundry house, I waved to Mrs. Hemple, the laundress, who was hanging linen on the drying line. "Afternoon, Mistress Abigail," she called as she balanced precariously on some boards laid over the morass of mud in the back portion of the yard. Surrounded by a cloud of steam rising from the warm, damp laundry, I thought she looked like a rosy-cheeked, middle-aged cherub.

Inside the washhouse, the fire had been allowed to burn down now that the tubs of water were empty. Two irons sat heating amidst the coals while Miriam Ilon used a third, smoothing napkins in rapid strokes. A neat pile attested to her work.

"Thank you for readying the linen," I told her. "We would have been serving on bare boards tomorrow, had you not anticipated our need."

"Can't have our guests doing without table linen, can we? If they didn't have napkins, they'd just use their sleeves and then expect us to get the grease out of their coats, probably with their arms still in them," the maid replied. "This is far the easiest way."

Miriam assisted with ironing and sewing several afternoons a week, after she had cleaned the tavern rooms. There was too much laundry for Mrs. Hemple to tend single-handedly, a fact she repeatedly called to the attention of anyone within earshot. Having Miriam work with her was supposed to have been a temporary solution to placate her when the redcoats moved in, but I had left the arrangement, not in small part because I hoped it would limit her shrill complaints. Cherub she might appear in the steam outside, but behave like one she did not.

"If you think this is so easy, Miriam, you do the washing tomorrow," grumbled Mrs. Hemple as she came through the door with her empty wicker basket. "I'm so tired I'll likely fall asleep right when I gets home and miss my sister's birthday."

I ignored the complaint, knowing that if I responded to it, there would only be more said. However, Miriam nodded in agreement, and Mrs. Hemple simply returned her nod with a short bob of the head.

"Give your sister my felicitations," I said to Mrs. Hemple, as I turned to leave. "I'll ask Matty if any gingerbread remains after all that Uncle Samuel devoured. It would make a fine surprise for your supper tonight."

"I'd deem that most charitable of you, Mistress, and so would my sister."

Mrs. Hemple lived with her widowed sister and worked at the tavern as daily help. Their house was little more than three rooms. The one facing New Street was used for her sister's dressmaking business, while they resided in the two rear rooms. It did allow Mrs. Hemple some measure of privacy and gave the rest of us respite from her constant dissatisfaction.

"Mrs. Hemple, I have a small token for your good sister, if you would be kind enough to deliver it to her," Miriam said. "I brought her a piece of lavender soap, knowing that was her favorite."

"Wherever did you find such a rarity?" I inquired.

"Oh, I found it some time ago, before the British came, when luxuries weren't so dear." A small smile tugged at the corners of Miriam's mouth.

"I was hoping you had found a secret source," I added, the vision of holding a whole bar of lavender soap in my hand popping like a bubble.

"Certainly can't find anything like that these days, not without snuggling up to some lobsterback. Probably have to be an officer, at that," said Mrs. Hemple.

Miriam caught her breath, her eyes wide. "Watch what you're saying," she cautioned, looking pointedly from Mrs. Hemple to me.

"You know what I'm saying is true," said Mrs. Hemple.

"Not about me it's not and don't you ever hint that it is," Miriam said. "And anyway, even if what you say is true about some others, that doesn't mean that you have to talk about it in front of the whole world. You and I know more about how the world works than some people ever will." Miriam looked directly at me and I understood she included me in the naive portion of the population. After years of running this tavern, I would not have considered myself so.

I said my good-byes and turned for the door as Mrs. Hemple was complaining about finishing the day's work.

"We'll get it all done and in time for you to leave early to celebrate with your sister," Miriam responded. "You fret so much. I think you'll find something to complain about to the Almighty on Judgment Day."

"There's a thing or two I want to talk over with Him, that's for certain."

I walked back into the warming kitchen to seek out any remnants of gingerbread, although my mind was still on the relationship between the two women.

"Now what's you shaking your head about?" Matty asked.

"Any gingerbread?"

"You shaking your head about gingerbread?"

"No," I said, pausing on my way to the pantry. "I'm continually confounded by the friendship between Miriam and Mrs. Hemple. I can see no similarity between them."

"They's right different, that's true. Miriam, she's quiet, too quiet if you ask me, and Mrs. Hemple, why I doubts she ever stop to think of what she's saying."

"And Miriam is meticulous about her hair and dress, regardless of the meanness of her clothing."

Matty laughed heartily. "Not exactly what you'd say about Mrs. Hemple, is it? Why I thought she was gonna pop right out of her shift the other day what with the buttons missing on her blouse. Weren't she a sight to see?"

"I wonder if my friendships with you or with Rachel seem as strange to others? They make perfect sense to me." I shrugged. "Miriam's with Mrs. Hemple probably makes sense to her also."

"I been blessed with friends and I thank the good Lord for them. Can't rightly imagine my life without you or John, or that rascal uncle of yours. This life ain't easy for nobody, but having friends makes a difference. It's good for Miriam that she's got at least one friend. She ain't the easiest person to make friends with. Never wants to gossip." Matty went into the pantry and reached behind a large keg to retrieve a cloth-covered plate.

The smell of cinnamon and ginger wafted about the room as she cut us each a piece. A large enough piece remained to give Mrs. Hemple's sister. I picked at the crumbs on the plate while Matty poured coffee.

"I remember how hard we both worked to befriend her when she first arrived," I said. "I think Grace tried also. We didn't have much success. Miriam keeps to herself."

Matty shook her head. "She got a whole lot hidden behind that sour expression of hers, but she were never going to share her burden with me. Maybe it were something she and Mrs. Hemple could talk about."

"You think Mrs. Hemple is a more sympathetic listener than we are?" I asked.

"Maybe as far as Miriam's concerned. I hear them talking sometimes, when they thinks I'm not listening.

Miriam's got a heap of anger about something that happened to her mother and to a baby."

"Her mother's baby?"

"I suppose so. Miriam got right white-lipped when I asked her. She weren't gonna tell me nothing, but I could see the fire in her eyes."

"And that fits with Mrs. Hemple's incessant anger about life," I said.

"Maybe." Matty munched her cake for a while, then said, "That much bile's not good for the soul, twists it into ugly shapes with sharp edges. I knows, I been there. Ain't nothing but pain comes from wrath like that."

I had but to pay a bill that was due, then I could retreat to my room and the investigation of my secret papers. I walked the few steps from the warming kitchen through the back hall and into my office under the front hall stairs. The stairs wound around two sides of the office, allowing the room ample height. The only shortened space was directly under the stairs and it was used for storage and for the safe, all discreetly hidden behind oak paneling. To the left of the door as you entered was the beautiful Chippendale desk Uncle Samuel had left for my use. It had a base of two locking drawers topped by a slanting lid which folded down to make a desk. When the desk was opened a glorious multitude of compartments and small drawers was revealed. I delighted in the touch of its smooth walnut wood and in the golden-brown finish reflecting the candlelight by which I paid my bills and kept my ledgers. The office had no window, but I had become accustomed to its perpetual twilight and found that a small price to pay for the privilege of a private, quiet space in which to work. Managing a tavern is a relentlessly public office and even when I am not hostessing, I am having commerce with my staff or vendors. Thus, the ability to work in peace, and even with the door closed at times, is a great facilitation to my work and my sanity. This afternoon I left the door open and had barely settled in my chair before there was a knock and John peered around the door frame.

"I has some money for you, Mistress," he said, placing coins on the desk. "Mr. Jamison was in some hurry to leave for Princeton. Asked me to give this to you as he rushed out the door. Looked about the right amount to me."

A quick glance and I could see the payment was more than adequate. "I'm surprised he left. He said last evening that he would be here another couple of days."

John shrugged, causing the candlelight to glint off the highly polished brass buttons on his thigh-length black waistcoat. With his lanky build and straight bearing, John wore his clothes with enviable grace. "Don't know why he changed his mind, but he had his horse saddled and said he was on his way to the constable's office to check if he could leave, what with the murder being so recent. Guess Constable Grey must have said it were all right because Jamison didn't come back here."

"What time did he leave, John?"

"It were just a bit after Master Samuel rode out, and that were near ten, I think. You frowning, Mistress. What you worrying about?"

"I'm not sure, John. Maybe nothing." I paused, trying to verbalize a feeling that flitted around the edges of my mind but refused to solidify. "Jamison seemed honest enough, certainly a likable and hardworking person, which I suppose he would have to be as a salesman. It just strikes me as odd that he was here at exactly the right moment to identify Lee, and then leaves, earlier than he had planned, but at the same time my uncle is heading off on the constable's errand."

"Could be just a simple coincidence, Mistress Abigail."

"You're probably right. You didn't find anything about him that seemed a bit, oh, I don't know, a bit strange, or out of place?"

John paused for a moment, his eyes focused on the flickering candle flame. "He did say something that I wondered on as he left this morning. He offered to take Lee's horse and goods to Philadelphia."

I was still for a moment, considering the implication of John's comment. "How did he know the horse was here?"

"He most likely thought the horse was here because Lee's body's here."

"I suppose that's possible. Just because we know the horse had been taken and then returned doesn't mean Jamison would have known that. John, yesterday, when you left the stable to get Constable Grey, after Captain Phillips arrived, was there anyone else about?"

"Let's see, you and me was there. Amos Warren had brought the horse from his stable where he said Mr. Schmidt had brought it in, and then Captain Phillips came in, and I run over and got the constable. I suppose somebody could have seen me when I went to get him. Didn't notice anybody though. Who else you wondering about?"

I shrugged, feeling a bit foolish, the memory of the shadow in the doorway seeming less of a telltale than it had been yesterday. "It's probably nothing. Jamison's asking to take the horse to Philadelphia just seems strange to me."

"I see what you getting at, but I ain't got nothing more to add to it one way or another. And maybe we all still kind of riled from finding the body." John looked at me intently, as though measuring my level of anxiety.

"You're probably right, John. After wishing this had never happened, my second futile wish is that it was all long past and a simple memory."

"Amen to that Mistress."

I sent John to deliver the payment note to Chandler's Mercantile, closed and locked the desk, blew out the candle, and was about to lock the door, when Beth approached me.

"Mother, I was looking for you. Can you wait here, please, just a moment? I have to get someone and then we have a question for you." She scurried around the corner, returning shortly with Lieutenant Reade in tow.

He banged into Beth when she stopped more abruptly than he had anticipated, but he managed to compose himself sufficiently to bow and wish me a good afternoon.

"Oh, Mother, I didn't know where you'd gone, and I couldn't find you, and it's so important that we just couldn't wait to tell you, well, that is, to ask you." She paused to take a breath and then hurried on, "Alan has the most wonderful idea and I just know it would be so enjoyable, everyone would have such a splendid time."

Alan? I thought, although my frown at the use of the lieutenant's Christian name seemed to affect neither of them.

"It's about the dance that you're giving next week, Mistress Abigail," Lieutenant Reade said. "And we, that is, I, thought it would be most entertaining if it were a masked ball. I have been to several in London and have enjoyed them greatly."

"I think it's a bit late for that, Lieutenant," I said.

"But, Mother," Beth began to protest, her cheeks flushed, her eyes wide with excitement.

"It is not that I dislike the idea, Beth. But the broadsides have already been published and posted around the county. It is simply too late to change at this time."

"But it would have been so delightful to hide behind a fancy mask and have everyone guess who I was." Beth pouted, a child not getting what she wanted.

"It's not possible, Beth," I said. "I agreed to hold this dance against my better judgment, when you and Lieutenant Reade proposed it several weeks ago. I am still not sure this winter in the middle of a war is the best time to celebrate with festivities."

"It will be very good for morale, Mistress, what with the rain and rationing and all that," Lieutenant Reade said. "I'm sure we will have a most congenial evening."

"So you said, and I gave my consent. But it is too late to change the nature of the ball and make it a masked ball, regardless of how fine the idea."

Dances had been commonly held at Raritan Tavern before the British had arrived. It was a part of our role in the New Brunswick community to host plays and various entertainments as well as town meetings. Uncle Samuel had been astute when he added the ballroom to the side of the tavern years earlier. Our ability to accommodate many townspeople gave us a distinct advantage over smaller taverns. But I was nervous about how peaceably a social event could be held while the British were here. To say nothing of the fact that all the officers who were billeted in the ballroom would have to evacuate that room for a day, not a minor upheaval, although the young officers seemed willing enough to sleep in tents for one night.

Reade accepted my response graciously, thanking me again for agreeing to the dance, and asking that I consider a masked ball for the future. As they headed toward the dining room, I noticed he put his hand at the small of Beth's back. This pleased me not one iota.

NINE

Late afternoon was often a quiet time about the tavern, the supper soup simmering in the kitchen, the next day's bread cooling in the bakery, the evening drinkers still at their work. At that time of day most travelers were still on the road and wouldn't appear until later, when the sun met the horizon. After I had taken a brief turn through the first and second floors and found all to be quiet, I retired to my room and locked the door behind me. Silently, I retrieved my stolen treasures from their hiding place, the blue pocket I had hung from a nail in the storage space under the eaves. I had waited anxiously through the seemingly endless afternoon for a discreet moment to examine the contents of the leather envelope, but now that I held it, I felt oddly reticent about proceeding. That I had taken something that did not belong to me was without question, although I justified the theft as rescuing the material from the British. My hesitation was purely emotional, a confused sensation of enticement and foreboding. For a fleeting moment, I contemplated not opening the packet, leaving the knot in the leather thong that closed the flap and wound about the envelope. But to what end? If I didn't open it, I would not know what it contained and thus to whom it should be passed, for surely it needed to be in appropriate hands. If it were business letters, for example, it would need to be returned to the manager of Mr. Lee's business. So, reaffirming my good intentions and ignoring my thumping heart, I reached for the parcel.

It was oblong, approximately five by eight inches, and quite flat. The brown leather was scratched and stained; the well-worn hide felt soft in my fingers. Untying the thong, I found the contents further wrapped in thin oilcloth, probably to protect the contents from moisture. Inside the oilcloth were three letters on stiff, creamy vellum. The top one was folded in thirds and then in thirds crosswise but was unsealed, while the bottom two were sealed with red wax.

Neither side of the unsealed letter revealed a name or address. This greatly surprised me as the paper was obviously costly, appearing to be of a quality that is used for legal documents or other important correspondence.

I was about to open the top letter when the other two slid off my lap. Picking them up, I turned them over and set them faceup on my apron. I glanced at the name on the top letter. It took a moment for my startled mind to accept what my eyes saw. John Hancock, President, The Continental Congress, Philadelphia. Some giddy bubble broke through my thoughts. Ah, the other is sure to be for General Washington, I told myself. With a finger, I pushed the letter aside to read the name on the one concealed. Indeed, I was correct. I was so terrified that my breath came in erratic gasps. What had I done by purloining these confidential letters? I didn't know what I had expected the small packet to contain, a hint of a murderer perhaps, a love letter condemning a married man, a last will and testament leaving an illicit fortune. Not this. Not letters directed to heads of state, valuable, secret, and certainly not intended for British eyes. I was far, immeasurably far, beyond my depth in this murder and rued my confounded curiosity that had led me to hide these letters.

I resolved to take them to . . . Ah, yes, that was the rubbing point, was it not? To whom would I take the letters now that I knew their intended destination? Assuredly not the British, although I was certain Captain Phillips would gladly relieve me of them, and without doubt, the British would pay me dearly for their possession. Constable Grey seemed logical until I wondered again if his neutral behavior was genuine. If he was truly neutral, would he be willing to get the letters delivered safely? My uncle was, of course, the perfect answer, except that he was on his way to Philadelphia. How regretful I was that I had not looked at the packet before he left. Perhaps I could take them out to the farm and give them to Benjamin, Uncle Samuel's manager. Surely he would be in my uncle's confidence and know of reliable men who could be trusted with the letters.

In my consternation, I shifted on the rocking chair and the stiff parchment of the unsealed letter opened enough for me to see writing, which I read automatically.

> *"Most Honorable Sir,*
> *Whereas the bearer of this letter is our trusted emissary,*
> *risking life and well-being at our behest in the service*
> *of our noble cause."*

Of course, I could not stop there. Rationality does not limit one's nature at moments like this. The letter continued:

> ". . . *Any assistance you may render our faithful messenger in the deliverance of these missives will be honored by us and by the God who blesses our endeavor.*
> *Your Most Humble Servant,*
> *Benj. Franklin*
> *Paris. 11th of January, 1777.*"

I swiftly gathered the letters and wrapped them in the oil-cloth, which I had to refold several times before it would fit neatly into the leather envelope. I was securing the thong around the package when I heard Beth's light steps running down the hall toward my room. Finding my door locked, she knocked, whimpering, "Mother. Oh, Mother, please open the door. Something terrible has happened."

Not now, Beth, I thought. This is not an opportune time for you to feel disconsolate.

Hastily replacing the letters under the eaves, the door slipped through my nervous fingers, closing with a loud thud. I feared the whole tavern had heard that sound and a redcoat would appear instantly to arrest me as a rebel spy. I would probably be hanged by sunset.

Shaking my head at the insanity of the situation I had created, I unlocked the door, bracing for Beth's hysteria.

"Oh, Mother," she cried, tears running down her cheeks, her light brown hair flying in all directions, as she had pulled off her mobcap and was wringing it in her hands. "Three of them are dead, and Lieutenant Southerland was shot in the leg."

Trying to remain calm myself, I drew her into my arms and waited for her sobs to diminish. When her crying subsided, I handed her my handkerchief and we sat side by side on the bed, my arm still around her, as she poured forth the story that caused her such distress.

"A foraging party of three hundred men went out this morning and Lieutenant Southerland, Alan's friend, was in command," she said, her voice hoarse. "They were returning to town with the carcasses when they were ambushed. Three of them are dead, Mother." Beth started crying again, quietly this time.

While I understood Beth's liking for the young men she saw and spoke with every day, it was worrisome how easily she forgot they were enemy soldiers.

"Did you know any of them?" I asked.

"No. They were all privates and lived out in the tents. Johnnie Southerland is the only one who stays here and I don't really know him. I tried to talk to him once or twice, but he's rather shy. Alan talks about him a lot. I think they are from the same part of England or something."

"Lieutenant Southerland is the tall one with the light curly hair?"

"Yes. Oh Mother, how could someone have shot him? They were only gathering food. I know they take it from our neighbors, but they share it with us, don't they?" She paused to wipe her eyes with the back of her sleeve—so much for my handkerchief. "They give us meat, don't they?"

I nodded, "They give us meat to feed their officers who stay here. But they are British officers and we are at war."

"Mistress Abigail?" Lieutenant Reade said from the doorway.

I hadn't noticed his approach and gasped, seeing a redcoat at my door. Gathering my composure, I rose to face him.

"How may I help you, Lieutenant?"

"Excuse me for interrupting you. I know I am not allowed on this floor, but Captain Phillips sent me to requisition a room for Lieutenant Southerland. He will heal faster if he is given the quiet and warmth of a private room." The lieutenant's face was a worried shade of gray, his anxiety for his friend overshadowing his usual too-smooth charm.

"We will have to see about the room," I said. "How fares Lieutenant Southerland?" My sympathy for the injured young man was genuine but did not lessen the anger I felt toward those who robbed my neighbors and friends in their foraging parties, and my antipathy toward the army here to steal our freedoms.

"He is in the surgeons' tent," said Reade. "They say his leg was badly shattered and may have to be cut off. I know Johnnie would rather be dead than a cripple. I would."

I heard the vehemence in his voice although I disagreed with the sentiment. Only youth could be vain enough to prefer death to physical imperfection, I thought. Somewhere in England there was bound to be a family or a lover who would want him back with just one leg, if he should be fortunate enough to survive the infection that was bound to set in once the leg was removed.

"My prayers will be with your friend, Lieutenant, that he will recover swiftly and completely. I will have to speak with Captain Phillips as I am unable to accommodate his request to house Lieutenant Southerland."

Reade looked at me blankly as if unable to comprehend what I had said. Beth was not long taken aback. "What do you mean, Mother? Surely we have room."

"We have room Beth, but . . ."

"Oh, good. I'll go light a fire to give the room some warmth. Come with me, Alan," she said, heading towards the stairs.

"Just a minute Beth, that is not what I meant. We are forced to feed and house the soldiers billeted here or else to leave Raritan Tavern in British hands. We are not obligated to be a camp hospital. And Beth, we are not able to tend a gravely injured soldier."

"Oh, but I could, Mother. I would take care of him."

"Beth, that would not be acceptable. You don't have the skills to nurse him . . ."

Again, she interrupted me. "You could teach me, or Miriam could help . . ."

"No, Elizabeth," I said, so sternly that she stood agape. "I don't believe it would be in the best interests of either Lieutenant Southerland or our tavern for him to be brought here. This discussion is over. Lieutenant Southerland will not stay here and you will not care for him."

She nodded mutely, shocked by the firmness of my intention, tears spilling silently down her cheeks.

I headed toward the stairs, driving the redcoat before me. "Lieutenant, would you be so kind as to help me find Captain Phillips? And Lieutenant, I empathize with your distress over your friend and will overlook your breach of etiquette this once, but I must insist that you never come up to the top floor again."

Lieutenant Reade was silent during our two-block walk to the Stevens's house which was being used as British Headquarters for the Brigades of Foot. His behavior was proper, guiding me around puddles, helping me avoid horse droppings. His sullenness at my refusal to house his friend had not affected his manners. Escorting me into the entryway of the house, he went in search of Captain Phillips.

I had been a guest of the Stevens's on many pleasurable occasions, Florence Stevens being fond of entertaining and generous with her invitations. Today, the entry hall appeared barren. The dark oak table which always held an arrangement of fresh flowers or greens and the matching wall mirror had been taken by the Stevens when the house was requisitioned and they were obliged to leave. Florence had returned to her family in Allentown, Pennsylvania, while Mr. Stevens had established a small living area in the attic of his New Brunswick shipping business. It was rumored that Florence had fought mightily with him, demanding that she remain, but he was leery of the British and at last she had reluctantly agreed to move to the safety of her family home. The arrangement was not pleasing to either of them.

Mr. Stevens had removed the lushly colored carpet from the entryway where I now stood. The floor had clumps of mud tracked in from the streets. I was imagining the effort that would be needed to clean out the muck once the soldiers left, when a door opened down the hall and a redcoated officer paused in the doorway.

"Good of you to tell me, Phillips." I recognized the deeply resonant voice coming from inside the room as that of Colonel Oliver Belding, his Oxford education obvious with every syllable he uttered.

"My man should return from New York tomorrow or the next day and we will know what Lee was carrying," said Captain Phillips.

"You found nothing in his bags?"

"No, Colonel, there was nothing of interest, unless the constable took something, and I doubt he had time before I arrived."

"Bring word when you have further information, Captain," the colonel said as he left the room and headed further down the hall.

I was most intrigued. Phillips seemed cognizant that Lee had been carrying something of value. Letters to the heads of the provisional government, perhaps? Was it even possible that the captain had known Mr. Lee? If so, why would Phillips not have identified the murdered man when he saw the body? I doubted he would answer these questions directly and was fruitlessly pondering how I might obtain the information, when Phillips cleared his throat approximately one inch from my ear.

"Mistress Abigail."

I tried to cover my startled gasp with a feigned cough which sounded, to my ears at least, like a pig prodded with a pitchfork. Phillips's expression assured me such a raucous noise was not frequently heard emanating from English society matrons. I ignored his look, took a deep breath and hoped my heart would return to my chest so I could use my throat to speak.

"Captain," I said, and proceeded to cough genuinely and uncontrollably. One's body does betray one at the most inconvenient times.

"I hope you are not sickening, Mistress. I abhor being in the presence of ill people and will not have my officers coughing and rheumy."

"Thank you for your concern, but I am fine." My sarcasm was lost on Phillips, although, to my relief, he did retreat several paces.

"And what can I do for you, Mistress? Have you found another dead body at Raritan Tavern?" he asked.

"No, Captain, one murder a week is all we allow ourselves." The change of expression on Phillips's face from derision to uncertainty pleased me greatly. I continued before he could reply, "I have come to discuss the problem of accommodations for Lieutenant Southerland."

"And how, Mistress, can there be a problem?" he asked.

"As I am sure you understand, Raritan Tavern is not a suitable place for the injured lieutenant."

Phillips's brown eyes narrowed, a crease appeared between his brows. "And why is that, Mistress?"

"Captain, Raritan Tavern is just that—a tavern. We provide accommodations, food and drink for travelers. We are not a camp hospital and have neither room nor nurses to tend the severely ill or maimed."

"In this case, Mistress Tavernkeeper, you will," Phillips said, and turned to walk away.

I reached out and grabbed him by the sleeve, shocking myself as much as him. "No, Sir," I said. "Raritan Tavern will not tend your young lieutenant. I have not sufficient nursing women to tend his grievous injury. The other officers and guests would be disturbed by the moans and cries of a patient whose leg was amputated. We simply cannot accommodate your request."

"I am amazed at your lack of Christian charity, Mistress," he said. "I had heard that the colonies were barbaric, but I did not think they would deny the needs of an injured man."

"I feed the hungry and give shelter to as many as possible. I also provide for those of my own household and keep them fed and clothed and rested so they may in turn serve you and your men. I do not have enough servants to add the care of sorely wounded soldiers to our current duties." I could see by his countenance that he was unmoved by my argument.

"Then you will add more to accommodate my demand," Phillips said, leaning over me, using his height as a threat. "This is exactly why women should never be put in charge. They can't find a solution for a most basic problem in logistics."

"That is because there is no workable solution. I am not unsympathetic to the needs of the young lieutenant, but I can not and will not care for him."

"Yes, you will, as I have ordered." Phillips drew himself up to his considerable height, towering over me, his hand resting on the hilt of his sword, his face flushed as a boiled beet.

"No, I will not," I responded, my arms akimbo.

The silence between us held for a short eternity. I heard footsteps in the hall behind me; there was a pause and then they continued toward where I was standing.

"Mistress Abigail?" asked Colonel Belding.

I turned around so rapidly that my skirts flared out. "G'day, Colonel."

"May I be of assistance?" he asked, looking directly at me.

Phillips answered, his tone sarcastic. "The good Mistress has forgotten her Christian charity and is refusing to see to the nursing of Lieutenant Southerland as you had ordered."

"As you had ordered?" I stammered, looking from Phillips to the colonel. Refusing Phillips was one thing, refusing the British commander who reported directly to General Howe was an entirely different kettle of fish.

"Of course, Mistress," Phillips said, enjoying my discomfort. "Lieutenant Reade was but relaying the Colonel's message at my behest."

"If you would come to my office, Mistress," the colonel said, "we can discuss your qualms." He placed his hand under my elbow and led me down the hall. Phillips followed. At the door the colonel paused, "Captain, if you would be so good as to seek some refreshment for my guest."

I knew from the look on Phillips's face as he turned toward the back of the house that he was insulted by the colonel's rejection. I also knew he would find a way to redirect the insult in my direction. Insufferable man.

Colonel Belding escorted me to one of two burgundy leather wing chairs placed on either side of the fireplace. He stood against the white mantel filling his pipe, then bent to light it with a switch from the fire.

"You are ill at ease with my orders for young Southerland," he said.

I explained my objections as I had to Captain Phillips, though with more tact. "So you will understand, Colonel, that I am sympathetic to the young lieutenant's plight. Any young man must suffer tremendously from having a leg amputated, physically as well as in his mind, when he anticipates the future, but I feel he would be better served in your camp hospital than at the Raritan Tavern." I left unexpressed the conflict in my mind over whether I should act patriotically and refuse to aid the enemy or act morally and succor one who was ill. I continued to find the ethics of war perplexing.

"Southerland was perhaps fortunate," the Colonel said, sitting opposite me. "The surgeon did not remove his leg as the leg was not shattered, although it may never heal properly. I say perhaps fortunate because I am concerned with the possibility, no, the certainty, of infection. Our surgeons have found that a mangled leg cut clean off and cauterized has a better chance of healing than when the bone remains. However, as I am sure you know, even after an amputation infection is very common."

"All the more reason, Colonel, why Southerland should remain at the camp hospital where they are familiar with such injuries."

"Perhaps. But as we both know, Mistress, army surgeons are butchers and I believe often do more harm than good. I have been very fortunate during my service to never come under their scalpels or I think I would not be here chatting with you."

I was taken aback by the colonel's honesty.

"You seem startled that I would confess my thoughts to you."

I nodded.

Colonel Belding leaned forward resting his elbows on his knees, playing distractedly with his pipe. "Lord Southerland is a friend of mine since childhood. Our families are close, have been for generations. I promised Southerland that I would look after his son when the young man was commissioned and until today, I had managed to keep him out of serious harm. He is a good lad." The colonel sighed deeply. "I think his best chance for life is outside of the camp hospital and that is why I am asking you to take on his care."

"But Colonel . . ."

"I believe it probable that he will succumb to infection, but at least he will die in as comfortable surroundings as we can provide, and that is a responsibility we have to each other as human beings, Mistress Abigail, regardless of our political differences. I am certain you will find a way to ease his way."

"Sir, your confidence in me is misplaced as I have no skills with healing, but I will mull over your command to see if a solution can't be found that will be acceptable to both of us."

"That is all I ask, Mistress." He smiled. "We will, of course, compensate you for your efforts. As to your skills in healing, with your tenacity, I know Johnnie would not dare to succumb to infection."

Tenacious was I? Such a gentlemanly compliment and I took it quite to heart.

TEN

During my walk back to the tavern, I reluctantly came to the decision to house the injured Lieutenant Southerland in the kitchen storeroom. I prayed for a miracle to convince Matty that infringing on her hallowed kitchen space was in the best interests of the tavern. Then I said a second prayer that local patriots would remember it was Uncle Samuel's tavern, and not burst in and kill us all. I went directly to the kitchen, where the aroma of potato and bacon soup for the evening meal filled the air and made my stomach rumble. The three kitchen women greeted me as I entered. I could hear Matty talking in the storeroom.

"Now why can't I find that pan when I needs it? Ain't nothing ever in the place it belongs?" Standing in the storeroom doorway, I watched Matty bend down searching for something on a low shelf. "There you are," she said, reaching behind a large kettle, "thought you could hide from me, did you? Well, you wrong. I found you anyways." She straightened up, firmly gripping a small three-legged skillet, as though it had a life of its own. "Been looking for this here spider," she said, when she noticed me. "Don't know how it got behind that kettle. Truly amazes me how things gets misplaced in this kitchen; you'd think it were all just some jumble."

I looked around the kitchen at the scrubbed tables, the long-handled cooking utensils hanging neatly on the wood surround of the fireplace, the shelves along the wall with their carefully nested bowls, and baskets. Bunches of herbs—thyme, oregano, parsley, and others—hung from the exposed rafters, near to hand for cooking. Everything ordered and clean down to the swept wood floor.

"Doesn't look like much of a jumble to me, Matty," I said, as she came out of the storeroom.

She waved the cast-iron spider. "I been missing this since yesterday, and today I couldn't find my good paring knife for, well, for at least a couple of hours. Just plain irritating when you can't find what you needs."

"It is indeed, Matty, and I have the perfect solution. We'll just give your kitchen a good neatening right now."

Matty set the spider down gently on the worktable that dominated the center of the room. "What you want, Mistress?" Her eyes squinted slightly.

"Pardon?" I tried to appear as innocent as possible, but couldn't look Matty in the eye. Instead, I took off my navy cloak, hung it by the door and rolled up my sleeves to work.

"I know your favorite job ain't cleaning and neatening, so what is you up to?"

"Well. I need to make some space in the storeroom. And this seems the perfect moment because it will neaten the room for you at the same time."

"Are we getting new stores that needs room?" Her question was porous with suspicion.

"As a matter of fact, Colonel Belding is sending us two hogsheads of salted meat as well as some spices, and tea and coffee."

"Ah. And why this sudden generosity? I ain't aware any ship come upriver for the British, not since they was stopped by them cannon last Wednesday."

"No, there hasn't been one. We're going to do the colonel a favor and it's part of the payment."

Matty peered at me, knowing I was withholding something from her but uncertain if she should ask more with the kitchen maids about.

Time to bite the bullet. "We're going to take care of a young soldier who was wounded and for whom Colonel Belding feels responsible. I'm planning on putting him in the storeroom."

"My storeroom?" Matty was incredulous. "You putting a wounded British soldier in my kitchen storeroom? Now I ask you, how you expect me to make enough food to feed this army you got staying here and also give up my storeroom. No way I can do that, you know I'm short of room as is. Good Lord only gave me so much patience, Mistress Abigail, and you sorely trying it today. Now you better find another place because I ain't giving you my storeroom."

As I had thought, sacred space. "It really is the best place. It's always warm because you bank your coals overnight, and there's someone here most of the time, and it's far enough away from the sleeping quarters that his moans of pain won't keep everyone awake. I do think it's about as perfect as we can get." One look at her glowering expression and I hurried on, "Unless you have a better suggestion."

Matty thought for a long time, a frown on her face, her fingers idly following the oak grain of the worktable. Back and forth, back and forth. "How bad is he hurt?"

"Pretty badly, I gather, although I haven't seen him. The colonel will not hold us responsible should he die, which speaks to the severity of the lieutenant's wound. I think Belding wants to be able to tell Lord Southerland everything possible was done to save his son, but there seems little expectation for recovery."

"That don't sound very good, not to have hope for the boy."

"No, it doesn't," I said, praying Matty's inherent good-heartedness would overcome her common sense.

"And you sure there ain't no other place for him?"

"Not that I can think of."

"Well, let's see if we can't make room." She walked toward the storeroom to survey her peaceful fiefdom before chaos struck. Looking over her shoulder, she said, "I ain't no nurse, Mistress, so I'll need to have Miriam for a few days."

"Colonel Belding gave me funds to hire an additional woman to nurse the lieutenant. I thought I would get a camp woman from the British."

"Well then, at least get Miriam to supervise his care; she's more talented in healing than anyone I ever knowed."

Beth looked up from the pot she was stirring, "Where did Miriam learn so much about healing?"

"She's a midwife," Matty answered. "Lots of women what works here takes their complaints to her, and probably half of those what work in New Brunswick. She's good as Dr. Dillon for lots of things and only charges a fraction of what he asks."

"I thought you had to be licensed to be a midwife," Beth said.

"Her mother was a skilled midwife, and Miriam learned from her," I said. "Miriam's not licensed, so she's not able to have her own business. That's why she works here. Miriam's especially good with women's problems. She gives me a tea that makes my monthly courses easy."

"Most of what she does is using herbs and roots," said Matty. "You ain't never looked in her room?"

Beth shook her head.

"It's filled with drying plants and jars and baskets. She's got more stuff hanging from her rafters than I do," she gestured to the herbs hanging from the kitchen ceiling. "'Course, lot of the stuff she collects you wouldn't use in cooking, it may be good for you, but that don't guarantee it taste good."

I nodded in agreement.

With the help of two stable boys we set to work re-ordering the storeroom. The table which sat against the wall was cleared of jugs of Florence oil, linseed oil, and English catchup from India, wood boxes of coffee, cocoa, and the less expensive spices like Jamaican pepper and ginger. It took six of us to get the table through the doorway and out to the stable to be stored. Four casks of salted pork and beef, each weighing over 200 pounds, had rested beneath the table and were now moved into the kitchen proper. The lye-making barrel, and the butter churn, along with the candle molds, were moved to a corner of the bakery. With all of us working under Matty's careful scrutiny, it took just a little over an hour to clear enough space for a narrow bedstead. I was too busy to give the Paris letters, as I had come to think of them, more than a passing thought.

Miriam and Grace arrived, arms laden with rags and blankets just after the stable boys had placed an old straw mattress on a bed frame. "Pull the bed out from the wall a little," Miriam ordered, "so I can get to him from either side. Good. That still leaves room for my rocking chair. We can put my chest on that shelf and a lamp next to it." Grace nodded in agreement and began clearing the small table which included the locked spice cabinet.

"Mistress Abigail, where do you want the spices taken?" Grace asked.

Spices like cloves, cinnamon, nutmeg, mace, and vanilla were bought from the English, who imported them from India and the islands of the Far East. Thus, they were expensive and kept under lock and key. In many households only the mistress held the key for the spice chest; at Raritan Tavern, I shared the responsibility with Matty.

"Move it to this shelf," I said, clearing a large space on one of the waist-level shelves. "It'll be in plain sight for Southerland and we can give him the special charge of guarding it while he recovers. Make him feel useful."

A rocking chair was placed next to the table, an oil lamp lit, its glass chimney reset. Miriam placed a dark wooden box on the table. I had never seen Miriam's box before, though I knew it to be a medicine chest from having seen Doctor Dillon's. It was about a foot wide and tall, though not so deep, with a thick leather carrying strap. Miriam opened the top and folded down the front to reveal small compartments filled with a variety of bottles and containers, scissors and scalpels such as a surgeon would use. At least a million questions ran through my head about where this box had come from and what mysteries it contained, but Miriam was hurriedly making the bed from the rags she and Grace had brought. Even now we could hear moans coming from Southerland as the litter bearers neared the kitchen. My questions would wait.

Southerland cried out as he was moved onto the bed, but his eyes then closed and he seemed unconscious. His face was sickly gray. Sweat had washed rivulets through the blood and dust smeared on his face. The metallic smell of blood filled the room.

"Careful, you louts," said Lieutenant Reade, who had accompanied his friend from the surgeons' tent. The bearers ignored him, folded their stained canvas stretcher and left. Their faces betrayed no feeling, the war having already hardened their expressions to masks.

Southerland's leg was wrapped with blood-soaked rags. Two wooden splints were tied along the young man's lower limb.

"We will have to change these dressings immediately. They're filthy." Miriam had donned an old, though clean, work apron and rolled her sleeves up above her elbows. She began to untie the knots holding the rags in place. Grace placed water and clean cloths within her reach. "Lieutenant, what did the surgeons do?" she asked Reade.

"Well, they didn't. . .didn't. . .um. . .cut off his leg." Reade leaned against the door frame, in shock himself, looking from me to Miriam to Grace and then back to Southerland. Reade's face was so white I thought he would faint. Matty shoved a stool behind his knees, forcing him to sit and Beth placed a glass of sherry in his hand. He swallowed it unthinkingly and a bit of color returned to his cheeks.

I looked directly into his eyes. "Lieutenant Reade, what did the surgeons do to Johnnie's leg? We need to know."

Reade swallowed hard. "They cut down nearly to the bone to look for the bullet and shrapnel, and he screamed a lot, even though they had given him rum to drink first. Then they pulled on the leg to set the break and he fainted."

"Is the bone shattered?" Miriam asked.

"No, that's why they didn't have to cut his leg off, but they hurt him something awful digging around like that."

"The bullet must not have hit the bone," I said "That's good news, Lieutenant. Miriam and Grace will look after him now. You go wash up and have something to eat," I said, hoping to get him out of the kitchen before Miriam started her work.

"No, I have to stay with him." Reade moved to pull his stool closer to his friend but swayed against the door frame. Beth grabbed the glass from his hand a moment before he would have dropped it. She put her arm around his waist and turned him toward the door.

"Come, Alan, I'll walk you over to the taproom. There's nothing you can do for your friend that Miriam and my mother won't do and right now you're spent. We'll get John to find you a glass of that special whiskey he keeps hidden, and after you've eaten you can come back and look in on him. He'll be resting comfortably by then, you'll see." I heard her murmuring to him all the way across the courtyard, her voice only stopping when the back door closed.

"G's blood, this is an unholy mess," Miriam swore. As she was not a swearing woman, I knew her exclamation did not bode well. "This is beyond my ability, Mistress. The wound is very deep and still bleeding. You'd better send for Doctor Dillon so he can suture it. How the camp surgeon could leave anybody like this is beyond my ability to understand. It's akin to murdering the poor lad."

The wound appeared gruesome. Dark powder from the gunshot surrounded the ragged hole where the bullet had entered. The surgeon had cut deeply and sloppily into the leg in search of metal fragments and to determine the extent of bone damage. Blackened blood pooled in the wound with bits of skin and dirt, but with the unwrapping of the leg, new blood, a brilliant red, was filling the wound. My stomach heaved and I had to look away from such an unnatural sight.

"Doc Dillon is tending an ill child out beyond Somerset," Grace said. "He told me at dinner he was going, and didn't know if he would get back to town tonight."

"That's too far. Southerland will bleed to death before we get the doctor back here. Come hold this closed till I can get a needle threaded," she said to Grace. "And, Mistress, I'll need more water."

After threading a needle with fine gut, Miriam cleaned the wound, meticulously cut away the damaged tissue, tied off several small arteries, and then sewed everything back together, first stitching the muscle layer and then the skin. Grace and I followed her orders and watched fascinated as she worked. An herbal poultice to prevent infection and a clean cloth bandage and she was finished.

"Camp surgeon who did this should be hanged before he kills someone else," she said. "Not that the British are likely to take my suggestion."

"I'll need an opium draught for him when he stirs," she continued. "It is not completely safe after all the liquor the surgeons gave him, but he will be in great pain at first. I'll give him small doses throughout the night so that he'll sleep without stopping his breathing. Tomorrow, after the alcohol is out of his body, we can use some more laudanum to help him relax."

"I thought opium was a poison," Grace said.

"Only when used in larger amounts. In a weaker dilution it is most beneficial. The same can be said of many medicines which are deadly if used improperly."

"Miriam, I am without words to express my admiration and appreciation for what you have done here," I said. "I never realized being a midwife required such skills."

"Thank you, Mistress. But I am not a midwife. My mother was a very talented healer and I learned from her when I was a child. This box was hers, brought from Europe when she and my father came to the colonies."

"Well, I knew you weren't licensed, but obviously you are very knowledgeable."

"Why aren't you licensed?" Grace asked. "You'd be a lot better paid if you were a midwife than being a maid of all work."

"To be licensed you have to be apprenticed to someone already licensed, and neither my mother nor I were allowed." Miriam's expression hardened as she spoke; the sparkle of enthusiasm that had lit her eyes while she worked on the wound had fled. In the blink of an eye, Miriam became the sullen woman I had always known.

ELEVEN

I fell into an exhausted sleep and dreamt about walking the streets of Paris which, in the way of dreams, changed into New Brunswick, although Benjamin Franklin continued to saunter beside me. He pontificated about the duties and responsibilities of republican citizenship, all the while flirting outrageously. I woke feeling charmed and at peace with the world. Too soon the details of the day before filled my mind and I struggled fruitlessly to find my way back to the serene companionship of that Philadelphia Quaker.

It was Saturday, the fourth day after the gruesome murder of Mr. George Fenton Lee had been committed in my tavern. Before opening my eyes I could tell that it had snowed during the night, for nothing so quiets the horse's clopping or the wagon wheel's squeak as does that white cottony carpet. Even the normal noises of the tavern seemed subdued. Dressing quickly in my blue and white striped wool dress, white apron and matching neck scarf, I hastened to the warming kitchen and relished the first sips of coffee as they slid down my throat. Matty cut me a piece of oat bread and placed it on the iron toaster before the fire. I watched with wakening eyes as the bread turned slowly to gold and by the time it was browned on both sides, I felt almost sentient.

"Mrs. Hemple came in early, complaining," Matty said.

"A normal start to the day," I responded.

"Said she don't know how she's going to get all the laundry done with Miriam nursing Lieutenant Southerland."

"How is he?"

"Miriam said he were sleeping soundly with the laudanum she gave him. She went to get some rest herself. Guess she were up most of the night with him flailing about and her worrying he would reopen his leg. Lieutenant Reade is with him now, and Miriam wants to be fetched if he wakes."

Matty slathered butter and blackberry jam on my toast, which I took from her hand before she could put it on a plate. After the first bites, I said, "I appreciate how hard everyone worked yesterday to get Lieutenant Southerland settled, you, Grace and Miriam."

"Your daughter, too. She were worried it all be just right. Seems to me, she got some interest in that handsome young Alan Reade."

"Not an interest I care to encourage."

"You encouraging it, less you puts a stop to it."

I was not pleased Matty had noticed the infatuation between Beth and Lieutenant Reade. I still hoped I was misinterpreting what I had seen, the touching hands, the first name, the appearance of Reade on the third floor. After Matty's comments, I knew I would have to rethink my approach with Beth.

Mothering a young woman was not easy when my livelihood came from running a tavern. There have always
been young men coming through the doors, and no father to watch over and guide a growing girl. The billeting
of so many young British officers in their brass-buttoned
red jackets and tight buff pants, with their gentlemanly
manners and soft accents, greatly increased the tempta-
tion for my attractive, although naive, daughter.

"Maybe I should let the British just take over Raritan
Tavern. Then you, John, Beth and I could move out with
Uncle Samuel and live off the farm. We could forget
about war, politics, and charming young British soldiers."

"I'm not certain Master Samuel would appreciate that
arrangement. He don't want us all under his feet. Can't
you just see him tripping over us?"

I laughed at my image of Uncle Samuel, muttering
curses under his breath, as he tried to make his way
through the farmhouse kitchen filled to overflowing with
the four of us, his farmworkers, and a dog or three for
good measure.

"I doubt I'd be too welcome if I surrendered the tavern."

Matty nodded in agreement. "Not without a good fight.
Master Samuel put a lot of years building this here business."

"So have we all, Matty." I brushed the toast crumbs from
my skirt as I stood. "Well, if I can't avoid the situation by
leaving, I best have a talk with Beth. Do you have any idea
where she might be?"

"I'd try the kitchen storeroom. I has to go out there myself."

Following Matty out to the kitchen, I found Beth standing at the fireplace. Her cheeks flushed from bending
over the fire, she radiated youthful well-being. "G'morn-

ing Mother. I'm brewing tea for Alan, who's sitting with Lieutenant Southerland. Would you like some? Alan says our tea is as good as that brewed at home. Isn't that wonderful, that we could make it to his taste? I'm glad he likes it, at least it's one comfort for him, all these thousands of miles from England." Beth would have nattered on, had she not looked at me. "What's wrong, Mother?"

I paused a tad too long, trying to order my thoughts.

Her tone changed from cheerful to irritated in the space of a glance. "Now what did I do wrong?"

"I'm not sure you did anything wrong, as you put it. You and I just need to have a talk."

Beth turned her back to me as she filled the cup with tea. "I'm caring for Lieutenant Southerland. Could we wait a while to *talk*?"

"What do you mean, *talk*?" I could feel my pulse quicken even as I tried to speak calmly. Children seem to know exactly how to irritate their parents, and with amazingly few words.

She turned to face me, her face contorted by an angry frown. "When you say *talk* like that, it means you want to lecture me about something I did, something you think must change. Of course, for my own good."

"I don't think I've ever used that expression, although it is true. Why would I want something that was not for your own good?"

"I don't know, Mother. Because you like telling me what to do?"

I literally bit my tongue to stop myself from responding rashly to my daughter's insufferable comment. From experience I knew that being rude would only escalate our discussion into an argument. We would not be able to discuss Beth's relationship with Reade while fur was flying.

"That is sufficient, Elizabeth," I said firmly enough to stop her rudeness. "Our discussion can wait until you are not so out of continence with me. I do, however, need your help today. Miriam is unable to work in the laundry as she is nursing Lieutenant Southerland and Mrs. Hemple requires assistance."

"But *I* am nursing Lieutenant Southerland," said Beth.

"You do not have the necessary skills. Miriam does."

"I could learn from her."

"Indeed you could, and hopefully you will, although not today. Today you are needed in the laundry."

"I must take Alan his tea first," she said, defiance suffused with pleading.

"All right. Then you will go to the laundry," I said.

Beth did go, mumbling about how oppressed she was. She slammed the door behind her. I sighed with relief that our skirmish had not become a full battle. I wondered how often my mother felt at odds with my contretemps. I didn't recall what she had said the day I threatened to run away from home if she made me continue the detested sewing lessons with Widow Jenkins. I do know the lessons stopped and to this day I am unable to sew a straight seam.

Later that morning, my attention was caught by the sound of rapid hoofbeats stopping in front of the tavern followed by the opening of the street door. As I arrived at the front desk, a man in a black greatcoat and snow-trimmed tricorn hat was unwinding a woolen scarf from around his mouth and nose.

His indistinguishable first words ended with "Mistress Abigail," but soon the familiar smile of Bradford Jamison became visible. "A bit nippy out today. It's good to get inside."

"That was a quick trip to Philadelphia," I said, surprised to see him so soon after his hasty departure the day before.

"I never made it that far, only reached Princeton. I hope you have room for me for a night or two."

"Well, uh . . ."

"I could bunk down with the soldiers if need be. The inn I stayed at in Princeton was a horror, fleas in the blankets, and heaven only knows what the stew contained, mushy potatoes and no recognizable meat. I realize they are still rebuilding after the British ransacked the town, but it was not a pleasure to stay there and I am looking forward to a decent night's rest and some of Matty's superb meals."

I found his complaints passing strange coming from a person who made his living by traveling, fleas and no-name stews being a fair description of most accommodations. Perhaps he thought to distract me from asking about his questionable reappearance. "Although the dormitories are completely full with the British, the private room you occupied before is still available. Had we known you would be returning so soon, we would not have changed the sheets."

"Excellent, Mistress Abigail. Just excellent," he said, ignoring my barb.

"I will have your horse stabled and your saddlebags brought inside."

"Thank you. I will take the horse myself as I want the stable boy to give her a good rubdown and I prefer to handle my own bags. So you see, there is nothing more you could do to indulge me." He started to walk away, then turned, "Oh, has your uncle returned from Philadelphia with someone to claim Lee's body?"

"How did you know Uncle Samuel had gone to Philadelphia?"

"Constable Grey told me when I offered to take Lee's horse and effects."

"It's a good thing he went, considering you never got past Princeton." I wondered if I had succeeded in keeping the suspicion out of my voice.

"I would have gone all the way to Philadelphia, had I been the constable's messenger," he said. "I take my commitments quite seriously."

"I'm certain you do," I said, certain of no such thing. "No, my uncle is not back yet. As you know, it's a full day's ride each way, so I would not expect him this soon."

"Surely it would not have taken him more than a few hours to find someone from Mr. Lee's household or business who would be able to come to New Brunswick to claim the body."

"You seem most interested in this affair, Mr. Jamison."

His hands flew up as if to ward off my suspicion. "Just curious, Mistress Abigail. After all, I was the man who identified him."

He smiled most disarmingly. "If you would be so gracious as to excuse me, I really must see to my horse. I rode her rather hard from Princeton and it would be irresponsible should I not have her brushed down."

As he shut the door behind him, I wondered why he had returned to New Brunswick at a pace that would lather his horse.

I was not the least surprised that Mrs. Chandler appeared at dinner for her daily dose of gossip. She and Fanny conversed in a most animated fashion over the rabbit stew. When her dessert of apple cobbler had been served, she motioned to me.

"Mistress Abigail, if you have a moment, I would truly appreciate your ear. I have heard the most distressing news and would feel remiss not to share it with you."

Knowing I could say naught that would stop her, I nodded, but remained standing in the hope this would shorten her exposition.

"Oh, do sit down. Dinner is over. Surely your staff are able to finish the cleaning up without your supervision. Fanny," she called to the young serving maid, "bring your employer a cup of coffee. She is joining me for a while."

"I really must . . ."

"You really must hear what I have to tell you." She waited until I was seated and Fanny had brought me coffee before continuing. "You have a young daughter. Thank goodness mine are well grown and married and far from here. I should suffer so if I had to worry about a girl right now. It is truly too much to be borne, our lives being this disrupted." She sighed, pressing her hand to her breast. "But let me tell you what my sister's letter said. Such a tragedy, a real tragedy . . ."

"What did your sister write?" I asked, to shorten the lamentations.

"Well, there was a British soldier on duty in Penns Neck," she leaned toward me, resting her hand on mine, and whispered "who forced himself upon a young maiden in the village. She became with child."

I shook my head in sympathy.

"But, my dear, that is not the worst." Her eyes widened in feigned shock at the delicious horror of her story. "She thought the soldier would marry her, and take her to Mother England, where none would know of her shame. But after his company fled before Washington's troops, he marched away with them and left her."

"We have heard this story all too often," I said.

"Not this grievous story, for it does not end there. The young lady, muddleheaded if you want my opinion, became distraught and one night, after her parents were asleep, took a rope to the barn and hanged herself. She died and the unborn babe with her. She has two lives to answer for when she stands before Divine Justice," Mrs. Chandler said with righteous, unpitying indignation, her eyes raised as though she would see the Almighty through the wood ceiling beams. "I tell you this woeful tale, my dear, so you may be sufficiently prudent for your daughter's well-being. Surely a tavern must be a most dangerous place for the suitable raising of a young lady of refinement."

"Indeed, it is not without its pitfalls," I said, adding, "although I do find it preferable to being hungry and shelterless, especially in winter."

I was deprived of her reply by a booming voice that shattered the after-dinner hush, "I am seeking the owner of this fine establishment." The speaker was tall, the bass voice coming from the depths of a broad chest. He was clad in an exquisite dark gray greatcoat with a beaver tricorn of the same color. My instant impression of wealth was but confirmed when I noticed the intricate chased silver top to his walking stick.

Rising to greet him, I said, "I am Abigail Lawrence, tavernmistress of Raritan Tavern. How may I be of assistance?"

Removing his hat with a flourish, he bowed, gracefully making a leg. "Mistress Lawrence, I am indeed come to the right hostelry if so fine a lady as yourself is the manager."

This flowery speech might have gotten my back up for its condescension had I not observed the amused glint that shone from his winter-sea blue eyes. I nodded in appreciation.

"My man and I are in need of lodging for a night or so."

As I neared where they stood, I did notice the second man. His slightness and the indistinguishable blandness of his clothing made him almost invisible next to his flamboyant master.

"I have a private room that may meet your needs, if I may show it to you?"

"Robert will have a look, although I am certain it will more than exceed our simple desires."

With his curled and beribboned hair, his highly polished black boots, and the exquisite embroidery visible on his waistcoat, the visitor's desires would never be simple, of that I was sure.

"As for me, I am quite famished, my dear lady. Would it be a great imposition for your cook to find a bit of dinner for us?"

"None at all, Mr. . .uh. . ."

"Whitworth. Charles Elbridge Whitworth, at your service, Ma'am."

"Are you the novelist and writer of travel journals, Sir?"

"That I am, Mistress Tavernkeeper," he said, bowing again.

I barely refrained from responding with an absurdly inappropriate curtsy.

Again, that insouciant glint shown in his eyes, the subtle acknowledgment of a fellow games player. A look I was coming to enjoy injudiciously.

Robert approved the room for his master. After supper, Mr. Whitworth insisted he be allowed to express his profoundest appreciation for her stew directly to Matty. I don't recall ever seeing her blush so under that chocolate skin. When he left to walk about New Brunswick, the tavern seemed unnaturally silent.

TWELVE

I had resolved to take the Paris letters from Benjamin Franklin and the book Mr. Lee had been carrying to Rachel Morton. Surely she and Nathaniel would have the means to see the letters delivered into the appropriate hands. I felt greatly relieved, having finally determined how to rid myself of the evidence of my thievery, and was on the back stairs, nearing the third floor to collect the book and letters, when Grace, the head waitress, accosted me. She said that Dr. Dillon had sent a message and requested I attend him at his office. Since I was unsure of the urgency of his summons, I followed Grace downstairs and threw on my cloak, inwardly bemoaning the intrusion into my plans. I pulled on my foul-weather boots which were copied from a pair belonging to my deceased husband. They had proved far more practical than pattens, those raised metal platforms into which women place their shoes to lift their feet out of the muck.

Crossing snow-covered Albany Street and walking partway toward the river, I reached Dr. Dillon's office. The door opened before I was able to knock. Constable Grey stood in the doorway, his brow furrowed in a frown.

"G'day," I said, and heard him mutter something in response as he shut the door behind me.

He escorted me back to the doctor's private rooms, took my cloak and pointed to a wing chair near the fire where I was to sit.

"Mistress Abigail, thank you for coming promptly," Dr. Dillon said, entering the room with a tray of cups and saucers and a pot of coffee, which he set on a low table near the fire. "Would you be so good as to pour us all some refreshment while I get my notes?"

I poured for the three of us, handing the constable's coffee to him where he stood warming his hands at the fire.

"The doctor insisted you be included in this discussion, Mistress Abigail, as the murder happened at your tavern," Josiah Grey remarked, sounding annoyed.

"And because she was the one who figured out that the wine contained poison," the doctor added, shuffling his papers about on his lap as I handed him his coffee. "Very impressive hypothesis, Mistress Abigail. You were correct and I'll tell you the details in a minute." His approbation dispelled the annoyance I might have felt at my hurried departure. Dr. Dillon looked at me. "I hope you will not be discomforted at the discussion of my findings. This is not a conversation for the fainthearted."

"I appreciate your concern, Doctor. However I am not of a delicate disposition nor have I pulled my stays overly tight. And I did find the body, you will remember."

"Very well. As you had surmised, Mistress, when we examined the body in situ, George Fenton Lee did not die from being stabbed. He was already dead when the sword was thrust through his chest."

"You're certain of that?" the constable asked.

"Yes. If he had been unconscious, his heart still pumping, blood would have spurted when the sword pierced his heart. We found little blood, as you will recall."

"Could it not have been washed off after he died?"

"I don't think so. There would have been blood spattered about the room as well as more in the wound than we saw."

Constable Grey shook his head. "Why would someone stab a dead man?"

"That I can't tell you," said the physician.

"You have concluded that Mr. Lee was poisoned?" I asked.

"Yes. Lee was poisoned with cyanide. Stephen Scudder, the apothecary, and I first thought he had died of a heart stoppage, not related to the sword in his chest. Then we found salts in his stomach that were definitely cyanide. His dilated eyes, and the vomit from the chamberpot are consistent with that poison. Also, the typical bitter almond smell was most noticeable when we did the autopsy."

"How do you think the murderer would have given the cyanide to Lee?" Constable Grey asked.

"It's a salt and can easily be diluted. That we found it in his stomach means he ingested it somehow, in a liquid or possibly in food. It might have been concealed in a brandy or a toddy, or even in something medicinal like a cough syrup or tonic."

"So the wine I found hidden behind the lamp contained the cyanide?" I asked. "It didn't smell like bitter almonds. Had it been sitting for so long that the odor had dissipated?"

"No. And this was most surprising, Mistress Abigail. The wine you found contained another poison."

"What!"

Dr. Dillon nodded. "We were just as surprised. In fact, it took us some time and a great deal of arguing to agree that we had found two poisons, one in Lee's body and a completely different one in the glass you found."

"What was the second one?" I asked.

"Yew."

"From the tree?"

"Yes. The tree is poisonous, especially the black seed inside the berry, though the red berry itself contains no poison."

"Two separate poisons and a sword through the chest," I said, shaking my head. "Someone was taking no chances that Lee would die."

"I agree," said the doctor.

"So the yew was just sitting on the mantel, and you think Lee never ingested it?" I asked.

He nodded.

"This passes belief, Doctor." I said, aghast that two poisons and a sword had been used in my tavern to cause a death.

"Where would someone have obtained these poisons?" asked the constable.

The doctor rose and paced back and forth in the confined space, preparing to lecture. "Cyanide is obtained from the pits and seeds of a variety of fruit such as peaches, apples, and wild cherry. It is an old poison. The Roman Emperor Nero is said to have murdered his mother, brother, and several wives using cyanide. Today, it can be obtained from an apothecary and is used to poison rats."

"Has Mr. Scudder sold any recently?" I asked.

"He said he had not sold cyanide within the past few months, though he did sell some to Mrs. Chandler last fall to use in a warehouse after their cat died. He does not carry yew."

"Could yew be acquired in New Brunswick?" I asked.

"Scudder said many midwives have it in their pharmacopoeia, as it is known to cause abortion when administered properly. The problem is that desperate women try to administer it themselves and don't always know the correct dosage. The results are often fatal."

"So, in a large enough dose, yew is a poison?"

"Yes."

"And this would be common knowledge for a midwife?"

"That was my impression from what Mr. Scudder said. You would have to ask him for more details. I personally know of midwives who do carry yew, though I have no idea how often they use it, if they use it at all."

I recalled the many compartments of the medicine chest Miriam had opened in the kitchen storeroom. Was yew contained in one of the neatly labeled packets?

"Did you find anything else during the autopsy?" Constable Grey asked.

"No, that's all. I seem to have confused your investigation even more."

"How *is* your investigation progressing, Constable?" I asked. "Have you had any results from the men you sent out?"

"We have had a bit of luck, Mistress Abigail. It seems Mr. Lee and his companion, whoever she was, stayed the night at the King's Jester Tavern in Amboy. Joseph Coats, the tavernkeeper, said the couple arrived Saturday night and remained just the one night, informing him that they were on their way to New Brunswick the next morning.

His description exactly matches Lee and also matches the skirt and petticoat we found in the room at your tavern."

"Did Mr. Coats know where they were coming from?" I asked, pouring more coffee for all of us.

"Seems Lee was quite talkative once he had a few whiskeys and told Coats he was on a secret mission to escort 'the lady' from New York to Philadelphia. Coats didn't believe a word Lee said, so it's difficult to know if any of the story was true."

"We do know that they managed to arrive in New Brunswick, so that part was correct," I said.

"One other thing Coats said caught my man's attention. He reported that the couple had a vicious fight. The wife was screaming so loudly, a traveler in the next room complained to Coats that he thought the woman was being murdered. Coats went to investigate and got them to quiet down. But he was glad to see their backs the next morning."

"Did he know if Mrs. Lee was injured?" I asked, remembering a strangeness on the night they arrived.

"My man didn't say. I don't know if that means he didn't ask Coats or if Coats didn't know."

"It would fit with what John and I both observed when they arrived here. We thought Mrs. Lee walked awkwardly, and that would certainly be the case if she had been beaten the night before, wouldn't it, Doctor?"

"Certainly could be, Mistress Abigail. She might have been very sore and her walk would have appeared stiff. Did you see any bruising about her face?"

"No," I said, casting my mind about but coming up with naught.

"Mistress Abigail, were there any arguments or noise coming from their room Sunday night?" the constable asked.

"Not that I'm aware of, but I'll ask my servants and let you know if they heard anything."

"I would appreciate it, Mistress." Josiah Grey said. "The sooner we find this murderer the sooner I'll get a good night's rest."

A statement I agreed with most heartily.

I returned to the tavern in time to act as hostess for a calm and blessedly uneventful supper. Later that evening, the tavern began to fill, a common occurrence when the nights were bitter cold and the warmth of friends and tavern highly prized. In addition to the British officers living at Raritan Tavern, officers from the disparate battalions and brigades quartered about New Brunswick congregated. The stable boys had spent most of the afternoon chopping wood and we were well supplied. John was filling beer steins and refilling glasses with port at record speed, a rate that should have set off a tocsin in my head. I was in the kitchen refreshing the spices for mulled wine when I heard the shouting.

"You cheated!"

"I did not. You're a sore loser, just like all you damn Hessians, yelling foul when you don't get what you want."

"Shut your mouth, you Newgate nightingale!"

"Watch what you say, you Jager nickum!"

Unable to reach each other across the broad table, the two antagonists had grabbed whatever ammunition was to hand. The redcoated officer picked up the heavy oak chair on which he had been sitting, raising it over his head. The Hessian grabbed the fireplace pike, and lunged, ripping open the redcoat's arm. The chair the redcoat held over his head landed on the Hessian, break-ing his arm, and then smashing the table in two pieces.

Friends of both combatants rose in aid, and we would have had a melee without the prompt intervention of Constable Grey, Dr. Dillon, our new guest Mr. Whitworth, Captain Phillips, and John. Phillips hustled the redcoated soldier away immediately, threatening dire consequences should any of his men continue the fracas. In turn, the constable rushed the German mercenary out the door, heading for the Hessian Jager encampment and the com-pany doctor, to set the man's arm.

"Excitable group tonight, Mistress Lawrence," Mr. Whit-worth said, approaching the bar once order had been re-stored.

"Thank you for your assistance," I said. "You saved a life or two. The only fatalities seem to have been my furni-ture."

"I am bound by oath to rescue damsels in distress. But it is thirsty work," he said holding up his empty glass. "If, that is, you trust my degree of intoxication."

"Your agility a few moments ago would suggest you had consumed naught but water. Let me recommend a brandy to mellow the evening."

He sipped from the glass I placed in front of him. His eyebrows raised in surprise.

"Nectar of the gods."

"Appropriate for a true knight after an act of fearless bravery."

The glint I had come to enjoy was back in Whitworth's fathomless eyes, though only for a moment, as his attention was drawn to his servant, who had just entered from the street. Robert was bundled against the fierce cold. He nod-ded once to Mr. Whitworth, then scurried up the stairs.

"Fair lady, another tot of this liquid fire to warm the chilblains of my undeserving man, and I shall bid you a fond good night."

He was on the stairs by the time I could mutter, "Good night, sweet prince."

THIRTEEN

Sunday morning, Beth and I walked out the back of Raritan Tavern and two blocks along Nielson Street to attend a special Presbyterian service being held at the First Reform Church. Our usual church was currently unavailable, as it was filled with billeted British soldiers. I had been raised in a Presbyterian household and my father had been a minister. However, the passion of his life was education. He had looked upon his appointment to Princeton College as a professor of philosophy and logic as though God had personally led him into the promised land flowing with milk and honey, or in this case, ideas and intellectual discussion. Our house in Princeton was perpetually filled with college men come to borrow books and to debate. In turn, my mother attempted to fill the ever-empty stomachs of the many young scholars. The continuing horde was one reason she had hired Matty to cook for us after the Quaker community in Princeton had bought Matty's freedom, and then John's a few years later.

Although I had been raised a Presbyterian, it was within the Quaker community that I had made my spiritual home after being educated at the Quaker school, Mistress Chapin's. Both boys and girls were welcome at Mistress Chapin's, for Quakers hold that all men and women had God's light within them and that God speaks directly and quietly to each of us. They are against slavery, believing that if people demand liberty for themselves, they must then see that liberty extended to all others. Even as a child, I could see no reason why I should be born free while Matty and John were born slaves. In Quaker meeting I found support for my belief.

However, the Quaker prohibition on taking a life proved problematic for me. I believed in the value of human life as God-given, but I had difficulty reconciling that prohibition when there was an army camped literally on my doorstep, with soldiers who killed my friends and neighbors. I fervently hoped I would never have to make a decision about killing someone. Even with a murder occurring in my tavern, I had not been called on to respond in kind, and that was certainly a relief.

I did not regularly attend Sunday services. New Jersey, thankfully, had no laws such as those of Virginia requiring church attendance. But this week had tried my soul and today I wanted to be part of the community of worship. I had sought the comfort of the Presbyterian service as there was no Quaker meeting in New Brunswick. Also, I loved singing the hymns, a very non-Quaker behavior.

As I descended the church steps at the conclusion of the service, Mrs. Amariah Chandler pranced up to me, bedecked in a gold wool gown, a wide hoop revealing the heavily embroidered white on ivory petticoat to utmost advantage.

"My dear Mistress Abigail," she said. "You have no idea how thrilled, simply thrilled, I was to hear that Charles Elbridge Whitworth is staying with you. Imagine someone of his literary stature coming to our humble town. I am almost breathless with anticipation of the wondrous account of New Brunswick he will write for his *Traveler's Journal*. Or perhaps, he will remain here to compose another of his thrilling novels? Surely there are some charming and comely young ladies whom he could use as models for his next heroine. And he has so many choices among the handsome young British officers for his next hero." She accentuated each comment with great wavings of her leather-gloved hands until I thought she should fly away in her enthusiasm.

"You are planning to have a reading, are you not?" she asked. "Such a glorious opportunity. I can't wait to write my friends in Philadelphia and Boston. They always say we are so backward here in New Jersey and now they will be most envious, I can assure you. When will he be able to address us?"

"Mr. Whitworth has said nothing to me about a program, Mrs. Chandler."

"But surely you asked him." She paused, trying out several expressions of disbelief before settling on one of mild condescension. "You do know that Charles Elbridge Whitworth is an internationally renowned author, do you not, Mistress Abigail? It is rather akin to having Shakespeare in one's humble home."

I could not refrain from smiling at the comparison.

"I am familiar with Mr. Whitworth's work and I have enjoyed his essays about his travels through the colonies. In fact, Beth read one of his novels recently."

"You allow your daughter to read his novels? I am scandalized, Mistress. I had not thought such passion appropriate to so tender a mind. Why there is even, even . . ."

"Kissing, even kissing. But that is all Mr. Whitworth describes and surely Beth knows that men and women kiss. To answer your original question, I have not spoken to Mr. Whitworth about a reading. I generally do not wish to impose on my guests."

"But he is renowned."

"So are General Howe, and General Washington, and Dr. Franklin, all of whom have dined or stayed at Raritan Tavern."

"Well, we are on the major road between New York and Philadelphia."

"And I have found even notables have to eat and sleep," I said. "However, Mrs. Chandler, I feel it is my duty to give them the privacy and civility they seek, unless they indicate otherwise."

"I wouldn't want to be thought uncivilized, you understand," she said. "Oh dear, what shall I do? I had so hoped to tell my friends I had heard him."

"When I next see him, I will mention that one of our leading citizens has asked to speak to him about a reading and see how he responds."

"Yes, yes. Thank you, Mistress Abigail. Thank you so very much," Mrs. Chandler said, giving me a small, queenly wave as she left the church grounds.

Sunday was often a quiet day at the tavern. We served dinner to far fewer of our usual diners, as the residents of New Brunswick who were with us during the week generally ate with family or friends on Sunday. We did feed the British officers and any travelers who were staying at the tavern. After the work of dinner was completed, I sent a message to Rachel asking if she was free for a visit. I then headed into the warming kitchen while I awaited her reply.

Beth and John were sitting side by side on a bench, reading an old newspaper spread out on the table in front of them, their heads almost touching. Beth was teaching John to read. So intent were they on their work that they both jumped when I greeted them.

"Oh, Mother, this is so baffling. Every week, there are notices in the *Gazette* from employers who want the return of their runaway female servants." Beth pointed to a small section at the bottom of the page. "Why would a woman run away, and if she did, why would her employer want her back? She was obviously unhappy or she would not have run away, and then why would she want to go back if she was unhappy?"

"They're probably indentured. The employer wants them returned so he doesn't lose his investment," I said.

"You mean these women were thieves?" Beth's eyes widened in surprise.

"Not exactly. If a young woman wants to come here from somewhere in Europe but doesn't have the money for the ocean voyage, she can contract her services in exchange for her transportation. The employer is supposed to train her so she can be self-supporting and provide her with clothes when she has completed the contract. She owes the person who paid her transportation four to seven years of work or she breaks their agreement. If she runs away, she's stealing from the employer the years she agreed to work as a servant, or a cook, or a seamstress."

"It sounds like a fair bargain. So why would she run away?"

"Masters ain't always nice to their help," said John, slowly shaking his head.

"But these women aren't slaves like you and Matty were, are they?"

"You're right. Slaves ain't never free, except somebody buys them and then frees them like the Quakers did for Matty and me. But indentured servants can also be treated cruel if they gets a mean master. A few people is just plain bad, Beth. And they use any excuse to hurt others. There is times I wonders if some people is human at all. Maybe they is part devil, the way they acts. Maybe it makes them feel powerful. Seven years with a master like that can seem an awful long time. The ones that is treated well don't get their names in this here paper."

"John, do you know any indentured servants?" Beth asked.

"Course, and so do you."

"I do?"

"Mrs. Hemple, who washes the clothes, was indentured. I think her husband bought out her contract just before they was married. And Miriam, . . ."

"Miriam Ilon? Our Miriam?"

John nodded. "She were indentured to somebody in Philadelphia when she were real young. She don't talk about it much. I think she had a bad time. And Amos Warren, the blacksmith. He were indentured long time ago to a smith in Amboy. They're good friends to this day."

There was a brief knock at the back door and my friend, Rachel Morton, entered.

"Seemed silly to send Whit back with the message that I was free when I could tell you myself," she said, pulling off her black cloak and hanging it on an available hook.

"Oh, I am so glad to see you," I said, taking her cloak down from where she had just hung it and giving it back to her. She gave me a puzzled look, but took the garment. "You might need it . . . ah . . . I thought we could have coffee up in my room so we don't disturb John and Beth."

"Abigail, what's wrong? What's happened?" Rachel asked as we reached the landing on the second floor.

"Wrong? Nothing. Really . . ."

"Well, you're acting queerly."

"I'll tell you in a minute, Rachel, as soon as we get to my room."

When we reached the third floor, I hurried down the hallway to my room. Setting the cup on the floor, I reached into my pocket for the key. I had been extra careful to keep the door locked since I had taken possession of Lee's account book and the Paris letters. While I was fumbling with my skirts, Rachel depressed the door latch and the door opened. I stopped breathing, my mind scampering through memories of what I had done that morning. Could I have forgotten to lock the door on my way to church? I didn't think I had, but I preferred that explanation to the alternative.

"Abigail, what is going on?" Rachel asked.

"Just a minute, I'll explain. Come in, and shut the door."

Rachel picked up my coffee, entered my bedroom, set both cups down on a trunk, and closed the door. She watched me as I moved my rocking chair, and then opened the door to my secret passage.

I reached for my blue pocket, which was hanging on its nail, and could tell immediately by its lightness that something was missing. I turned back toward Rachel, pocket in hand. "I've been robbed."

FOURTEEN

I sat dejectedly on my rocking chair, my shoulders slumped, my hand still holding my blue pocket. "I think I just lost the war," I said to Rachel.

"Perhaps you could start a bit further back in the story so I could appreciate your misery, as well as your startling proclamation," Rachel said, gently handing the coffee to me.

"As you know, George Fenton Lee, the wealthy owner of a fleet of ships that ply the Atlantic and Caribbean, and a man of uncertain reputation, was murdered here last Tuesday night. He was a widower, so the person who accompanied him was not his wife, although they had been traveling together and had stayed at the King's Jester Tavern in Amboy the previous night. Mr. Lee had told Mr. Coats, the tavernkeeper, that he was on a secret mission. However, that is questionable as he was stewed at the time. Apparently three different people wanted him dead, because three different methods of killing him were used."

"That's not possible!"

A faint smile crept to my face. "Two poisons and a sword through his chest that pinned him to the floor. He was most thoroughly dead when I found him."

"Two poisons weren't enough? They needed a sword also?" Rachel said. "This sounds more akin to one of those novels Mrs. Chandler likes to read than something that would happen in New Brunswick. Do you know whose sword it was?"

"The sword belonged to some officer who Captain Phillips said had nothing to do with the murder," I answered, secretly enjoying that Rachel was enthralled with my implausible story. For once, I had a tale to rival Uncle Samuel's.

"Don't you think Phillips would lie to protect his man? He'd probably give him a medal for killing a colonist."

"Dr. Dillon said that Lee was killed by poisoning, not with the sword, though I still wonder if there isn't some connection between the sword and the actual murder. Besides, running a corpse through with a sword is bizarre and I am curious why someone would do that."

"Have you any idea who could have poisoned him?"

I was silent for a long time. "I suspect someone who lives here had access to one of the poisons, but until I'm sure that person knew Lee and had reason to kill him, I'll bite my tongue."

"And what if this despicable person poisons you because you know all this?"

As I raised my hand to brush away her suggestion, I realized I was still clutching my pocket. While it felt lighter than it had been, it was not completely empty. I moved to the bed where Rachel was sitting and turned the blue pocket on end. Out fell the account book, a handkerchief of mine, the nub of a pencil, and an earring. The packet of letters from Paris was gone.

I sighed, my moment of hope ephemeral as a rainbow.

"Let me tell you about the letters." I described how I had found the letters in the saddlebags of Mr. Lee's horse, which had been wandering about on the road to Princeton and Philadelphia. And how I had sought to keep the letters from Captain Phillips and had hidden them under the eaves. Then I explained that the letters were addressed to John Hancock and George Washington and that I had read the unsealed letter from Benjamin Franklin.

"How could I have been so foolish, Rachel? Truly, I meant to save whatever they were from Phillips, but I had no idea of their import. Now they're stolen and I don't know who might have taken them."

"Had you not taken them, the British would have had them on Thursday. At least you delayed that for a couple of days. It is my impression that messages of such importance are usually sent with more than one courier anyway, in order to guarantee at least one set reaches its destination."

"But what damage will these letters do once they are in British hands?"

"We can't really predict the effects as you didn't read all the letters." From her arch expression I could tell she would have read them, sealed or not. "I doubt the war is lost because of their theft. I think most important messages are written in some sort of code, anyway."

"Even if they were sent with a trusted messenger?"

Rachel shrugged. "Even trusted messengers can be ambushed, Abigail."

"And why would a messenger from Paris take a ship that landed in New York or in Amboy, British controlled ports? Why not take a ship directly to Philadelphia? Wouldn't that be safer?" I asked.

"I would think so. Could it not have been blown off course?"

"Lee told Mr. Coats, the tavernmaster in Amboy, that he had met the lady in New York. He wouldn't know to meet her there if the ship had been blown off course."

"You're right."

I rose from the bed and headed to the window, staring out. Over the rooftops of the nearby buildings, I could see the Raritan River, empty of British sloops as it had been since they were fired upon five days earlier, the day of Mr. Lee's murder. "We don't know anything about Mrs. Lee, except that Lee wasn't her real name. Maybe she was carrying the letters from Paris, but for some reason couldn't leave from France. Perhaps the only ship she could get left from England, and then, of course, it would need to land at a British port."

Rachel continued my hypothetical scenario. "The mysterious woman lands in New York and is met by Lee who is to escort her. To where? Philadelphia?"

I nodded.

"They come as far as New Brunswick, the last town on their route controlled by the British, and then Lee is murdered."

"The British must know about the letters and they decided to kill Lee to get them," I said. "And somehow, Mrs. Lee escapes on horseback with the letters heading for Philadelphia and taking Lee's horse to use when hers tires."

"And we would have won the war if she had thought to put the letters in her own saddlebags, rather than in Lee's," Rachel said.

I had been pacing up and down my small room, feeling more agitated as our conversation progressed.

"Abigail, please sit down. You've figured out that Lee must have been killed by the British. Now all you have to do is determine which of the officers did the deed and turn him over to Constable Grey. Or just tell the constable what you think happened and let him figure out which officer is guilty."

"I'm not so sure, Rachel. I can't imagine why a British officer would poison Lee. If they thought Lee had the Paris papers, wouldn't they just arrest him and hang him for treason? Make a lesson to all the rebels in New Jersey. Or if they wanted him dead for some reason, why use poison? It seems very unmanly to me. I can imagine they would run him through with the sword if Lee had put up a fight. But no one heard anything that night that would indicate a fracas."

"Would one of the redcoats tell you if he had heard something?"

"I doubt it."

"I think you're making this more complicated than need be, Abigail."

"Probably so," I said, fingering the items that had fallen out when I emptied my pocket on the bed. I picked up Lee's account book, turning it over in my hand.

"What's that?"

"The robber left Lee's account book for me to decipher."

"Decipher?"

"It's written in a code. It would have been lovely retribution to have the British become addlepated over it. The thief must have known it had nothing to do with the murder or he would have taken it also."

"I'm sure you will figure out Lee's code. You're usually quite astute at solving puzzles. No one can work those horrors Amos Warren makes better than you."

"I only glanced at it briefly. I'll wager we could decipher it together."

Rachel took the book from my hand, a frown developing as she read page after page. Needing to do something so as not to fidget, I went downstairs to refill our coffee mugs. Rachel drank half of the second cup before closing the book.

"I agree this is an account ledger of some sort and with Lee's name on the cover page it would seem to have belonged to him. Some entries are clear, lists of goods by the ship that transported them. It includes the price paid at the port of departure and then the price Lee received for the goods when he sold them. He certainly made a good profit. It's the other entries that are puzzling. As you said, they do have a regular pattern, and some of it is clear."

"It reminds me of something I have seen before, Rachel. A voting list, no, that's not right." I shook my head in frustration. "Some kind of list . . ."

"It begins with names," she said, reopening the book. "Names, and then some abbreviated information."

"Yes," I agreed, sitting on the bed next to her and looking at the page she held open.

"And these abbreviations are what you thought were code."

I nodded.

"How did Lee make his living?"

"Bradford Jamison said Lee was a shipping merchant involved with transporting indentured servants and, as you can see in the ledger, other kinds of goods." I could feel the solution to this puzzle just outside my grasp. If it would come just a bit closer. "I've got it. This reminds me of a ledger I saw on a farm in Pennsylvania, a list of the owner's slaves, their ages and monetary worth. Look at the pattern."

23 August, 1746, Johan Schmidt, m.s.24.lab.53.
Peter Cullen, Phila. 430.

23 August, 1746, Gustav Hindler, m.s.22.far.47.
Charles Boyle, Balt. 400.

"First there's a date, next a name, and then probably the sex of the individual." I pointed with my finger.

"Schmidt, then Cullen, though only Schmidt has a sex, male," Rachel said. "What does that make of Cullen?"

I ignored her last comment. "I think the two lines go together. See how the second name of each entry is indented."

"All right," Rachel said, following my finger. "Then comes Phila., which is usually the abbreviation for Philadelphia. Balt. for Baltimore?"

I nodded my agreement. "So we have Schmidt, male, then probably *s* is for single. Could the second name be the buyer of the servant's contract and where he lives? Might the number be the price that was paid for the contract?"

We continued decoding the book until we had hypothesized that the first entry of each pair was the date the person's contract was acquired, then the name, sex, marital status, age, and an occupation such as *lab.*, meaning laborer, while *far.* signified farmer. The last number may have represented the monies spent to bring the person across the Atlantic. If we were guessing correctly, the profit Lee made from each individual was substantial and when you took into account the many years recorded in this book, the amount was overwhelming.

"A wealthy merchant may have been an understatement," Rachel said. "The fortune Lee amassed must be staggering."

"If you and I could just go sailing the seven seas, we too could make a fortune. I could stop worrying about the cost of replacing tables broken by drunken soldiers and you could dress in something other than black."

"And not be acknowledged as eccentric and odd? How would I maintain my reputation?" My friend gave me a wink.

Sunday night was the slowest night of the week. Grace Plough, the head waitress, and I spent most of the evening sitting behind the bar, catching up on the week's gossip. She was knitting a wool scarf in stripes of red, white and blue yarn. The British officers assumed it was in honor of the Union Jack, although Grace told me a new patriot flag was being designed in Philadelphia using the same colors. I sat working on the Traveler's Bane puzzle. I had gotten no further in solving it. It required a certain degree of concentration to figure out one of Amos Warren's puzzles and my mind was occupied elsewhere.

Charles Whitworth sat by the fire drinking Madeira and writing at a small round table. Actually, he spent more time staring into the fire and sharpening his quill than putting ink on paper. Finishing his wine in one swallow, he approached the bar, glass in hand.

"I fear fair Calliope has deserted me tonight, Mistress Abigail," he said.

"Surely not, Sir Author. The muse of heroic poetry must be about somewhere. One moment, let me look." I reached under the shelf for the bottle of my finest whiskey, the Bushmills Uncle Samuel hoarded for his own use. Turning my back, I poured a goodly amount into a clean glass.

"Let us see if a toast to the fair muse with this liquid gold will not entice her hence," I said, giving the glass to Mr. Whitworth.

He eyed the golden liquor with interest, sniffed at it once, then again, his eyebrows raising in surprise. He took a small sip and a look of astonishment came over his face. "Fairest Mistress Tavernkeeper, you overwhelm me. How could you possibly have a bottle of the finest Irish *aqua vitae* to hand?"

"You recognize it, Sir Author?" I asked.

"Of course, though I have not had its inestimable fragrance on my tongue for, well, for at least an eon. You are most truly a sorceress, Mistress, to possess the epitome of civilization, a bottle of Bushmills, in the midst of this war's blight and privation."

I bobbed a small curtsy. "Actually, it is my uncle's personal bottle, but he would be loath to see a good man separated from his muse."

"My undying appreciation to your Uncle . . .ah . . ."

"Samuel."

Whitworth raised his glass for a toast. "To the elegance of Uncle Samuel's drink and to the generosity of his niece." He took another drink of the whiskey.

"I would be most pleased to buy you a glass of this glorious delight, Mistress, should it please your fancy."

"Thank you, Mr. Whitworth . . ."

"Charles."

"Charles." I repeated. "I am not an enthusiast of malt whiskey."

"Something else, then. If you would join me by the fire, I am certain you could charm my muse to reappear." His eyes challenged me to accept.

"Perhaps a bit of bourbon for me," I said answering the challenge. "Have you tried any of our colonial whiskey?" I poured myself a glass and joined Charles at the table by the fire, taking the bottle of Bushmills along.

"Yes, gentle lady, I have."

"Abigail," I said.

"Fairest Abigail," he said clinking glasses with me. "Yes, I have tasted many of the local whiskeys on my travels. Some of them are quite promising, which is not surprising considering all the Scots and Irish who are settling in the colonies. I find bourbon an interesting taste with that hint of burnt oak, but there is nothing here yet to compare with a real Irish whiskey."

"I must confess, Charles," I said, pouring another generous portion into his glass, "I have a request I am loath to burden you with, and I am using this incomparable bottle as a bribe."

"Ask your heart's delight, fairest of the fair, and I shall count it as but a sign of your true affection. Certainly not as bribery."

"One of our town's most memorable citizens has discovered your presence and seeks to approach you about a reading of your works. I had thought to protect you from such importuning, but she is most insistent and will pester you herself should I not broach the matter."

"Fear not. I am accustomed to memorable leading citizens, as you so aptly call them. After all, they do buy my books and put pence in my pockets. I would gladly perform," he raised his hand in a cautionary gesture, "but only if you will promise to attend. Without your presence, a reading would be pleasureless."

We set the date for the next Sunday in the afternoon and spent the remainder of the time talking about books such as *Tom Jones* by Henry Fielding and Lady Mary Wortley Montagu's *Letters Written during Her Travels in Europe,*

Asia, and Africa. It was a challenging and informative discussion for me as Charles had met both of the authors, though he claimed modestly to know neither of them well. There are advantages to living an educated and privileged life in England that cannot yet be equaled in the colony of New Jersey.

FIFTEEN

Dinner on Tuesday was finished by 2:30 P.M., an excellent meal of broiled beef and browned potatoes, with carrot and onion pudding. Matty had made lemon cheesecake that was so popular we were forced to limit each guest to two servings. The postprandial cleaning was well under Grace and Fanny's control and I had just closed the strongbox with the dinner monies when I heard shouting outside the warming kitchen door.

"Matty. Abigail. Someone come rescue this old man from the disgrace of his infirmities." Soon knocking commenced and then more shouting. I flew to open the door and was confronted with the wet nose of a heavily breathing horse, its front feet on the top step while its rider reached his rifle butt for another round of noisemaking. Uncle Samuel had returned. Seeing me, he smiled broadly and backed his horse off the steps.

"My darling niece, how winsome you look, except for that frown on your lovely countenance."

"And how would you look were you to find a horse about to charge into your kitchen?" I asked. "You teach your horse bad manners, Uncle." But I was delighted to find him back from his travels, uninjured, undaunted, and thoroughly unchanged.

"Now, Abigail, you know Horatio is the most well-mannered of beasts, a refined gentleman of the equine family."

"I don't know that. He eats my pansies in the summer and my apples in the fall, to say nothing of terrorizing the stable boys."

"But has he ever given you, yourself, a moment of dismay?" Before I could frame my retort, he continued, "You see, he has a taste for the finer things in life. Now dear, if you would just call John, I am grieved to request assistance, but I am stuck fast to this saddle, having ridden farther than these ancient bones can tolerate."

"John is at the stable, Uncle, as you probably saw when you and Horatio trotted past on your way to greet me." Uncle Samuel shamelessly waved and gave greeting to the soldiers, maids and stable boys who crowded the courtyard to watch his noddy-headed behavior.

Shaking my head in amused disgust, I said, "I will see to preparing a liniment for your weary bones."

"Thank you, my dearest. A large brandy should do nicely. Forget that smelly stuff you and Matty concoct to torture discomforted men." My uncle headed toward the stable, still waving and looking not the least bit tired.

I poured Uncle Samuel a large brandy at the bar and returned to the warming kitchen where I found him dismounted, though still cloaked, giving Matty one of his bear hugs and demanding to know where she had hidden his cheesecake. "You did save me some, did you not?"

"Now how I to know you coming home today, Master Samuel?"

"You always know these things, some sixth sense you inherited from your ancestors."

Samuel was rooting around in the pantry as he spoke.

"Be kind of warm if I kept it in there," Matty teased.

"Oh, faithless servant, to make me hunt for my own cheesecake." Uncle Samuel headed down to the cold cellar, emerging triumphantly, although a bit stiffly, a few moments later. "She thought she could hide this from me, Abigail, but I am much too clever for her."

Matty reached for the cake to cut him a piece, I handed him the brandy and removed his cloak.

"A true welcome. Cheesecake, brandy, and the company of my two favorite ladies."

"Three," a lighter voice announced and with a flurry of skirts Beth ran to greet her favorite relative.

"Three," Uncle Samuel agreed. "Come join me, Beth, and tell me all that has transpired since I left." They sat at the side table while Matty served him the prized piece of cake.

"Oh, Uncle, one of Alan's friends was shot in the leg and he is staying in the kitchen storeroom. Miriam is teaching me to nurse and she's very good." Beth explained the details of Lieutenant Southerland's injury at length. Samuel asked an occasional question of my pretty daughter but had ample time to finish several pieces of cake and to wave his empty brandy glass at me as the story unfolded.

"And now you are learning the healing arts, a most womanly and valued skill, Beth," Samuel said, taking her hand and folding it in his own. "I wonder if I might beg of you a small favor that would take you away from your nursing for a short time? I need to speak to Constable Grey, but am content to sit here and rest my weary old bones. Would you go to his office and ask him to join me here? Perhaps he would be persuaded by a piece of cheesecake."

"Of course, Uncle. I would gladly fetch the constable." Beth took her cloak from its peg and departed through the warming kitchen door.

I handed Samuel his refilled brandy glass. "Much more of this and you'll not be feeling anything, Uncle."

"I truly am stiff all over, Abigail."

"So I noticed as you bounded down the stairs in search of cheesecake."

"Heartless woman," Samuel said, but the laughter and the gentle voice he had used with Beth had gone from his voice. "This soldier was wounded while foraging among our neighbor's cattle?"

"So I assume, Uncle, though I don't know exactly where the ambush occurred. Three British soldiers were killed from the three hundred that went out."

"And you were ordered to tend this wounded soldier?"

I nodded. "Colonel Belding wanted him cared for here. He had little hope the boy would survive and felt an obligation to the lad's family. I did not think nay-saying the colonel would be politic so soon after our murder."

"You are probably right in that. How does the boy?"

"Well, so far. He is awake most of the time now and seems in good spirits. He enjoys all the attention he receives in the kitchen. There's no sign of a spreading infection, which Miriam says is an encouraging sign."

Leaning over, I lowered my voice, "When I went to British Headquarters to speak with Colonel Belding, I overheard a conversation between Captain Phillips and the colonel. I gather they had known George Fenton Lee and had sent someone to New York for further information about him."

"How interesting," Samuel said. "That fits with what I discovered." Samuel rose, stretched, and poured himself a cup of coffee. "I didn't anticipate Beth would become so interested in these young officers. I still think of her as a child. She's only . . . what . . . fifteen? Do you think it is a good idea for her to remain here? She could come out to the farm with me, at least for a while."

"It has taken me by surprise also. But so far her romance seems to be a young girl's enthusiasm, nothing more. Her friends are all in town and I think she would feel put upon if I moved her to the farm."

"If you change your mind, she is welcome." Samuel pensively took a sip of his coffee. "You are welcome too, Abigail. When I left you as tavernkeeper, I never expected that you would have to cope with thousands of British soldiers wintering in New Brunswick. You have a young daughter to protect above all, and this may not be the best place for either of you, not with a houseful of redcoats, to say nothing of a murder and the attention that has brought to you."

"Attention to the tavern, not to me directly, although I do feel a need to help hasten the resoluton of the murder, lest it give Captain Phillips cause to take over the tavern completely. However, I would feel even more vulnerable at the farm with only a few servants to keep marauding forces at bay. Whatever happens here is quite public and witnessed by individuals of various persuasions, and some of no persuasion at all."

"As you strive to appear."

"One of us has to give the appearance of being neutral or we will lose Raritan Tavern. Your patriotism is sufficient for the whole family, Uncle."

"Indeed, if one of us is to be hanged for spying as Nathan Hale was in New York, I would prefer it be my scrawny neck that be stretched than yours."

"Nobody in this family will be hanged, if I have anything to do with it," I said. "We are not the stuff of which heroes are made. I wish only to find out who murdered Lee and get on with keeping both a tavern and an uncle with good reputations."

Constable Josiah Grey arrived and, after a facetious argument over ownership of the remaining cheesecake, settled with his portion and a cup of coffee. "You are home promptly, Samuel. I hope you were successful in your quest."

"Indeed, Josiah, I was able to find out much. It does seem that our body is that of George Fenton Lee. He was expected in Philadelphia on last Wednesday night and has not returned. His butler and his business manager gave a physical description that match our corpse. Someone, probably Obediah Fitch, the business manager, will be along soon to claim the body and possessions."

"Which of Lee's family did you meet?" I asked.

"There is no real family. Bradford Jamison was correct that Mrs. Lee had died a number of years ago and there are no legitimate heirs."

"Legitimate?" asked the constable.

"Lee had a reputation for fathering a number of children on the wrong side of the sheets, although there were no children from his marriage, which apparently, was not very happy. Mrs. Lee came from a wealthy, landed family who almost disowned her when she married someone so far below her class. He used her name and social influence to bolster his fledgling shipping business, and quite successfully, I might add. The relationship between them had mortified until they had even stopped speaking to each other. And then she died, under rather suspicious circumstances."

"What did the inquiry determine?" Josiah leaned forward in his chair, intent on Samuel's story.

"There was no inquiry, Josiah. Whatever happened to Mrs. Lee was a secret interred with her," Uncle Samuel replied.

"There were no servants, a lady's maid, or someone loyal to her?" I asked.

"Lee sold the slaves Mrs. Lee brought with her as part of her dower. Then he let go her servants, including her personal maid, replacing them with servants loyal to him."

"That alone would sicken a marriage, I would think. Women can become very close to their maids."

"Mr. Lee seemed not to have cared what his wife, or anyone else, thought of his actions. He had a reputation for being a successful businessman, but that is all, there was no mention of kindness or generosity from any with whom I spoke. In fact, the opposite, for he was said to be shrewd, ruthless, if not an outright thief. One person described him as 'willing to sell his mother to the devil for a guinea.'" Uncle Samuel spoke solemnly and, I thought, portentously.

"Marriage to someone like that must have been a torture." A chill passed through me at the thought of what some women endure from those who have vowed to love and protect them. My husband, Jared, had been the exact opposite: a truly loving and protecting partner and as close to perfect as I am likely to find in this life.

Samuel nodded. "Lee had another merciless way of taunting his barren wife. He kept for himself the contracts of the most comely indentured servants he transported. These nubile young women were forced to work out their seven years in his home and at least three gave birth to his get. Then he would add years onto their contract for the time they were with child or nursing."

"It sounds like Mrs. Lee would have had good cause to murder him," I said. "And perhaps a few of his indentured servants were similarly motivated."

Further discussion of Lee's depravity was interrupted by the pounding of boots in the hallway. The door was flung open as Captain Phillips and two other officers hastened into the kitchen. The angle of his chin alone, stiffly raised and jutting out, warned us of his temper.

"You have done it again, Sir," he said, directing his stare at the constable.

Josiah Grey rose slowly to his feet and faced the infuriated officer. Josiah appeared more puzzled than alarmed. "What concerns you, Captain?"

"You are again withholding information from me concerning this murder. Your informant returns from Philadelphia and you have not the courtesy to call upon me, to notify me that I might share the evidence he brings. I find this very suspicious. How long have you been here, Mr. Holt? And why was I not told of this meeting?"

"It's not exactly a meeting, Sir," responded Samuel, "more, a repast with cheesecake. It's too bad you gentlemen didn't come a few minutes earlier before we ate it all; it was quite remarkable."

"Don't try those colonial manners on me, Sir."

"Someone here needs to have some, Captain," Uncle Samuel said.

The captain's face turned the color of his uniform, but he would not be deterred from his purpose. "I think it will be necessary for you to accompany me to headquarters, Mr. Holt."

"I'm quite fatigued from my journey, old man that I am," Uncle Samuel said. "I would be honored to inform you of my findings on the morrow after I have rested."

"Taking your infirmity into account, it would be easier for you to talk with us now rather than having to return from your farm tomorrow. I must insist, Sir, that you accompany us now."

"Come, Samuel," the constable said. "You can lean on me and hobble down the street. I will accompany you, Captain. It will save Samuel having to retell his story to me."

"Thank you for the cheesecake, Abigail. I shall return to fetch my horse before I leave for the farm," Samuel gave me a kiss on my cheek.

"I'm coming also," I said.

"I think not, Mistress," Captain Phillips said. "This is not a matter for ladies."

"But certainly it is a matter for a tavernmistress who found the corpse in one of her bedrooms."

"No. It is not." Phillips and his two guardsmen surrounded Samuel and Josiah and headed out the door.

This did not bode well for Uncle Samuel or for my continued residence at Raritan Tavern.

Sixteen

I was angry and hissing like a penned goose. How dare Captain Phillips think it appropriate to exclude me from his discussion? How like him to think of me as a supernumerary to be ignored when the choice scenes are being played out. Would I not add constructively to his discussion? Would I not have a thought or two that would further the investigation? I paced up and down the kitchen pondering these thoughts.

"You about to wear a furrow in that floorboard, Mistress," Matty said after watching me for several moments.

"I'm so angry I could scream. That imbecile thinks he can ignore me whenever he's of a mind to do so, with no thought to how I might feel about it, with no concept of what I could add to his manly conversation. He doesn't even think twice about it, so certain is he that his ideas are the right and proper way of the world. It is infuriating to be ignored so; I am not superfluous just because I wear skirts."

"Men does have a way of taking over when they's a mind to. And I'm certain that murder's one thing they thinks no woman should be involved with."

"But it's my tavern," I said. "They wouldn't dream of excluding Uncle Samuel."

"No, they included him, all right."

I heard Beth's light footsteps rapidly descending the back stairs. "Mother, what's happened? I just saw Uncle Samuel walking down the street surrounded by Captain Phillips, two other soldiers, and Constable Grey. Is something wrong? Where were they going?"

Lieutenant Reade appeared at Beth's side before I could respond to her questions. I had to admit they were a handsome couple, which at the moment only added grease to the fire of my anger. "I am sure all is well, Beth," he said. "Captain Phillips must want to ask your uncle about his trip." Reade pulled Beth to him, draping his arm protectively about her shoulder.

"Let go of my daughter," I said, my temper having found a suitable target. "This display of affection is as unseemly as it is spurious." I felt righteousness in every bone and marrow of my body, a most marvelous experience after suffering humiliation from another redcoated officer. "I demand you refrain from further contact with Elizabeth or I shall evict you from this establishment."

Reade's expression subtly changed from astonishment to anger to a sneer. "You delude yourself if you think you have that authority, Mistress." He turned to face Beth, grasped her by both shoulders and firmly kissed her.

Beth did not resist the kiss, but she gasped as he released her, then blushed the color of Reade's coat.

"Get out of here this instant," I said, pointing toward the door.

With a defiant smirk, Reade strode out the warming kitchen door into the courtyard beyond.

"Alan, wait," said Beth, flinging open the door to follow him. She looked around and closed the door slowly when she couldn't see him. I knew from the lightning in her eyes that a storm was about to disrupt our household.

"Mother, how could you? Alan was being nice to me and you treated him quite rudely. Now what will he think of me? He'll never talk to me again. I just know it. And it will be all your fault." She stared at me in undisguised embarrassment, twisting her freshly pressed apron into a knot until she burst into tears and fled up the back stairs.

Infuriated now beyond reason, I strode to where my navy cloak hung. Pulling it about my shoulders, I had my hand on the door latch when Matty grabbed me by the shoulders, turning me around to face her.

"Now, where you going in such a temper?" she asked.

"To get that young Lothario out of this tavern before I cut off certain of his bodily parts."

"And just how you gonna do that?"

"With a sharp knife, I expect. You're the expert at carving. How would you do it?"

"I mean, how you gonna get Reade to leave this tavern?"

"I'm going to go to British headquarters and insist that Colonel Belding move him to another location. Belding owes me a favor for looking after Southerland and I'll demand payment."

"An' you think this here's a good time to talk to the colonel?"

"Matty, I'm in a hurry. What are you getting at?"

"Just make sure you says hello to Master Samuel when you gets to the colonel's office."

With that, I slumped back against the door. It was as though she had poured a pail of water on the fire of my anger, which became a puff of smoke rapidly dissipated in the air. I hung my cloak back on its peg and moved to stand next to the fireplace where Matty was pouring hot water into a teapot.

"Thank you, Matty," I said. "What would I do if you weren't always there to stop me from jumping off the precipice?"

"You just gets heated up some times, especially when you afraid that child of yours is getting herself in trouble. Once Master Samuel's home you can shout at those red-coats for all you worth. I'll refuse to do any more cooking 'til they gets Reade out of here, if it'll help."

I reached around Matty's ample shoulders and gave her a hug.

"Maybe you best think about sending that young lady out to the farm, like Master Samuel suggested," Matty said.

"I certainly need to figure out something that will curb her interest in these redcoats. She's too young to under-stand the consequences of a romance with an enemy sol-dier. How can I protect her and also keep the tavern? To solve one problem seems to demand that I give up on the other and I am not willing to let go of either."

I poured a cup of tea, symbolic not of a lack of patriotism but of my need for comfort, and removed myself to the solitude of my room. Beth's door was closed when I passed and I could hear no sounds except the occasional squeak of her bedstead. I needed to think about sending her safely away and didn't want to confront her before I knew my own mind. And until I could speak with her calmly, without my temper reigniting.

I had always had a temper. I remember my mother throwing up her hands at my "most unwomanly" tantrums when I was four or five. At Mistress Chapin's School, I was counseled with a Quakerly plea for godly patience. Later the word "shrewish" was attached to my outbursts, with a warning that no man would want such a wife. Fortuitously, Jared had thought my behavior spirited and remained equitable in the face of my anger. Over the years, I had learned that tact would obtain what I wanted far more often than a blistering tongue. But today the heady intoxicants of rejection, fear, and anger had overwhelmed my sense of caution. I had not been able to strike back at Phillips, so I had struck out at his subordinate, who had then sought to defend his manly superiority at my daughter's expense.

I debated every possible place I could send Beth, every friend and relative I knew, but each had as many disadvantages as advantages. By the time I thought of my sister in Philadelphia, I realized I was spinning in fruitless circles, and my mind wandered to another resident of that city, George Fenton Lee.

If, I hypothesized, he was as despicable a man as Uncle Samuel had portrayed, could he have been murdered by someone upon whom he had worked his peculiar brand of evil? Someone whom he had abused during his or her contract of servitude? Some indentured husband who was cuckolded, or even worse, whose wife was forced to bear and raise Lee's bastard? There must have been many whom Lee had cozened over his years in business, whom he had exploited as he had his poor deceased wife.

As dusk crept in, I lit a candle from the spark of a tin-derbox and, sitting on the bed, began again to study Lee's account book. I read several pages trying to further dis-cern the abbreviations he had used: name, sex, age, occu-pation, then a number that Rachel and I had guessed was the amount paid for the contract of indenture. The sec-ond line was consistently a name, place and a second amount, possibly that of the purchaser of the contract and the amount he paid Lee. My eye was caught by one entry, Baby Hartmann, a boy, who apparently was sold in 1771 for £200 to Roger Cochran. I thought I had come across that name in an earlier entry. Searching back through many pages, I found it. Martin and Ilona Hartmann, and their daughter, Miriam, ages 29, 28, and 7 had come from somewhere in Germany in July of 1760. Lee had pur-chased their indenture for £15 and £9 respectively, the child apparently included. The second line of the entry differed from most, noting that Martin Hartmann died aboard ship and that Ilona was now responsible for the contract.

I knew this to be the legal practice, that if one spouse of a married couple died before fulfilling the contracted in-denture, the surviving spouse was responsible for repay-ing both contracts. In this instance, for example, Ilona Hartmann was legally bound for both her own and her husband's indentures, a total of either fourteen years or the monetary value Lee would have made on the sale of both contracts. I didn't know how the child's passage was paid.

My mind refused to recognize what, even then, I sur-mised. The first candle sputtered and only awareness of the flickering light drew my attention in time to replace it. I was caught in a timeless place of appalling malevolence.

But there it was, pages later: in 1760, Ilona Hartmann was indentured to the household of G. F. Lee as an assistant cook. In 1771, Baby Hartmann had been sold from Lee's own household.

I know not how others react when confronted by evil. I felt empty to the depths of my being and wondered if I would ever feel complete again. For all that I had heard from pulpits across New Jersey, I had never truly been exposed to the handiwork of Satan. I had thought him a metaphor, a symbol for that piece of all of us that is selfish, or mean, or brutish. I knew now that I was mistaken. True evil does exist, its sadistic issue shown here in this ledger, the record of a devil who played out his will on a hapless young widow and then sold her child for £200.

My reverie into the works of the devil was broken by the sound of familiar footsteps outside my door. A brief knock and the door was flung open to reveal my friend Rachel, her hands laden with a tray from which wafted the enticing scent of honey-laced tea. Rachel busied herself settling the tray on the trunk next to the rocking chair. After handing me a cup, she sat in my rocking chair, her tranquil rocking at odds with my riotous feelings.

"Thanks," I said, savoring the warmth of the tea that slithered down my throat with the first sip.

"Matty tells me you're on the warpath."

"My temper got in the way of my sense." I sighed. "But what worries me more is that after my outburst at Lieutenant Reade, he felt it necessary to use Beth to display his inherent superiority. And she did not protest. Rachel, I am responsible for having her live in a tavern filled with

British officers. If I had kept her away from here, she and Reade would never have met. I have been thinking about where I could send her now that would be safer, but I have been unable to find any place that would be acceptable to both of us. God's blood, Rachel," I swore. "How I wish we didn't live in a world where we must concern ourselves with our young women being abused by an invading army of youthful bum-ticklers. I have begun to think that Uncle Samuel is right, I should send Beth to the farm with him, though she would be most aggrieved. I know not how to protect her anymore."

Rachel rose to put her arm around my shoulder. "Your day would try the most steadfast of souls. I think Beth would become accustomed to the country, although you are correct she would be vexed at leaving here. And I wonder if it would truly be safer than in town."

"I have always told myself she would be safer here where I can watch her, but now I'm not certain as being here puts her in daily contact with the British soldiers."

"With their polished manners and handsome uniforms," Rachel said. "Had you thought to send her to your parents in Princeton? The fighting is over there for the moment."

"For the moment," I said. "But for how long? At least if she's here I do know what's happening and don't have to wait a week for a letter to tell me of some misfortune. I would worry so. And Rachel, I would miss her greatly." I shook my head at the terrible quandary of Beth's safety. "No, for now, I guess she's as safe here or with Samuel as she would be anywhere else."

Rachel poured us more tea, then returned to her rhythmic rocking. "I saw Samuel and Constable Grey in the company of Captain Phillips and several soldiers. That was a fast trip to Philadelphia. Was he able to find someone to claim your corpse?"

I winced at her referring to Lee as my corpse. I explained what Uncle Samuel had told us before Phillips had taken him away.

"No wonder you were so ired at Phillips. He didn't let you hear all the bloody details." She paused in contemplation, and then added, "So Lee was a most foul individual. That does change my ideas about the murderer."

"Truly, it does," I said and told Rachel how I had concluded that Lee had sold the baby he had forced upon Ilona Hartmann.

Rachel was silent for a long time, shaking her head slightly. "I am without words, Abigail. How is such evil possible?"

"It would take the wisdom of Solomon to understand how a man could sell his own son."

There was little more to say about the sale of Baby Hartmann, neither of us being philosophers who could make the irrational even a bit understandable. The conversation returned to something we could comprehend, Phillips taking Samuel to British headquarters.

"Didn't Samuel go at the constable's behest?" Rachel asked.

"Yes, it was Josiah's commission."

"Then what did Phillips want?"

"I don't know and that troubles me. I don't understand why the British are interested in this murder at all. At first it seemed that their only concern was that there might be some threat to the officers billeted here. Then I overheard Colonel Belding and Captain Phillips talking about sending to New York for more information about Lee."

"New York?" Rachel said, raising an eyebrow.

"Yes, and I thought it strange too. What could their headquarters have to do with Lee?"

Rachel shook her head. "Abigail, I have no idea. I can ask Nathaniel, although at the moment he seems to have more questions than answers."

We sat for a while in silence thinking about possible explanations until Rachel spoke up. "Nathaniel wanted me to ask you about Charles Whitworth."

"Don't tell me Nathaniel's heard about the reading already?" Rachel looked puzzled until I told her about Mrs. Chandler's request on the church steps and Whitworth's agreement to read publicly on Sunday. "Would Nathaniel like to attend?"

"I doubt he would pass up an opportunity to meet such an accomplished author. Nathaniel is not fond of Whitworth's novels; however, he finds the journal writing excellent. How do you like Whitworth, personally, I mean?"

"Quite charming, actually," I said.

"Is he attractive?"

"I think so. He appears the veritable paragon of British sophistication and snobbery until you see the insouciant gleam in his eye and realize his manner is but a façade, a game he plays with the world."

"If the light weren't so poor in here, I would think you're blushing, dear friend. I wonder if I should not warn Josiah Grey he has competition for your affection?"

"I'm much too old to blush," I said. "And, as you know, my relationship with Josiah has never been more than a cordial friendship."

"Putting your obvious infatuation of Whitworth aside, Nathaniel wants to know why he is here at all."

"I assume to add to his travel journal, though I don't recall if he mentioned that specifically. What makes Nathaniel curious?"

"Whitworth has a companion, does he not?"

"His man, Robert."

"What does Robert look like?"

"He's . . . actually, he's rather hard to describe. I have only seen him in Whitworth's company and he is but a wisp of smoke next to his flamboyant master."

"Nathaniel described someone as 'thin, medium height, slouch-shouldered, in a dark cloak with a tricorn worn low."

"It could be him, Rachel. The 'slouch-shouldered' would match Robert's habitual stance, though I had not thought to describe it so. Why?"

"Nathaniel saw someone of that description entering and then leaving British Headquarters this morning and was curious who the person might be and what he was doing there."

"I don't know. There may be an obvious explanation. Since Whitworth is English, perhaps his man knows someone stationed here." I shrugged and thought no more of it until after Rachel had left, when I remembered the conversation between Captain Phillips and Colonel Belding about sending a soldier to New York for information about Lee. But that conversation had taken place in the late afternoon on Thursday and Whitworth had arrived about noon the next day, much too soon for a rider to have reached New York and an investigator from British Headquarters to have returned. I was surprised at the relief this conclusion brought me.

SEVENTEEN

Nigh onto five o'clock, as I was lighting candles on the taproom chandelier, I glimpsed a familiar figure walking past the front window. I beat Uncle Samuel to the door, throwing my arms around him in a catharsis of unacknowledged anxiety. He allowed my public exhibition, hugging me in return, chuckling.

"What are you in such a twit about?" he asked, leading me gently toward the warming kitchen. "Is there any more cheesecake?"

"No, you ate it all this morning." My attempt at a cheerful smile felt false on my face. "I was worried about you, Uncle."

"Whatever for?"

"It's not every day that you are taken away under British escort," I said.

"Ah, you were concerned for my safety. I thought you were merely aggravated to be left out of the discussion," he teased. My uncle is most sagacious.

"Of course I didn't wish to be left out of the discussion, but you remained with the British so long I had become quite anxious. Did you find something that they want? Why are they even interested in this murder?"

"Get me something to wet my throat, please, Abigail, and then we can discuss it." He made a gesture of clutching his throat.

I filled a glass with a heady, ruby-red port from a supply I keep in the warming kitchen pantry, while Uncle Samuel removed his greatcoat, scarf, and tricorn, depositing them in a heap on the ladder-back chair in the corner. He took the wine, drinking it down in one long swallow. Perhaps he was not as assured about his meeting with the British as he would have me believe.

"Not the way to appreciate a good port, or so my uncle always taught me," I said. A slight upturn appeared in one corner of his mouth, he gave me the glass for refilling. I returned the glass to him as he stared at the flickering of the fire's magenta and orange flames.

"Let me tell you what I told Phillips," he said, breaking from his reverie. "Lee appears to have been a man without any moral constraints, whose only goal in life was to dominate those around him. I already told you about his boorish behavior with his wife and the hushed suggestions that he was somehow behind her premature death. Apparently, his mental abuse and subjugation were not limited to his household, but extended to his trade. I was able to talk to those who should be most loyal to him, his business manager, Obediah Fitch, and others who profited greatly from his schemes, and yet, his behavior had been so despicable that even they were willing to talk openly about his excesses."

"He *is* dead," I observed ironically.

"And the general reaction to that news was relief. I found it odd to have his business partners bemoan their loss of income and at the same time express deliverance as though from a great burden. His partners were all scared witless of him, Lee having intimidated them thoroughly."

"How did he do that?"

"An example. One of his partners, a Mr. William Godwin, told me of his involvement with Lee. Godwin, a successful young cloth merchant, had sought a partner to help finance the shipping of tobacco, rice and indigo from the Carolinas to England and on the return voyage to transport English cloth to Philadelphia, hoping to control his shipping costs. Lee agreed to invest 40 percent of the capital needed to buy and operate a ship for a return of the same percentage of the profit of each trip. It was a satisfactory and remunerative arrangement for several years allowing Godwin to greatly enlarge his own stock of fabrics, as well as selling cloth to merchants in Boston, New York, and Charleston. Then his ship was pirated at sea, and while there was no loss of life or of the ship, there was no profit from that voyage. Lee insisted he still be paid his 40 percent, not of the profits, but as a set price. Godwin had to sign over a partial interest in his store as payment. According to Godwin, Lee took malicious glee in besting him."

"Horrible man," I said. "But, surely Godwin had a written contract detailing the agreement between himself and Lee."

"Indeed he did. But the contract was kept in a strongbox at Godwin's home, which suffered from a fire that destroyed half of the house before it was extinguished. And in the panic of that night the strongbox went missing."

"Didn't Lee have his copy that could be referred to?"

"Lee's copy stated that the agreement was for a set, yearly fee, and," he held up his hand to forestall my next question, "it was signed and stamped, though Godwin swears he never signed it."

"So it was forged."

"Probably."

"How does Godwin fare now?"

"He and his family were forced to sell their house and move into the rooms above the store to pay Lee, but their business may survive as they have begun importing Dutch silks and satins to replace the boycotted English goods. Mrs. Godwin is a favorite milliner in Philadelphia and she has been quite innovative in introducing some of the recent styles from Europe. Godwin spoke enthusiastically about their prospects, though he swears he will never again have a business partner, except his wife."

"And were there other similar stories?"

Samuel nodded. "A persistent pattern of tragedy and misfortune which put citizens at Lee's mercy."

"All of which he caused?" I asked.

"Probably not, though we will never know, now that he is dead. Regardless, he used whatever transpired to his advantage."

"So there are a great many people who disliked Lee."

"Hated enough to kill him, I think, is more accurate, Abigail."

"And the devil must have shouted 'Huzzah' when Lee arrived at the gates of hell."

"Not all men are kind of heart. You know that, despite your quixotic desire to find the good in everyone. You have seen men who rob you, who take drinks or lodging without paying, who steal blankets or metalware outright from the tavern."

"Of course, but that is petty thievery."

"And what of the two horses that were stolen from the stables last year? We were sore pressed financially for several months to replace them, and we have a most profitable tavern. A theft of that magnitude would break most families."

I sighed, confounded by the ills and vices so pervasive in human nature. And yet, it seemed to me there was a difference between the kind of misbehavior we saw at the tavern and the malfeasance Uncle Samuel attributed to Lee. "I know that men steal, women too for that matter, as things go missing from our kitchens and the laundry. And sometimes there may even be pleasure in the theft itself, the success in not getting caught, in being clever at sneaking a free drink. But what you describe is another magnitude of wrong, it is a vicious, deliberate enjoyment in causing another pain."

Uncle Samuel just shook his head and added another log to the fire.

I still did not understand how my corpse could possibly concern the British. Even if Lee had cheated a member of the English nobility, why would they care how he died? I paced in front of the fire trying to piece together the puzzle, but could find no pattern, just a random thought here and another there.

"There must be something else besides Lee's villainy." I realized I had spoken my thought aloud when Samuel responded.

"Yes, there is something else, though I am not sure where it leads." Uncle Samuel motioned for me to join him on the bench where we could speak quietly. "Lee was a spy."

"Surely for the British?"

"This is where it becomes confusing. I spoke with several reliable patriots who swore Lee was an American spy. They told me of specific information he had given them concerning British troop movements, transportation of supplies from England, and even of reading letters stolen from British officers stationed in the colonies."

"Lee seems an unlikely rebel, certainly not one motivated by noble ideals."

"Exactly my thought. So I questioned more widely and started to hear hints and whisperings that he had sold information to the British, nothing as specific as what I was told by the patriots, but then I am not as welcome in loyalist houses. I mulled this over on my ride back and I have a guess, though little proof to substantiate it. I would wager that Lee sold information to whoever would buy it, probably under the guise of being a patriot or a loyalist as the situation demanded."

"Are our leaders that gullible?"

"No, I think Lee was a very persuasive liar. People have talked about his exploitiveness and almost demonic enjoyment at anyone's suffering, yet none spoke of being forced into association with him initially. I think he was a master at manipulation, at showing everyone what they wanted to see until he had them at his mercy."

"So," I theorized, "he would tell the patriots he had information about the British gathered from the captains of his ships, or heard in the markets in Paris, or Bristol, or Jamaica, and that he would give . . ."

"No, sell," Uncle Samuel corrected me.

"That he would sell them the information. Who buys such information and how would they know to trust the person who was selling it?"

"We know that General Washington pays for both his own spies and for specific information from other sources he deems reliable."

"Really?"

"You sound surprised."

"I always assumed that spying was done gratis."

"Ah. And how would spies pay for their food and clothing to say nothing of supporting their families. Or do you think they are all wealthy bachelors?"

I quickly gave my uncle my idea of a recruiting broadside: *Wanted: Bachelors of Means to Spy for Your Country.*

He ignored my levity and continued, "As for how anyone would trust Lee, he may have given accurate information. As you just mentioned, he cast a wide net with his commerce and could easily have had ears in many ports. In fact, considering his Machiavellian nature, I don't see how he could have resisted doing so."

"And I suppose he could have told the Americans he was spying for them and then told the British he was pretending to give information to the rebels but was really gathering facts for the loyalist cause. And the payment he received would be used for his expenses, for bribery, or for posting men to uncover information, or just to make money." My impressions of George Fenton Lee were getting more complicated by the moment.

"Yes, I think it plausible that Lee was a spy for both sides," Uncle Samuel said. "I am just not sure this had anything to do with his murder, though Colonel Belding, or someone, seemed to want me to make that connection."

"How so?"

"Do you remember the sliding doors between the parlor and the dining room at the Stevens's house, where the British currently headquarter the Regiments of Foot?"

I nodded, recalling the mellow gold of the birch used in the doors and door frames and fashioned into the magnificent wainscoting of the dining room.

"Constable Grey and I were questioned by Colonel Belding in the parlor. I told him what I had found in Philadelphia, leaving out the spying. After a while Belding went into the dining room and closed the doors tightly behind him.

When he returned, I noticed that the doors were left slightly ajar. This to'ing and fro'ing went on for a good while before I realized there was another man in the dining room."

"Could you hear what was being said?"

"Not really, just fragments having to do with 'the ship from Bristol' which 'the spy was on' and then something about letters or dispatches. I knew Belding's voice, but I didn't recognize the other man's. He said that he had lost 'them' in Amboy and was most upset when the colonel blamed the 'whole bloody cock-up' on him."

"Then what happened?"

"After the colonel and the Voice stopped shouting at each other, Belding came back and asked me questions specific to Lee's trip to New York. All I knew was what Obediah Fitch, Lee's business manager, had told me: Lee had gone to New York to meet a boat from England and he was to have returned to Philadelphia on Wednesday. Fitch wasn't sure if Lee was to have met someone or to have picked up something but he said that Lee had been anxious about getting there before the boat arrived. I told Belding what I knew, but he became very agitated and kept pressing me about New York."

"Did you ever see who was in the dining room?"

"No, the draperies were fully closed and the room was in darkness."

I wondered if we would ever figure out all the mysteries connected to this murder. Every day seemed to add new pieces to the puzzle rather than allowing us to find one meaningful pattern.

I told Uncle Samuel about the letters I had found in Lee's saddlebags, how I had stolen them, and about their disappearance from my hiding place under the eaves.

"I can appreciate wanting to obstruct Phillips whenever possible, Abigail, but you were taking quite a chance."

Samuel gave me a fierce, scolding look. Then shaking his head as though he recognized the impossibility of changing my actions once I had determined a course of action, he continued, "From what I overheard, it would seem likely the British stole the letters you had secreted in your room, although our side would have wanted them as badly."

I thought for a moment. "It could be possible that a person, 'the spy,' brought these letters from Dr. Franklin in Paris to Bristol, crossed the Atlantic, and planned to deliver them to General Washington and to John Hancock at the Congress in Philadelphia. But that leaves us not knowing who 'the spy' is, who 'the spy' works for or who Lee would have approached with the letters. So you are right, Uncle, this may or may not have anything to do with the murder."

We heard steps in the hall and John came through the door.

"I got your horse saddled like you asked, Master Samuel. If it's all right with you, I'll ride with you out to the farm. I ain't seen Benjamin for ages and thought I might pay him a visit."

Uncle Samuel and I both knew that visiting my uncle's manager was an excuse; John wanted to be certain my uncle arrived home safely.

"Good idea, John," I said. "Why don't you spend the night there? Then you and Benjamin can get caught up on all the latest news and you won't have to ride back in the dark."

Uncle Samuel and John left, cloaked against the cold. It was much later that I realized I had forgotten to ask my uncle if he would be able to recognize the Voice if he ever heard it again.

EIGHTEEN

Wednesday night supper was under way, the fragrance of warm, buttered cornbread and chicken stew with sweet herbs filling the dining rooms. Grace, Fanny and I were serving when I looked through the open doorway to the taproom and saw Captain Phillips sit down at one of the tables. Teapot still in hand, I hurried to speak with him.

"Good evening, Captain," I said. "May I serve you something to drink? Or would you care to partake of our chicken stew?"

"I've eaten. I would like a glass of sherry, if John could fetch it for me," Phillips responded.

"John's not here this evening, but I will be pleased to get it for you." I filled a glass and brought it to his table. He was laying out a game of solitaire.

"I have something I need to discuss with you, Captain."

He continued turning over cards and would have ignored me had I not held the drink he requested. Taking the glass from my hand, he sipped. "Yes, Mistress, what did you wish to say?"

"I must request that you remove one of your officers from this tavern. His actions toward me and toward my daughter have exceeded the boundaries of gentlemanly behavior. I will gladly fill his place with another, so you will not be greatly inconvenienced, but for the comity of the household, he must leave."

"And what, pray tell, did he do that was so insulting to you and your daughter?"

"He kissed her."

Phillips sputtered, sherry spewing onto his cards. "You're telling me that I must find another billet for one of my officers because he kissed a tavern wench?"

"No. I'm telling you he must leave because he behaved in an ungentlemanly fashion and I will not abide advances toward any of the women at my tavern, much less my daughter." I realized I was on shaky ground.

"Many an English girl would be thrilled to be kissed by one of my officers. You again astonish me with your hidebound, provincial ways. Who was this young gallant whose advances, as you call it, have so incensed you?"

"Lieutenant Reade."

The supercilious smirk on Phillips's face changed to anger as he rose to his feet, upsetting the table, cards and wine glass flying. "I told you, Mistress, that Reade had nothing to do with the murder of Lee. I questioned Reade myself and he assured me he was soundly asleep when his sword went missing. I find it offensive that you will not accept my conclusion, but to then demand I remove him from these premises is an insufferable insult to my command. I will not hear another word against that young man. Do you understand me?" He turned his back and stomped toward the front door.

I was about to respond when I heard Matty shouting for me. I don't remember Matty ever raising her voice before that night.

"Hurry, Mistress. They needs you in the kitchen," she called from the doorway. Rushing out the back door and through the courtyard I could hear Miriam yell, "Hold him down, he'll tear the stitches."

Other voices cried out: "Grab his leg."

"Hold his shoulders down."

"Bloody hell, he's strong."

"Ow. He bit me."

As I approached the kitchen storeroom, I could see four officers trying to pin down the flailing patient, a tangle of arms and bodies in the cramped space. The wavering light from the single candle cast weird specters on the shelves filled with pots and pans.

"Talk to him, Beth," Miriam said, when she spotted my daughter in the doorway behind me. "Help him remember where he is, so he'll calm down. And get another candle or two for more light," she told one of the kitchen maids. "Mistress Abigail, would you open the outside door? We could use some fresh air."

I did as she asked, allowing cold air to gush in, refreshing the room, clearing out the stuffiness and smoke I had failed to notice earlier. Even I could breathe more easily. But pleasure in the fresh air was soon accompanied by shivers as my skin registered the temperature of the night air.

"Good," Miriam told me, indicating she too felt the cold entering the room. After shutting the door, I watched Beth crooning to Lieutenant Southerland whilst she gently massaged his head. "It's all right, Johnnie. You're doing fine. Just relax. Your leg is healing nicely, not even a bit of infection. You're going to be walking in no time." As she went on in such a vein, Southerland calmed visibly under her ministrations. His fellow officers stepped away from the bed one by one as his thrashing ceased, waiting nearby should restraint be needed again. He blinked several times, then focused on Miriam who had approached the bed with a cup of water.

"Where am I?" he asked, as though he had not spent the last six days in this very room. Miriam and Beth raised his head to help him sip the water.

"You are in the tavern kitchen, remember? You've been here since you were shot. Miriam and Beth have been taking bloody good care of you," one of the soldiers replied, continuing to talk softly to his friend after the other soldiers had moved out of the cramped space of the storeroom. A moment later, Miriam followed into the kitchen proper to thank them for their help, reassuring them Lieutenant Southerland was healing well and there was no infection.

I stepped after them to hear what she was saying. "What happened?" I asked, when the soldiers had left.

"It was a reaction that laudanum sometimes causes." Miriam stood collectedly, her hands clasped at her waist. As I had seen on other occasions when Miriam was nursing, she was self-possessed and calmly in charge, only the pinkness of her cheeks betraying emotion.

"Very dramatic," I said.

"And my fault," she said, shaking her head in disgust. "I am ignorant of the dosage of these medicines. I could have killed him."

"How so?"

"Laudanum is more powerful at soothing pain than any other medicine we have, but given in too high a dose it can cause a man to stop breathing. I wanted to keep the lieutenant comfortable, but because I was afraid of harming his breathing, I guess I gave too small a dose. Between the pain and the drug and the dark room, he must have woken feeling crazed, not known where he was, and acted in a panic. It is really just an effect of my misjudgment with the laudanum."

"Is there not a prescribed amount that is safe to give? I certainly don't want a British patient who was healing well to suddenly die of an overdose of laudanum."

"It depends on many things such as the strength of the laudanum, the build and age of the patient, and how much pain you are trying to overcome. Unfortunately, I never learned enough from my mother. But that's obvious isn't it?" she said, biting her lip. "You must find someone else to minister to the lieutenant. My lack of skill could bring the wrath of the British on our heads and I have no desire to hang for inadvertently killing one of their officers."

"Miriam, your skill has been most admirable. Lieutenant Southerland is healing well and it is close to a miracle he has not developed an infection considering how deep his wound was . . ."

"After they mangled it in the torture chamber they call a hospital."

"The very reason Colonel Belding wanted him here and you have proved him correct. Is there not someone who could help you determine a safe dosage? Could you not ask Dr. Dillon? Surely he would know. I will get Whit from the stable and send him for Dr. Dillon, though only to consult with you, Miriam. You are to remain in charge of Lieutenant Southerland's care."

Beth's light footsteps sounded behind me. She slipped her arm through mine, gently patting my hand. "Are you all right, Mother?" she asked.

"Yes, I'm fine. I want you to know that I am proud of what you just did. You walked into that chaos with a cool head and contributed greatly to calming Lieutenant Southerland. I am impressed with the maturity you demonstrated."

Beth blushed at the compliment, though she truly did seem more adult at this moment. "I was rather frightened. He was thrashing around so."

"All the more notable, that you had the courage to do what was needed." I gave her a hug and was pleased when she warmly returned it, a sign our somewhat rent relationship was on the mend.

Later that evening, I went to the taproom to assist Grace. She had offered to stay beyond supper to tend the night-time drinkers as John was still at the farm with Uncle Samuel. I found she already had an assistant, Beth again. My aproned daughter was laughing with a group of officers while they passed around the punch bowl she had brought to their table. I was struck as by lightning that my daughter had indeed become a young woman, the days of her childhood having passed without my taking note.

"She makes an excellent tavern wench," Grace told me when I reached the bar. "Spills not a drop, and the men are drinking more than their usual just to have her flash her sparkling eyes at them."

I had to admit Beth was a most pleasing picture: her tiny waist embraced by the ties of the white apron, her budding breasts peeking from under her neck scarf, her hands clasped to her pink cheeks as she laughed at something one of the men said. She knew she had an attentive audience and was playing to it, although she had about her the innocence and sweetness of the maiden. I too was captivated by her flirtations until motherly concern intruded, reminding me again of the dangers for innocent girls in an occupied town. War brings with it a constant pressure of worry that intrudes on even the simplest of pleasures. I sighed.

"That is a sigh with all the worries of the world in it," Charles Whitworth said from somewhere just behind me.

I whirled to face him, embarrassed at being overheard.

"My dear gentlewoman, come sit with me at that corner table and tell me what detestation could possibly have caused such a sigh. Since the gods of misfortune must have been abusing you, I shall hear your sad tale and hearten you." The essayist grasped my elbow gently but firmly, ordered two sherries from Grace, and led me to the table. He was dressed fashionably, as I had come to expect, his cravat perfectly tied at his neck, the black embroidery about the buttonholes of his waistcoat matching his black coat. The only indication he was relaxing in a colonial taproom rather than spending the evening in a fashionable English tavern was his lack of a wig, his dark hair being tied neatly with a black ribbon at his neck. My heart skipped a beat or two at the very sight of him.

Our wine delivered, he raised his glass in salute, "To the most captivating woman in New Jersey, may your days be dazzling and your worries fleeting."

I smiled back at him, sipped my sherry and returned his compliment, "To the most flattering writer of journals, may your travels be entertaining, and your stories always in demand." Another sip.

"Ah. That is better, a smile on your lips and a twinkle in your eyes, enough to bring joy to the heart of a travel-weary scribbler such as myself. Now, think of me as a comfortable older brother and tell me what has you sighing so deeply?"

I laughed outright. "It is beyond my ability to imagine you as anything like a comfortable older brother. And as for the sigh, it signifies very little more than the weariness that intrudes on us all at the end of a day."

"Oh, I think not, fair lady," he said. "I saw you watching that delicious daughter of yours and I would hazard a guess that she is the cause of your worry. It is perhaps not a felicitous time to be the mother of such a glorious bud of womanhood."

I responded in a trice without censoring my thoughts. I know not what led me to believe I could confide in Charles Whitworth, only that I felt a surety and ease in his presence.

I stared into those deceptively soft blue eyes. "If only her father were alive to protect her, for these are strange and frightening days." I explained my concerns about the attentions Beth had received from Lieutenant Reade and Captain Phillips's refusal to have Reade removed from the tavern.

"I have thought to send her away to another place, but am unable to determine where that would be. What do you think? Is there somewhere the war won't touch, a place where she can grow to womanhood with only the usual problems to overcome?"

Whitworth listened closely, then reached across the table to cover my hand with his. "Truly Madam, you raise a problem of the greatest magnitude, and I fear I have no suggestion worthy of your consideration, for the world seems no safer to me. Have you no male relative who could protect her?"

How typical of a man to ask about other men to make life safe for Beth, I thought, until I remembered I had started the conversation bemoaning the lack of a father. "Uncle Samuel, out at the farm."

He shook his head immediately, "No, not safe at all." A frown gathered his dark eyebrows into a straight line across his forehead.

"I think it is not that bad, and perhaps less tempting than here. There are fewer attractive young men about."

"And how would your fair daughter enjoy living on the farm with her great-uncle?"

"Probably not at all." I grimaced and proceeded to the next option, "My parents in Princeton."

"The fighting still threatens all around us. General Washington is a wily fox in his strategy and I don't trust him to keep his troops confined to their Morristown winter quarters. Have you no one beyond New Jersey?"

"My sister and her husband are in Philadelphia."

"Glorious lady, this becomes more dire with each relative of whom you speak. I am unable to conceive of a way Philadelphia could escape being attacked by General Howe, short of the Congress disbanding and Washington calling a truce."

"Oh, if only that were to happen," I fantasized. "Then the British would leave New Brunswick and Beth would be permitted the normal experience of growing up."

Whitworth laughed, a sound from deep in his chest that could only be answered by a smile. "With her winsomeness, I think Beth will never have what you are calling a normal experience. Should all these young Englishmen leave tomorrow, there will remain enough hot-blooded New Jersey lads for you to be concerned still for her welfare. But I think she is safer in your keeping than anywhere else."

I started to disagree, but he held out his hand to ask my leave to continue.

"She is but an incomplete copy of her mother, and you are not a simpering, whaleboned woman in need of protection. I would gladly pit you against the remarkable General Howe and stand back to watch the sparks fly."

I laughed at the image, but was flattered sufficiently to feel my toes warm. I noticed the lines that crinkled about Charles's eyes when he smiled broadly, a veritable map of past enjoyment that tonight brought me delight.

"Can you tell me truly that your life was full of normal experiences when you were her age?"

"I considered it decorously proper and mundane, although I must admit there was a continual parade of students through our parlor and kitchen, supposedly to consult with my father about their readings or to be fed by my mother."

"Ah," he said in satisfied victory. "And those young men just happened to find time to spend with you."

I was unable to resist the chuckle that arose with my memories. "There was one student who thought himself quite the young buck, and pursued me incessantly, as though I was his prerogative. I tired rapidly of his possessiveness but was unable to dissuade him politely."

"And how did your impoliteness manifest itself?" he asked, exhibiting more than casual interest, I thought.

"It was a very warm spring that year and the students were fond of spending afternoons swimming in the river. One day that young man's clothes went missing while he and his friends were cooling off in the water. He managed to return to town in a borrowed shirt, somewhat embarrassed that his knobby knees were exposed to public purview. His embarrassment was greater the next day when the dean of the college, in front of the assembled students and faculty, demanded to know whose clothes he had found flying from the roof of his porch. I sent my erstwhile suitor a note offering to lend him an old dress of mine, but he never responded. Rather rude, I thought."

"And how old were you at the time?" Charles inquired.

"Fourteen," I responded, "though I may have been a bit immature and unladylike for my years."

"Most audacious lady, I am certain that Beth is as protected in your formidable care as she could possibly be anywhere. Have you ever told her this story?"

"No," I said. "I have no desire to encourage her with the adventures of my intemperate youth."

"I am relieved you have put such prodigal behavior behind you." He leaned forward to ask quietly, "You are certain there is no need for me to tell Robert to guard my breeches with his life?"

I sat up ramrod straight, raising my chin a bit, "Sir, I am a mature and dignified woman; your breeches are safe as long as they are about your person." We both burst out laughing, and were instantly the focus of every pair of eyes in the tavern, Beth's the widest of all. Mature and dignified indeed. I did feel young at heart for the moment and tired no more. Grace came to refill our glasses and as she poured the sherry, I remembered I had a question for my companion.

"Do you know if Robert was at the Stevens's house today?" I asked after I had reseated myself.

"Where?" Whitworth looked puzzled.

"Regiments of Foot Headquarters," I clarified.

"I don't know, though it is possible. I was there."

"You were?" I asked, my heart stopping at this unexpected reply.

"Well, yes. You seem surprised."

"I probably shouldn't be, you are English after all."

"From York actually, although I've lived in London since I finished at Oxford. I found I had a talent for writing while I was there, thought I would become the next Shakespeare or Marlowe, you know: 'But stay! What star shines yonder in the East'. . . . The lodestar of my life, if Abigail."

"Shakespeare?" I asked, puzzled.

"No, Marlowe. *The Jew of Malta.* Sounds like a line from Romeo and Juliet though, doesn't it?"

I nodded.

"I fear the muse of poetry alighted on another's shoulder, although I can pen a fair journal about the dangers and delights of distant places like New Brunswick."

"And will you spend the rest of your days traveling the earth in search of exotic experiences?" I knew quite well I was flirting shamelessly, a behavior I had not enjoyed for a very long time.

"Most gentle lodestar, if you would marry me, we could live ever more on the banks of the River Ouse at York. I would write glorious poetry in your honor and you could steal my breeches with impunity."

"A most startling proposal, kind Sir, although I fear I can only accept offers from those with muses already seated on their shoulders. Perhaps you could approach me again on Friday."

"Ah," he said "at the ball. I do hope you will do me the honor of dancing with me, even if you would spurn my proposal tonight."

"I think you will find our upcoming festivities to be a cornucopia of strange savage behaviors to write about in your journal and if, in the midst of it all, you find a moment to dance, I would be pleased to be your partner." To my ears, that reply sounded sane, sensible, and proper. And not the least bit dangerous.

Nineteen

Thursday morning I went out to the bakery and kitchen to see how the preparations for the next night's ball were progressing. The sky was that brilliant blue we get on very cold, winter days, and it was indeed very cold, little white plumes forming at my every breath. The cold boded well for the ball as the roads would freeze, making a firm bed on which the carriages and wagons could travel. An evening like this usually attracted between two and three hundred people. While we had posted our broadsides throughout the county, we wondered how many would brave the British encampment for this ball. We expected many British officers and hopefully a few women of loyalist or neutral persuasion to partner them. Of course, a few patriot spies might also arrive seeking information from the relaxed and possibly drunk soldiers. Unlike other balls, tonight we would not be housing overnight guests as our rooms were filled with billeted men. The scarcity of overnight accommodations in New Brunswick would also limit the number coming from any distance to those having relatives or friends in town. I wondered if those staying with relatives would include the two Cooper women from Kingston, who usually attended our balls. I hoped they would come as I had questions for Lydia Cooper.

I opened the door to the bakery and was enveloped by a glorious mélange of scents—cinnamon, ginger, vanilla, and others indecipherable to my nose. Eleanor Granger, our baker, was covered with a fine dusting of flour up to her eyebrows. Two New Brunswick women, Mrs. Tate and Mrs. Lishman, were assisting her, all three neighbors and members of the same quilting circle. I spent a few moments admiring the products of their hard work: several dozen loaves of bread, trays of cherry and lemon tarts, bread pudding and plum pudding, two shelves of orange cake and sponge cake soaking in rum, and a dozen different kinds of cookies.

"Who made these beautiful apple pies?" I asked, for the pies were worthy of a painting. They were made without a top crust, and every thin slice of apple had been aligned perfectly making a swirl that became smaller until it reached the center. The pies had then been coated with honey and sugar and baked to golden perfection.

"Mrs. Tate did those. Truly apple-pie order, are they not?" Eleanor asked.

Mrs. Tate looked up to smile at her friend's compliment and returned her attention to the gingerbread she was decorating with powdered sugar sifted over a paper lace cutout.

"Have you decided what you're wearing tomorrow night, Mistress Abigail?" asked Mrs. Lishman. "We were just talking about what we will wear. I have a lovely grey silk with a maroon petticoat that I think will be perfect. I am so pleased you decided to give a ball. It will give us all a much needed lift."

"Are Lydia and Maria Cooper coming up from Kingston?" I asked.

"Oh yes. My niece and her daughter will be arriving by the coach sometime this afternoon. I haven't seen either of them for months and I'll be delighted to have them with me."

"Wonderful," I said. "I look forward to greeting them." Kingston was a small town near Princeton and further along the road where George Fenton Lee's horse had been found. Constable Grey had sent a man in that direction looking for any traces of Mrs. Lee and he had returned empty-handed, but I thought it worth my time to inquire if Lydia Cooper, a local housewife and known busybody, had any other information.

After thanking the bakers, I headed for the kitchen, which was also bustling with activity. Just a bit more vinegar," Matty was saying to her assistant, after sampling the marinade that she was concocting for one of the next day's meats. Matty looked at me, questioning if I needed to speak with her. I shook my head and she went on about her work, the commanding general, calm and confident in her ability to produce a notable buffet for several hundred people.

I moved to the kitchen storeroom doorway to be out of the bustle and found Lieutenant Southerland propped up in bed, sharpening a carving knife.

"Matty put you to work, I see. No more playing with my tavern puzzles?"

"Indeed, Mistress, though I did certainly enjoy the ones you sent over. Some of them were quite hard to figure out. For now, I want to do whatever I can to help Matty. She told me she 'ain't wasting any good pair of hands today' or something like that."

"It's good to see you feeling better. You had us all a bit frightened last night."

"I am most sorry to have disturbed the whole house, Mistress Abigail. Sharpening knives doesn't begin to repay you for all the trouble I have caused."

"Lieutenant Southerland, the best payment you can give us is to see you back on your feet. Now don't look so dismayed. Dr. Dillon says the chances of your using your leg again are excellent."

"Really? He did?" Southerland sounded for the moment like the very young man he was. He tried to blink away the tears of relief that filled his eyes, finally wiping them with his shirt sleeve. For the first time in days, he grinned.

"Yes," I said, smiling in return. "He looked at your leg when he came last night and said it was healing very well, better than he expected. He wants you to try walking on crutches in a week or so, which he says is exceptionally good progress. And don't worry, Matty'll find you an endless supply of knives to sharpen that will more than earn your keep." That, plus the monies the good colonel would give us, I thought.

I started to leave, when a thought crossed my mind.

"Lieutenant, were you close at hand last Wednesday morning when Lieutenant Reade found his sword was missing?"

"Indeed I was, Mistress Abigail. And the language he used was not fit for a lady's hearing. He thought two of the men from across the hall had taken it as a prank, and he was furious when they wouldn't tell him where it was. Of course, they hadn't taken it and had no idea where it was. All of us were awfully surprised when we were told it had been used to murder that man."

"Do you have any idea who might have taken it?"

"I know Alan certainly didn't take it. Alan is an honorable man and he would never kill someone in that way. As to who did, I have no idea. Alan's bed is right by the door, so just about anyone staying at the tavern could have taken it; he keeps it hanging right on the bedpost. Wish I could help you, Mistress Abigail."

Bidding good-bye to the lieutenant and the kitchen women, I returned to the tavern proper, my thoughts focused not on the ball, but on murder weapons. Entering the warming kitchen from the courtyard, I found Miriam stirring some evil-smelling liquid at the fire.

"G'day, Mistress," she said.

"Lieutenant Southerland seems fit this morning," I said.

Her face was lit with one of her rare smiles. It made her almost beautiful. "Indeed, he is. Thank you for summoning Dr. Dillon last night. He was helpful with the laudanum dosage."

"He was most complimentary about your skills, Miriam. Have you never thought about becoming licensed as a midwife? You have a rare talent that could serve the whole community and you would earn a great deal more than working here as a maid."

Her countenance assumed its habitual dour expression; the corners of her mouth flat, the light gone from her eyes, her shoulders bearing some invisible load of sorrow. "I would have liked to become licensed, but I never had the liberty to pursue such a position, to say nothing of the money needed to be trained. And now I am much too old to even be considered for such training."

"You're not that old," I protested.

"I'm 24, Mistress. Midwives want apprentices who are eight or ten years younger than I am." She turned away from me abruptly and stirred the foul liquid to keep it from boiling.

I wrinkled my nose at the odor coming from the pot. "What is that witches' brew?"

"Just a decoction to strengthen the young lieutenant. It's the wormwood that smells so awful, but it's good medicine. It'll help relieve some of his pain, and Dr. Dillon suggested we try something milder than laudanum. By the time I've mixed this with wine and some other herbs, it'll be palatable." Her shoulders straightened a bit, a reflection of the pride she felt in her nursing skill.

"While we're on the subject of medicines, I have a question for you. I received a letter from a friend of mine whose daughter was violated by a soldier and tragically now finds herself with child. The daughter is still very young and my friend was talking about trying to end the pregnancy. She says there are medicines that would cause a miscarriage. Do you know anything about what they are and how to get them?"

Miriam paused and then spoke carefully. "Mistress, there are compounds which may sometimes cause a pregnancy to be ended, but they are very dangerous and oft times do more harm than good. They can damage the health of the mother severely and yet not stop the pregnancy. I would suggest that your friend think not on that course. My mother, who had much more knowledge than I, used such only in the direst of circumstances, and then I think she was never certain she was doing right."

I ignored this candid comment and proceeded to my real questions. "I've heard you can use cyanide in small doses."

"As far as I know," Miriam said gravely, "cyanide is only a poison, and quite a deadly one at that. You could ask Mr. Scudder, the apothecary, but I don't know of any beneficial uses to cyanide, other than killing rats."

"Do women ask you for cyanide to kill their rats?"

"Never. I wouldn't have it near me. It's too dangerous." She looked at me as if insulted.

"Then what would you suggest I recommend to my friend? I'm sure she doesn't want to poison her daughter."

Miriam paused, and said slowly, "Moldy rye or yew."

I tried to keep my voice steady. "I see. Well, it might be hard to find moldy rye at this time of year, but what about yew? Have you any in your box of remedies?"

Miriam put her hand against the fireplace mantel to steady herself. When she looked up there was great sadness and a furious anger in her expression, although her voice was flat. "My mother used yew to end a pregnancy that had been started by rape and which she felt must end at all costs."

"And did it?"

"Yes. Eight years ago, it killed both my mother and the baby she carried. She had come to find her life too painful to endure. I was sixteen." She pushed herself away from the fireplace, not meeting my gaze. "As with the lieutenant's laudanum, ending pain can sometimes result in death," she said as she removed her pot from the flame, and carried it out the back door. I watched her as she crossed the courtyard and entered the kitchen.

While I did not doubt the veracity of what Miriam had just told me, her telling being quite persuasive, she had not answered my question about the contents of her medicine chest.

Having determined that all preparations were progressing well for the ball, I donned my navy cloak to walk the several blocks to Aaron Jacobs, our local silversmith. I had gone but half a block up Church Street toward George, when I heard someone call my name. Turning, I saw Lieutenant Reade hastening to catch up with me.

"Forgive me for shouting your name in public, Mistress, but I must speak with you," Lieutenant Reade said. "I spoke out of turn yesterday and most humbly beg your pardon for insulting you. I hope you will forgive my boorish behavior and allow me back in your good graces."

It was a pretty little speech, but despite the charming smile that accompanied it, I wondered what had prompted the self-centered young officer to apologize?

"Thank you for your gentlemanly words, lieutenant. You understand I will not allow my daughter to be treated disrespectfully? She is not as wise in the ways of the world as you and your friends are."

"Indeed, Mistress, her spontaneity is one of her great charms, something lacking in many of the older, more sophisticated women of London. I will endeavor, henceforth, to demonstrate naught but the most honorable behavior in her presence."

Typical condescending Londoner, I thought. "I will hold you to that promise, Lieutenant." And wondering if my words to Captain Phillips last night had been effective, I asked "Oh, Lieutenant Reade, who ordered you to apologize?"

"Colonel Belding did," the young officer said through gritted teeth.

"Thank you, Lieutenant," I said turning to continue my walk toward George Street.

Was it not strange that Captain Phillips had told the colonel about the argument he and I had last night over Lieutenant Reade? Surely Phillips had too much pride in his ability to manage his soldiers to mention such an insignificant detail to his commanding officer.

Aaron Jacobs and his wife, Dinah, had a small shop on George Street. Samples of their silversmithing were displayed in the large multipaned window that drew admiring viewers. Today, a pair of candlesticks fashioned to resemble Greek columns with Ionic capitals captured my appreciation. A silver coffeepot with a carved wood handle and elegant engraving had been placed next to the coveted candlesticks.

I entered the shop to the ringing of the bell suspended over the door. Mrs. Jacobs hurried out from the workshop, still carrying a beautiful silver ladle and the cloth with which she had been polishing it.

"Mistress Abigail, how good to see you. And how is your charming uncle?"

"Uncle Samuel is his usual self, which is to say, in excellent spirits and making mischief wherever he can." Or so he would have people believe, and who am I to gainsay my uncle?

"And how may I be of service to you?" she asked.

I pulled the silver earring I had found in George Fenton Lee's room out of my pocket and held it out for Mrs.

Jacobs. "I was wondering if you could tell me anything about this earring."

Setting down the ladle, she picked up the earring, studying it with care. "First of all, this is silver over gold, as you may have noticed."

"I did notice the inside of the hoop looked gold, though I don't know why someone would cover gold with silver."

"It's been a fashion in France for a few years. Some jewelers believe it makes the diamonds appear more luminous."

"Those are real diamonds?" I asked.

"I think so, although Aaron could tell you better with his glass." She went to the doorway of the workroom and summoned her husband. He appeared with his jeweler's glass in hand.

"Mistress Abigail," he said. "So you have a bit of a puzzle for us. How wonderful of you to brighten up our day in this manner." Adjusting the glass to his right eye, he took the earring from his wife's hand. After a moment he moved closer to the window where he could see the earring in the daylight. "These are definitely diamonds, though very small. The French have made excellent paste jewels for the past sixty years, but these are not paste."

"And you are certain the earring is French?" I asked.

"Oh, beyond a doubt. Look here," he pointed to the small hallmark stamped on the inside, the gold side of the earring. "This is the hallmark of a well-known Paris house of gold and silversmiths, Thomas Germain. He died a few years ago, but I believe his house continues. Do you have the matching earring, Mistress Abigail?"

"No, this was left behind by a guest at the tavern. I wanted to determine if it was worth the expense of trying to return it to its owner."

"Most definitely," Mr. Jacob said. "She is probably heart-sick to have lost it. I expect she would reward you hand-somely for its return."

Which was exactly what I hoped for, although I had a specific reward in mind. If I could find this mysterious woman from Paris, I wanted her to tell me her story.

TWENTY

I woke Saturday to a rumble of sounds at first indistinguishable in my state of semi-sentience. A few more drowsy moments and I was able to sort out a male voice giving orders, some effortful grunts, and laughter. Preparations for the evening's dance had begun and I was still stretching sleepy muscles. A bang from the courtyard below and a shouted "Watch the window, you tom doodle!" had me on my feet without further ado. I dressed hurriedly, pulling on the blue striped wool dress I had worn the day before and a grey apron, suitable for the work I would be doing that day, and I twisted my hair into what I hoped resembled some order. As I descended to the tumult below, I noticed the coffeepot in the warming kitchen was empty. I scurried across the courtyard to the kitchen in search of my first morning cup.

"You best be getting the beef up from the icehouse so we can get it on the clockwork spit," Matty was telling one of her assistants as I entered the kitchen. "Tell Whit and Tom to carry it; it's too heavy for you."

"You managed to get it working again?" I asked. The complicated clocklike mechanism turned the meat on the spit continually, assuring the meat would cook evenly on all sides without someone turning it by hand. When it worked, that is.

"Amos Warren guarantees it's in perfect order. Says if it's not he'll eat one of his horseshoes. I'm wondering what kind of sauce I should make so the horseshoe tastes good."

I laughed as I poured myself a cup of the aromatic brew. Cooking the beef and several turkeys, and then adding the fish and the smoked hams for warming would take up most of the day for Matty and her helpers.

"Do you need anything from me?"

"Not before you had your coffee, I don't. You ain't civil til then. And anyways, things is going as usual, only a little jumbled, nothing I can't take care of." Matty dished up hot oat cereal with apples, placed the bowl on the table and went to find the maple syrup. "Now you take this over to the warming kitchen and eat it, and don't be arguin' with me," she said emerging from the storeroom. "It's gonna be a mighty long and tiring day and you won't stop to eat once you starts."

I acquiesced. Matty knew me too well for me to deny what she said. I ate my breakfast at the table in the warming kitchen, which was a little quieter than the ordered chaos in Matty's domain. After finishing every bite, I felt replete, sipping my coffee and watching the world hustle about me. Down the hall, British soldiers were emptying the ballroom where many of the officers were billeted. The first group carried collapsed camp beds, those ingenious foldable pieces of wood that raised the mattress off the floor and also provided a frame for the canopy that could be closed on all sides to give the officers a bit of privacy in their cramped quarters. Next, desks were carried out, their boxlike tops removed from their folding legs. Soldiers appeared, toting trunks filled with officers' clothes and personal belongings, locked for security. A very young soldier gingerly carried a camp stove containing hot coals. It was a flat piece of iron about eight inches square that rested on short feet and could be filled with coals when the iron-worked sides were raised. An officer had probably used it to keep his tea hot or to warm water for his morning shave. I thought to call out to the young man to suggest where he might safely put the coals when a redcoated officer came through the door waving madly and directing the young soldier toward the nearest fireplace.

For as long as I had been at Raritan Tavern, we had hosted balls and other community events such as town meetings, weddings, judicial proceedings, or anything that required a large room. Samuel had built this ballroom about ten years earlier. A glorious addition, 30' by 50', the room featured a raised alcove at the far end where a band would play, thespians perform, or a visiting judge dispense justice. The ballroom's wing stood perpendicular to the tavern proper, which allowed for a high-beamed ceiling and graceful windows on the two long sides. The walls were painted a soft dove gray, the wainscoting and other woodwork a rich ivory.

When the British officers arrived in December, occupying not only the second floor rooms, but the ballroom as well, we had to cancel our monthly dances, including the afternoon dance instruction given by Monsieur Guy Pierre de la Roche. I missed M. de la Roche's monthly visit from Philadelphia, not because I yearned for instruction in the latest Parisian dances but because no one else called me "Chère Mam'selle" when paying for lodging. Relations between France and England being what they were, de la Roche would not be coming today, despite the outcry from the mothers of young ladies of New Brunswick.

I would have been content to wait for the departure of our English guests before scheduling a ball, not only for the obvious logistical problems of having an army encamped on my dance floor, but also because I was naturally disinclined to mix the waging of war with festive cavorting. Persistent pestering from neighbors and handsome young English officers, in addition to threats from Beth that she would never speak to me again in this life, had finally worn down my resistance. Thus the hubbub about me.

By mid-afternoon, the ballroom approached cleanliness, although I had sharp words about the wax drippings, spilled wine, boot black and unrecognizable blotches that had ravaged the floor. Sanding and refinishing could never be finished by evening, so we swept, buffed and ignored that which we could not remedy. The two chandeliers were lowered, their brass polished to a glow and new candles added before they were raised aloft. Fires would be set to blazing in late afternoon to warm the room. However, the amount of wood would be lessened with the arrival of the guests, for too hot a room discouraged dancing while a moderate temperature fostered exuberant activity from which developed a fine thirst that could be slaked with the purchase of refreshment. It was from the sale of food and drinks that we made our money as we didn't charge anything to attend the ball.

By late afternoon, only the last details remained to be completed. Grace and I were smoothing a crisp white

linen cloth on the long table where we would serve in the
style of a buffet, when Beth entered the dining room, her
arms laden with newly pressed skirts and petticoats.

"I've finished all our skirts, Mother. I'll lay yours out on
your bed. Have you anything else for me to do before I
go?" she asked, excitement twinkling in her eyes.

"You have done a yeoman's service today, dearest, and
for that I thank you. There is naught else for you except
to primp with Lucy. Have you everything you will wear?"

I could almost hear her going through the list in her
mind until she looked at me with a rueful smile.

"Stockings," she said, "the new white stockings you gave
me for Christmas. I had put them safely away for a special
day and now I almost forgot them." She shuffled her shoe
slightly back and forth, remnant of a childhood behavior
that bespoke a momentary nervousness. "I had thought to
wear a heart-shaped patch on my cheek. Lucy has a star
and her mother said she could use it."

Grace stopped working on the table. "Why would you
want to wear a patch, Beth? You've never had the pox and
have no marks to cover. Your skin is perfect. You watch
tonight, there will be few women here who have near your
complexion." Grace shook her head. "I wouldn't cover an
iota of that skin if it was mine."

"Really?" Beth said.

"Really."

"I have no objection to one little patch, Beth," I said.
"I've never worn one and I hear they itch after a bit, but
the decision is yours. You will look very pretty with or without a patch. And don't forget the honey cake Matty made
for you to take to Mrs. Pratt."

With a smile, Beth left the room to assemble her
clothes. I was most grateful to Lucy's mother, Mrs. Pratt,

who had graciously included my daughter in preparations for dances and other fetes that were held at Raritan Tavern. I had neither the time nor the talent needed to curl and powder and primp to my daughter's satisfaction, while Mrs. Pratt was delighted to treat both Lucy and Beth like princesses off to a royal ball.

I was startled a bit later to hear the musicians tuning their instruments in the ballroom. Evening had arrived and I had been too occupied to notice even the lighting of the candles about the room. The tables were heavy with gastronomic treats that belied our winter wartime scarcities. The British had been generous with supplies of meat and we had ample vegetables from the farm's cold cellars. Fruits we had canned and dried the previous fall were used in beautiful desserts. Matty was checking the banked fires in the warming kitchen that would keep the cooked foods warm until they were served. She had changed from her work clothes into a clean skirt, white apron, neck scarf, and mobcap that she would wear to supervise the serving.

She looked up from stirring a meat gravy redolent with basil. "Look at you, you ain't even dressed yet and folks'll be arriving any minute. You can't be the hostess looking like a scullion."

"I'm too tired to play hostess tonight. Let's fetch Uncle Samuel and let him act the part."

"He'd never play the role of hostess with your style, Mistress." John responded as he entered the kitchen, dressed for the evening in black breeches, stockings, his matching waistcoat and frock coat with double rows of silver buttons imprinted in a leaf pattern. His black and grey hair was tied at the back of his neck with a velvet bow.

"Now ain't you a sight, John," Matty exclaimed. "I'm gonna have to watch you all night so some pretty young thing don't decide to take you home. You is right handsome, husband."

John walked to where she stood and embraced her. "Ain't no woman who could take your place, Matty. Lessen she be mighty rich, that is."

Matty pushed him away and waved the wooden spoon in his face. "You just watch out John, or I'll . . . I'll . . ."

"Drip gravy down your cravat," I said grabbing the spoon in time for the offending drip to fall safely to the floor.

"I thank you kindly, Mistress." John looked me up and down with a raised eyebrow. "That the latest fashion that you're wearing tonight?"

"I'm going. I'm going," I said, as I trudged up the back stairs, which seemed to have grown several stories since I had descended that morning. Had my bed not been covered with the clothes Beth had pressed for me, I would have crawled under the quilt. A knock at the door and Grace hustled in with a steaming pitcher and towels.

"Let me help you," she ordered. I was soon washed, perfumed, my cheeks rouged and my hair atop my head. Over my shift and corset we added a number of linen petticoats and finally the heavy ivory silk petticoat with its quilted pattern of flowers. The skirt of rose brocade was pleated gracefully over the sides and back but open across the front to show the intricacy of the petticoat design. The matching rose bodice had a square neckline and three-quarter-length sleeves, both trimmed with small white ruffles.

"You clean up very prettily," Grace teased as she secured the cap of delicate cream lace to my hair. "I think even Mr. Whitworth will approve."

I sputtered, unable to think of a suitable retort, which I attributed to my exhaustion until I realized that I was not nearly as tired as I had been but moments before.

"Ah, that is better, Mistress, a sparkle in your eye becomes you and all that you need now is a smile and you will win the heart of every man tonight, which will surely drive Mr. Charles to heights of jealousy."

"You're beginning to sound like him, Grace," I observed wryly.

She chuckled in response.

As we descended to the ballroom, I realized I had not thought about the murder of George Fenton Lee all day. That was until I reminded myself to seek out Lydia Cooper from Kingston.

The musicians were playing "Lady Mary Powis's Minuet" as I entered the already crowded ballroom. There were but five or six couples dancing, although the room was aswirl with color, light, and laughter. On the far side of the room, I saw Colonel Belding and went to thank him for commanding Lieutenant Reade's apology.

"It was the least I could do, after the care you have given young Southerland," the colonel said. "They tell me he may even regain the use of his leg. That is well done indeed, Mistress. Would that you could teach your secrets to my surgeons."

"It did surprise me that Captain Phillips would mention Reade's behavior to you."

"Phillips? Phillips said nothing to me." The colonel smiled, his eyes crinkling at the corners. "It was another friend of yours who brought it to my attention. He mentioned you were concerned by Reade's advances toward your daughter, as any mother would be. You let me know should you have any further problems with Reade." He bowed slightly and moved to speak to the Chandlers. Perched on Amariah Chandler's head was a powdered wig so ornate she could not turn her head, but needed to move her entire body in the direction she wished to face.

"Difficult to dance with that wig," said Charles Whitworth softly in my ear.

I whirled about and then stepped back for a better look at him. He wore a full-skirted black velvet coat with elegantly simple silver and white embroidery about the high collar. His waistcoat was lavender silk with the same embroidery in silver and black. White lace gently cascaded from his cravat and his shirt sleeves, wafting softly with each movement. He wore his clothes with a grace that could have been foppish except for his broad shoulders and vigorous bearing.

"No wig?" I said forthrightly, startled to note his dark hair was curled on the sides and braided in the back with a velvet bow.

"Fairest Lady, do I offend you by my lack of formality?"

"Indeed Sir, I am shocked that you would appear so attired." A frown appeared between his brows as though he could not determine the seriousness of my comment. "If you had only worn a formal wig, we could have honored you and Mrs. Chandler as Lord and Lady Periwig."

"Ah," he said, his frown having dissipated, "but then I would have had to sit out with Her Mopheadedness all evening."

"And into the early morning."

"And we could not have danced," he said. He made a leg, bowing deeply. Rising, he elegantly extended his right hand to me in invitation. "Lodestar of my life, it would give me great delight if you would honor me with a dance."

I curtsied, my rose skirt swirling out prettily. "It would please me exceedingly, gallant knight," I said placing my hand in his. The white lace from his sleeve cascaded over our hands, tickling, as he led me to the center of the floor as "King George the Third's Minuet" began. Minuets gave way to country dances as the night grew into morning. Beth and Lieutenant Reade danced occasionally, though, to my relief, she was also partnered by many other young men. At times, I had duties that needed attention and on my return I found Charles gallantly partnering Beth for "Miss Moore's Rant" or Lucy for "Lady Breast Knot". He even danced once with Mrs. Chandler, a sedate minuet that did not disturb her wig.

Breathless after twice dancing "The Duchess of Brunswick," I went to the warming kitchen in search of something to drink. Matty had finished with her work, the dining room table now laden with cakes, cookies, puddings and tarts. As she opened the door to leave, she wished me a good night. The cool draft from the night air felt most welcome and I followed her out to the back porch. The stars were bright and silent and I savored their peace until I became chilled. Coming back into the warming kitchen, I remembered I wanted to seek out Lydia Cooper.

I found Mrs. Cooper sitting against the wall in the ballroom. She was contentedly watching her lovely young daughter, Maria, dancing with a British officer.

"I want to thank you for having this ball, Mistress Abigail," she said when I sat down next to her. "It has been such a dreary and scarifying winter. How good it is to be able to forget the war, if even for an evening."

She prattled on with wearisome detail about their coach trip from Kingston, until I had almost concluded there was no local gossip from which I would benefit.

"We feel quite isolated in Kingston," she said. "We get very few travelers passing through to tell us the latest events, most prefer to go on to Princeton, or even Philadelphia than to stay in our village. It has been particularly difficult this winter with the war and all. And even when someone does show up at your door, likely as not they'll give you a fright."

"Did something happen recently?" I asked.

"Why, just last week Tuesday, well, actually it must have been early Wednesday morning, we were awakened by a pounding at our door. Nearly made my heart stop."

I was suddenly very interested. She was talking about the morning after the murder. "What did you do?" I asked.

"I was afraid to answer the door. I got down the gun my late husband, God rest his soul, kept over the fireplace. You just don't know what to expect these days."

"Frightening." Please, keep talking, I thought.

"Yes, and what do you know? It was some woman, dressed as a man, looking for the house of one of our neighbors. And at that hour." Lydia was fanning herself rapidly, frightened anew.

"Who was she?"

"I didn't recognize her, but I can tell you she looked very sick. A woman like that shouldn't be out at night. Gives a fright to honest folk."

I listened carefully to Lydia's tale. She related it had been dark at such an early hour of the morning and she had seen only a little in the candlelight, but the rider had been wearing a dark blue or black velvet cloak when she had knocked on their door.

A midnight blue cloak I remembered well, having last seen it draping the shoulders of Mrs. George Fenton Lee.

TWENTY-ONE

I am certain I undressed and found my bed sometime in the wee hours of Saturday morning although I have little memory of doing so. What I do remember and will most likely never forget is waking with a start a few hours later. I know not what roused me, because the house was preternaturally quiet, as it is oftentimes after a fete. Yet something was troubling me; something felt terribly wrong. My mother would have said angels had passed over my grave. I sniffed for smoke and found none. I listened for footsteps and heard none. Yet I was not able to relax and let myself float back into sleep. Instead, I felt both exhausted and wide awake. A few more moments of doubtfulness and I reluctantly lit the candle at my bedside.

I put on my robe and slippers to investigate the status of the household. I thought I would walk down the corridor to the main stairs and then return, use the chamberpot, and certainly fall back asleep. I passed Beth's room, holding my candle aloft, its small circle of light revealing nothing amiss. I heard Miriam snoring and Ruth turn over on the straw mattress in their room at the top of the stairs. I stood there for a few moments sniffing and listening, but there was naught but the usual creaks and groans of the tavern.

And yet the feeling of malevolence did not dissipate. I was halfway down the main stairs when I heard a slight sound like the mewling of a kitten coming from the hallway I had just traversed. My tired brain railed at the idea that Beth had brought a cat into the tavern. I was indignant to have been awakened from a sound sleep by an illicit pet.

Then came another sound, a cry, suddenly hushed into a whimper. Beth's room. She had long ago outgrown the nightmares she had suffered after the untimely death of her father and brother, but today had been a long and exciting day for her and I hurried down the hall thinking to soothe her. I now noticed a faint light coming from under her door. She cried out softly again as I reached the door and I heard the voice of another with her, a man's voice bidding her to be quiet. Startled, I stopped short and strained to listen. Whatever she responded I could not determine, only that it was cut off as though someone had covered her mouth.

Silently, I pushed down on the door latch. The bolt rose unobstructed. Still holding the latch, I pushed on the door and met resistance where there should have been none. When shoving harder did not budge the door, I realized a chair or some other object had been shoved under the handle of the door.

"Get off me," Beth said.

"Shut up, Beth. I'm not going to have you get me into trouble," Alan Reade said, his speech slurred with drink.

"But . . ." A slap followed. I could hear her begin to cry.

I had to calm my ravening anger so I could think straight. If I tried to break down the door and failed, I was afraid the bloody drunken bull would harm her further. And despite my wrath, my chances of success against the stout oak door were not great. My heart was pounding. I thought it surely loud enough to wake all of New Brunswick to its alarm, although no one raced to help me rescue Beth.

I silently lowered the latch back in place. Forcing my concentration on that simple action allowed my thoughts to free themselves from my roiling rage and a plan formed.

Hastening back to my room, I opened the door to the eave space where I had hidden the Paris letters, and retrieved the loaded flintlock pistol Samuel had given me. I was a better shot with a rifle, the Kentucky pistol's bigger brother, but did not have one to hand. Anyway, I was hoping surprise would be all I would need to chase Reade from Beth's young life.

The space under the eaves ran the length of the tavern. I bent over slightly to keep from banging my head on the beams of the lowered roof. The passageway was cluttered with barrels and boxes and trunks from years past, all covered with thick dust. Spiderwebs hung from the rafters, gossamer tendrils that I had to push aside with my pistoled hand to prevent the candle from igniting them. A few steps and I had raised enough dust to feel the tickle in my nose and throat. Don't sneeze, I told myself sternly. Whatever you do, don't sneeze.

Beth's room had been a windowless closet set between the hall and the undereave space. Like my room, it had access to the undereave storage by a door in the wall. I might not be able to break down a stout oak door, but on my soul, I could break past a door held in place by no more than a small wood bar.

I found the outline of Beth's little door and readied myself to break through it. Firmly gripping the pistol, I stepped back to gain momentum, and took a deep breath to steady my nerves. Too deep a breath, for I simultaneously sneezed, blew out my candle and broke through into Beth's room. Two pairs of shocked eyes, lit by a candle on her table, looked in my direction. Beth was lying on her bed undressed down to her shift, which was pulled up to her waist. Reade had one hand over her mouth and held her arms over her head with the other. His trousers were down about his ankles, his knees on either side of Beth's hips, his erect member jutting out from under his shirt.

"Get out," I snarled, in a deadly quiet voice even I didn't recognize. I aimed the pistol between his eyes leaving no doubt concerning the gun's accuracy. He scrambled to get off Beth and the bed. I grabbed his shirt and pulled; he landed on the floor atop his red coat and waistcoat, flattening his tricorn. He stood awkwardly, his breeches still about his ankles. I relit my candle from Beth's.

"Get out," I said again, poking the pistol sharply into his buttocks as he bent to retrieve his clothes and boots. Reade left his coat and hat, pushed aside the dresser that blocked the door and flung himself down the hall, tripping several times on his pants. He finally succeeded in pulling them off as he fell halfway down the main stairs, crawling the final steps to the second floor. I followed closely, my pistol aimed at his back. When Reade turned toward his room, I prodded him again.

"Out. I told you." I snarled at him. "Out of my tavern and don't you ever presume to show your face here again."

"But I'm billeted here; you can't just throw me out," he replied, his voice whiney with defeated pride.

"Seems I'm doing just that." I prodded him again with the pistol, and we proceeded down the stairs to the front door.

"But my clothes and belongings." He looked down at his shirt, the only article of clothing he was currently wearing. "I can't go out like this. They'll think me a bloody jack fool."

I shrugged. "That's nothing to what *I* think of you." I set the candle on a nearby table, unlocked the door and grabbed Reade's shirt once more causing it to rise up and leave him naked below the waist.

"I want to make certain you understand, Lieutenant. If you and your little dirk should ever return here, or have anything further to do with my daughter, I will use this pistol where it will do the most damage." Looking him directly in the eye I pointed the pistol at his now deflated member. He shivered and I think not from the cold. I let go of his shirt and he tumbled out into the night. I closed and locked the door behind me, then leaned my head against it, my courage gone.

I opened my eyes to see Charles Whitworth on the stairs, candle in one hand and sword in the other. Standing directly behind him was his man, Robert, also with sword in hand.

"I came to rescue a fair damsel in distress, but she appears as brave Boadicea, not needing the aid of mere man."

"Not very brave, merely desperate," I responded. I was suddenly very cold and could not stop shivering. Charles removed the fancy dress coat he had thrown over his nightshirt and placed it about my shoulders. Robert disappeared up the stairs.

"Let's find some brandy to warm you," he said, brushing at the cobwebs that adhered to my hair and clothes. "You must have some that isn't under lock and key."

"I really must check on Beth. I don't know if she is hurt or merely hysterical."

"Then I will get a brandy for each of you." He bowed graciously, seemingly unaffected by wearing only a nightshirt.

I told him where to find the brandy in the warming kitchen pantry and headed back upstairs. I had apparently disturbed the entire household, for many sought information about the noise as I returned to the attic floor. Robert spoke sharply to them and they retreated to their rooms.

Miriam was sitting on Beth's bed, holding her and rocking her slightly. As I entered Miriam rose and whispered to me, "She's fine, still virginal, though a bit shaken. That slap mark will disappear in a day or two and none will be the wiser for what happened. I'll make tea and put something in it to help her sleep." Miriam left just as John appeared in the doorway, carrying his rifle, and asking what was going on. He had seen candles moving about and heard the front door slam. Charles came with the brandy, Miriam with the tea, and eventually the tavern returned to its nighttime quiet. Beth and I settled down in my bed. She did not argue about sleeping in her own room tonight.

"I didn't mean for anything to happen," she said, her voice harsh from crying, her hair unkempt and twisted into strange knots.

"I know, dearest." I continued running my fingers through her hair, a gesture that seemed to calm us both. "It's more my fault than yours. I should have stopped that man from seeing you long ago. I was remiss in my duty to you."

"No, it was my fault. He was so drunk, playing like a little boy. I thought he would just walk me to my room and then go back down to his room. It all happened so fast and then I was trapped. I couldn't even call out." She shuddered but didn't start crying again. I could tell she was becoming drowsy. She yawned. "I had forgotten about the door to the storage area. I was awfully surprised when you popped through, all covered with dust and spiderwebs." She yawned again. "You were quite a sight, Mother. I've never been so glad to see you."

Beth got very quiet and soon her breathing slowed; she was asleep. My last thought before morning was that I would never fall asleep again.

TWENTY-TWO

By late afternoon the next day, the ballroom had been thoroughly scrubbed—one of the benefits of giving a ball is a sparkling clean room afterwards—and the officers were once again in residence. Lieutenant Reade's belongings had disappeared during the course of the day, presumably taken by a fellow-in-arms, as Reade was nowhere to be seen. Would that all my threats were as effective. Beth stayed by my side, a silent shadow, pale and listless, until I tired of tripping over her and sent her to work in the stable repairing and polishing harnesses, safe and comfortable in John's company.

Rachel came to share a cup of coffee and to lend her sympathetic ear to my self-recriminations over the events of last night. She felt Reade's previous behavior had not suggested he would behave in such an unseemly manner. I believed it was moot; I was still responsible for what had occurred.

"You did rescue her, Abigail," Rachel said. "Surely you can allow yourself comfort in that."

"And if I had not awoken? I have no idea what caused me to wake at that moment. What if I had slept through the entire night?" I asked, not wanting a response.

I told Rachel I had decided to send Beth to stay with Uncle Samuel at the farm. I was not completely satisfied with that choice, but it seemed the lesser of possible evils for the moment. He would be pleased to have her, and I hoped she would feel safe in a household of older, avuncular men who doted on her. One of Samuel's farmhands had recently married, so there would be another woman to talk to, although Beth would sorely miss Lucy and her other friends here in town. I had not told Beth of my decision yet, thinking I would give her a while to recover from the fright of last night. Rachel hugged me as she left. In the busy, noisy tavern, with people all around me, I felt very much alone.

With paper and pen gathered from my office, I sat in the warming kitchen tallying the profits from the ball, figuring which of my many debts I could now settle, but the heat and crackle of the fire was hypnotic and I dozed, my head on the table near the fireplace. I was running along the warm sand of the Jersey shore, the ocean waves tickling at my feet with my skirts raised immodestly. I was laughing as my husband tried to catch me, he was reaching for my shoulder and would kiss . . .

"Mistress. Mistress Abigail, wake up."

I started, knocking over the ink bottle. A gnarled black hand reached to steady the quill and ink before more than a few drops had spilled. That is not Jared's hand, I thought, and then remembered he was dead these ten years. The present reasserted itself and I found myself looking into the concerned face of Benjamin, Uncle Samuel's manager.

"Benjamin?" I asked, noticing that Matty, John, and Grace were all standing in the room. Beth had wedged herself between my chair and the wall, protected from whatever travail was about to occur.

"They's taken Master Samuel," Benjamin said in a breaking voice, "and I couldn't do nothing to stop 'em." He pulled at his short, gray hair, tufts of it now standing at all angles.

"Who took my uncle? What are you talking about, Benjamin?" I asked, still muddleheaded from my nap.

"The British. That Captain Phillips had a bunch of soldiers with him, too many for me to fight or I would of tried, Mistress, I swear I would have. And Master Samuel were yelling at me not to fight and just to tell you. So I be telling you, but I so mad at them British I would have taken them on myself if I had a gun at hand." Benjamin was pacing up and down, his back rigid with guilt and anger. "Never heard such nonsense in all my born days. Master Samuel didn't kill that man. I know he didn't, but them British don't want to hear nothing from me."

"They think Uncle Samuel killed someone?" I said. "Who?"

"That man Lee, what were killed here last week. How can they think he would have killed a guest in his own tavern, and with you here running things? No sir, that don't make no sense. Master Samuel'd never do that."

"Phillips thinks my uncle killed Lee?" I asked, hardly comprehending.

"That's what he said."

Beth started to cry softly, her adolescent emotions roiled again. Matty came to comfort her and I longed to be enfolded in those strong arms along with my daughter.

"Do you know where they were taking Uncle Samuel?" I asked Benjamin.

"To headquarters, they said."

As I rose from my chair, John said, "I'll go along. I don't want nothing happening to *you.*"

"No," I said. "I want you to go to the lawyer, Edward Pratt, and inform him we need his legal advice. Benjamin, you'd better go with John as you know more about what has occurred than any of us."

"I want to go, too," Beth said. "I don't know what I can do, but I do know Mr. Pratt better than anyone, as Lucy is my best friend."

"All right, but I want you to stay with Lucy should Benjamin and John accompany Mr. Pratt to British headquarters. I don't want you on the streets alone." Beth solemnly nodded.

My disbelief warred with my rage. I hoped for a moment that this was a nightmare from which I would awaken to find myself still concerned about paying debts. Alas, as I stepped out the tavern door and felt the sleet on my face, I appreciated that this new crisis was real and that I had forgotten my cloak. I retreated into the warmth of the tavern to wrap myself in a cloak of woolen righteousness and thus clothed against the villainous enemy, I slid up the precariously icy street toward British headquarters.

That Uncle Samuel would have murdered George Fenton Lee was not possible. Well, I amended the thought, it *was* possible, though not in the tavern. That was completely beyond reason, at least beyond my reason. Regardless of his patriotic leanings, Samuel would never have endangered Raritan Tavern. So why had the British arrested him? What possible evidence could they have that would connect him with Lee? And why arrest him now? Because no one had been arrested in the week following the murder? What had Uncle Samuel not told me this time? I had no answers as I stomped my feet clean of icy muck and the door to the Stevens's house opened.

"Mistress Abigail, come in, come in. It's frightful outside, isn't it?" asked Lieutenant Peter Fuller, one of the officers currently billeted at Raritan Tavern.

I started at the slamming of the door. Facing the red-coated officer brought back all the anger I had felt when I had found Reade in Beth's room. That anger, combined with my rage now that Uncle Samuel had been arrested, left me momentarily speechless. Fortunately, Lieutenant Fuller continued to ramble on, giving me time to calm down.

"I wanted to thank you for taking care of Southerland," the young lieutenant said. "He's a fine chap and we're all relieved that he's going to be all right. And also, I had a most enjoyable evening at the ball last night. I even got to dance two dances."

I muttered something which must have been at least tangentially appropriate, as Fuller nodded and gave me a toothy smile before setting off to announce my presence to Captain Edward Phillips. I recognized the captain's footsteps as he descended the stairs. He greeted me and motioned to take my dripping cloak.

"There is a great chill in this house," I said. "I prefer to keep my cloak about me."

Shrugging off my response as inconsequential he asked, "How may I be of service to you, Mistress?"

"I would like to see my uncle."

"I cannot help you with that," he said.

"And why not?" I asked.

"He is not here."

"But, I was told . . ."

"He was here, but after the colonel spoke with him, he was taken to the Johnson house. I can give you a pass to see him there if you wish." His voice dripped with his usual condescension.

"I don't want your pass. I demand you release him and then I can visit him whenever I please."

Phillips looked down at me, his mouth a flat line, his eyes cold. "I don't have the authority to release him, Mistress, and I wouldn't let him go even if I had."

"Then I will speak with the colonel," I said and turned toward the hall. Phillips grabbed at my arm, but having anticipated his move, I left him with naught but my sopping cloak. I knocked at the colonel's door and did not wait politely for an invitation to enter, propriety being of little import to me at the moment.

Two maroon leather wing chairs faced the blazing fire, their backs to me. On hearing me open the door, Colonel Belding rose from one and walked rapidly toward me. "Mistress Abigail," he said, his hand outstretched, "allow me to offer you some tea in the parlor."

"Thank you, Colonel, but I would disturb you for just a moment."

"Ah, but your cheeks are red, and surely you would like to warm yourself in front of the parlor fire." He turned to Captain Phillips who now stood in the doorway, water from my cloak making a puddle on the polished oak floor. "Captain, escort the tavernmistress to the parlor and order tea for her."

"Colonel," I said, planting my feet firmly, not understanding why he was anxious to have me leave the room in which we stood. "I have not come for a social visit, rather

I would speak with you about my uncle, Samuel Holt, whom you have imprisoned. It is not possible he killed George Fenton Lee."

The colonel frowned, though whether at my rudeness or at my persistence I did not know. "And how do you know this, Mistress?"

"Samuel spent the night at his farm and his man, Benjamin, will confirm this to you."

"I believe it was your uncle who manumitted Benjamin, was it not?" The colonel waited for my confirming nod before continuing, "I do not put much weight behind the word of a servant who owes his very freedom to his master. Have you other witnesses who might be less biased?"

"I would have to inquire, Colonel." My mind raced to think of someone, anyone, who could support Benjamin's statement but could come up with no one, although that did not prevent me from continuing my argument. "Let me add that I find it most improbable that my uncle would murder a guest in his own tavern. Even if he had some reason to kill Lee, and I know of none, do you think he would have endangered his very livelihood?"

"And your home and living as well, I believe."

"Yes," I said. "And all the more reason that Uncle Samuel would do nothing so witless as to murder Lee at Raritan Tavern."

"Witless indeed, Mistress," replied the colonel, "for property belonging to a man convicted of treason is taken by the Crown, which means not only that Samuel Holt will hang but that you and your daughter will be forced to leave Raritan Tavern."

"Treason. What treason? How, pray tell, do you consider killing a traveling merchant as treason?" I asked.

"George Fenton Lee was in the service of the Crown at the time he was murdered. Killing an agent of the King is treason."

"What did he do for the Crown?" I was sure I knew the answer.

"I am not free to discuss this with you, Mistress," the colonel replied.

"He was selling you information, wasn't he?" I demanded. Belding glanced away, and I surmised I had guessed correctly. "But this has nothing to do with Uncle Samuel."

"Your uncle stole something after murdering Lee and then delivered it to Philadelphia."

"What did he steal?" I asked, but my heart had stopped in midbeat knowing my uncle had taken nothing. I had.

"It is of no concern to you, Mistress."

"It is of no concern!" I shouted, incredulous. "You would turn Beth and me out of our home and you say this is of no concern. You haven't even apologized for what occurred last night, and now you're threatening to evict us." I moved toward the fireplace to put additional distance between the colonel and my rage, having discovered it's easier to yell at someone when he is not standing at your side. Walking around the left wing chair, I tripped over a pair of boots. Hands grabbed me about the waist and I was pulled back as I was about to fall headfirst into the fire. There was another person in the room and, with a shock, I knew immediately who it was.

"Charles, what are you doing here?" I asked harshly, too startled by his presence for any brilliant repartee.

"Abigail," Charles said, "come sit down."

"No. I think not. I am obviously interrupting," I replied, as I moved in the direction of the door.

"Abigail, wait. Listen to me. Let me explain why I am here." He paused, "At least look at me so I know you are hearing what I am saying."

I glared at him.

"Belding and I attended Oxford together. We have been friends ever since, and though our lives have moved in different directions, we have corresponded. I stopped in New Brunswick to visit with him."

"So you are old friends," I said. "And I suppose you were having a good laugh about how you danced with a traitor's niece just before he was arrested and she was thrown out of her home."

"Actually we were talking about you and your uncle, though not in the way you think."

"How then?" I demanded.

"Charles does not believe your uncle is guilty of Lee's murder and came to ask me to release Mr. Holt." The colonel held up his hand before I could interrupt. "I cannot do that without finding the person who is responsible for Lee's death and retrieving what was stolen from him."

My anger deflated in the impossibility of both those tasks. I had been trying to find the murderer with little success. As for the Paris letters, I hadn't one clue as to who had taken them from my room while I had been at church a week ago, to say nothing of where they could have gone since. I was quite glum when I left the colonel's office. He gave me a pass to visit my uncle and also warned me that Uncle Samuel would be taken to New York for trial as a traitor, should the letters and the murderer not be handed over to him before General Howe left New Brunswick the coming Tuesday.

Charles walked me back to the tavern. I thought not to speak with him, but my frustration and anger easily overrode my frayed self-control.

"Why didn't you tell me you were in that room? What possible entertainment could you have gotten from listening to me argue with Belding? I felt the fool, the doodle, putting on a performance for your enjoyment, and not even aware of it. How could you have been so rude?"

Charles stopped, the foot traffic having to move around us, took off his tricorn hat with a sweeping gesture and made a leg. "My profound apologies, I would not embarrass you for all the tea in China, nor for all the tea at the bottom of Boston Harbor," he looked up, appealing to me to laugh, but I was far too angry.

"Arresting Mr. Holt was not my idea," he said.

I had not considered that Charles would be in a position to influence the conduct of the British staff officers. Then I remembered the apology I had received from Lieutenant Reade.

"You were the 'friend' who told Colonel Belding about the problems I was having with Lieutenant Reade, weren't you?"

Charles appeared taken aback by my change of topic. "Yes, I was. Though obviously my efforts did not prevent further damage from being done and for that I apologize. Would that I had kept a closer eye on Reade last night. I admit to being distracted by a most charming lady." He bowed again. "How is Beth today?"

"Fine. The young recover rapidly," I said shortly. As we walked on I tried to determine what was happening. It seemed that my charming, flirtatious, game-playing Englishman was playing games more serious than our simple teasing. I wanted to know about those games as they now involved my uncle, and possibly even Beth and myself.

"Whose idea was it to arrest Samuel Holt?" I asked in as disinterested a tone as I could manage.

"The colonel's," he said, looked at me with narrowed eyes, evaluated me and then continued, "He is in a panic because General Howe has been waiting in New Brunswick to receive the letters Belding was to have obtained from Lee."

"Lee had something that General Howe wanted? I had wondered what caused the good general to return to New Brunswick so soon after his departure last December. At that time he had been so anxious to return to New York and the arms of his paramour, Mrs. Loring."

"Two days before the murder here, George Fenton Lee met a courier at the New York docks who was bringing messages from Paris to John Hancock and the Congress in Philadelphia."

I was mildly surprised that Charles, the traveling essayist, was so well informed, but I was shocked he would volunteer this information to me. And for the first time, I understood that my stealing the letters from Lee's saddlebags had ramifications that reached as high as the British Commander in America. If I masked my excitement at this information, could I intrude farther into Charles's confidence? "Were the letters about negotiations between Dr. Franklin and the French?" I asked, now not disinterested at all.

"Exactly. And Howe desperately wants to know about those negotiations, as they could involve us in another war with the French. We had enough problems with them during the Seven Years War to be leery of a reentanglement. Lee was to escort this courier and to retrieve the letters before they could be delivered. Somehow Lee was poisoned, the courier escaped, and the letters have gone missing. Belding was responsible for obtaining the letters from Lee and giving them to General Howe. That's why the general is waiting, impatiently I might add, here in New Brunswick. My friend, the colonel, hoped to receive a commendation, but instead now he has to go to Howe and explain that the letters are lost, the courier escaped and Lee poisoned. Belding's career is important to him, as he is a younger son who will not inherit. He is not as fortunate as I am and does not have an inheritance on which to live."

"So by arresting Uncle Samuel the colonel wants . . . what? To have him hang and therefore to placate an irate General Howe? And that based on the fact that my uncle went to Philadelphia at the constable's behest?"

Charles sighed. "Not exactly. We know that Mr. Holt didn't take the letters to Philadelphia. We also know that they haven't reached their destination by other means."

"How do you know that?"

"Not everyone in Philadelphia is disloyal to the King, Abigail."

I didn't even want to know how Charles knew that or who the "we" he referred to included. "But if you know Uncle Samuel is not involved, why arrest him?" And threaten me, I thought.

"Belding is hoping the letters will mysteriously reappear and save his career. He's desperate. He thinks arresting Samuel Holt will notify the rebels that the letters must be returned. I think it's an exceedingly poor plan, but he had already arrested Mr. Holt before I found out about it, and now he refuses to release him." He shrugged. "Perhaps it'll even work."

"Charles, the letters could be anywhere, even in British hands someplace."

"No, they're not in British hands."

"You're so certain?"

"Yes."

His response was such that I thought it better not to persist. "And if the letters were to magically appear?" I asked.

"Regardless of what he said, I don't think Belding cares who killed Lee, he just wants the letters to give to General Howe. And you never know, fairest Mistress. There may yet be a simple way out of this. Stranger things have happened."

As we had reached the tavern, Charles opened the door, bowed gracefully and went up the stairs to his room. I stood in the front hall, my cloak still dripping, understanding that Charles's confidences were but a request that *I* find the Paris letters and deliver them to British hands.

TWENTY-THREE

When I went to visit Uncle Samuel two hours later, the weather had warmed a bit, enough that my feet were now endangered by puddles rather than patches of ice. My uncle was being held in the Johnson house, for Mrs. Johnson had fled to relatives in northern New Jersey after her home was taken over by the British. Her husband, Colonel Johnson, was wintering with General Washington and the Continental Army in Morristown. Maggie Johnson had abandoned New Brunswick fearing for her life, perhaps unwarranted, and for her silver, probably more warranted.

The home was of a goodly size in the usual four up and four down style, with the stairs in the center hall. My uncle was being "jailed" in a second floor room, which was more than adequate for his comfort with its fireplace and two windows, although those had been shuttered and secured. The day being overcast and dismal, he wasn't missing anything scenic.

As I arrived, Uncle Samuel was entertaining his two guards with stories, elaborated to the point of fantasy from long telling, of his years among the Indians of New York. The guards, having never heard his stories before, were vastly entertained. The scene appeared more like a barroom than a jail. At first glance, my uncle looked his normal vibrant self, but I saw on closer inspection that he appeared drawn about the eyes.

The sergeant, a florid-faced, jolly man, and a very young, thin private politely left the room to return to their posts outside the prisoner's door, each amply supplied with bread, cheese and meat from the basket I had brought my uncle.

"And how do you like staying in a lady's bedroom, Uncle?" I asked, referring to the pink walls and lace-trimmed curtains.

"It would be fine my dear, if it only contained the lady. My two guards are good company, although they are inept at the finer arts of flirting."

He held out his arms to welcome me, an invitation I readily accepted. "You are looking well, my dear, but your cloak is dripping wet, and you are shivering. How do you expect to care for everyone else if you come down with a cold or the grippe?" Removing my cloak, he grabbed a rough wool blanket from his cot and placed it about my shoulders. It had not the feel of my good cloak, but it was certainly drier.

"You are very cheerful, Uncle, considering you're being held here on charges of murder and treason. The treason I can understand, you can be a bit outspoken, but murder?"

"Murder indeed!" Uncle Samuel said. "I never laid eyes on that chap, Lee, much less murdered him. These

British are such bloody fools, as though I would endanger you and Beth. Don't any of these cretins have families? Do they really think I would be stupid enough to kill someone in Raritan Tavern? Especially someone I'd never met. Nonsense, fool-headed nonsense."

Uncle Samuel stopped pacing and pulled a bench close to the fire. "Come sit, you'll be warmer here." We sat shoulder to shoulder, warming our hands. At this distance, he could speak to me in a whisper, a concern as the guards were just outside the open door.

"They can have no proof I killed Lee. I would almost think they want something else from me, though, for the life of me I can't imagine what that would be. I told them most everything I found out about Lee in Philadelphia."

"I'm afraid I know what they're after, Uncle. They want the letters I took from Lee's saddlebags."

"Do they know you had the letters?"

"I don't think so, and they certainly don't know the letters were stolen from my room. You were arrested because Colonel Belding hopes the word will get out that you are about to hang unless the letters are returned by some patriotic soul who wants to keep your neck from being stretched." Was this turn of events all my fault?

"Like bait in a trap."

"More like extortion."

"Still, I am a tasty tidbit, you'll have to agree." Uncle Samuel was positively gloating.

"I think I'll stick with gingerbread, if that's all right with you, Uncle."

"Speaking of which . . ."

"No, there's none in the basket. Now don't frown so. Matty's baking some at this moment and will undoubtedly bring it over herself as soon as it's finished. I hope you will be properly appreciative, as she had to start the oven up just for your treat, and you know how difficult that is."

"I'm always appreciative of Matty and her good works. She knows that," he hesitated, "don't you think?"

"You're sounding a little uncertain. You aren't possibly just a bit intimidated by being imprisoned and threatened with a trial and hanging in New York." Even though my uncle was in a dangerous position, I found it impossible not to tease him a little.

"For purely selfish reasons, I do hope it won't come to that," he said suddenly sober. "Edward Pratt feels there is naught to be concerned about, although I don't know of any lawyer who tells his client to worry. For the moment, I have no complaints about British hospitality. My jailers are fine fellows. I am relieved to know that Belding doesn't really think I killed Lee, even if it puts me in a rather uncomfortable position of hoping some patriot will be unpatriotic and hand over the letters."

He paused, staring into the fire. "Did Belding tell you how much Lee was being paid to deliver these missing communications?"

"No, only that Lee was in the employ of the Crown."

"Employ," Uncle Samuel said, with a snort. "Yes, I'm certain payment was involved. I can't imagine Lee being motivated by patriotism, or any such intangible reward."

I shrugged off the itchy wool blanket, the heat of the fire having warmed me down to my toes and reminded myself to send a softer blanket over from the tavern tonight. I leaned closer to Uncle Samuel to speak as softly as possible. "When you were traveling to Philadelphia, did you stop in Kingston to inquire about the missing Mrs. Lee?"

"Yes, I stopped to see Anthony Borrows at the Wayside Inn, but he and his wife were out and some neighbor was tending the place. Very unforthcoming, the old codger was, too. Couldn't get much information out of him, although he didn't say anything that made me suspicious. Why do you ask?"

"A comment one of the guests—a Mrs. Lydia Cooper from Kingston—made at the ball had me wondering, that's all."

"It may be helpful if you talk to Dr. Dillon about the letters. He can find out if anyone knows where they were taken after they disappeared from your room."

"Dr. Dillon." I said, loudly enough to be heard by any listeners who might have been about.

Samuel replied in laconic fashion as though we were merely discussing the weather. "He's most knowledgeable, Abigail, and he's known you for years. I don't think you should be afraid to consult with him. He's had wide experience and if he doesn't have a remedy, he can obtain assistance from a colleague. If I were you, I would consult with him immediately, tonight even. He's a physician. He'll keep what you say in confidence. And now, my dear, except for this small problem you will take to Dr. Dillon, is everything else well with you and with the tavern?"

Deciding not to mention Beth's encounter with Lieutenant Reade as irrelevant to our concerns at the moment, I discussed the success of last night's ball and the bills I intended to pay with the profit.

"A wonderful experience, paying debts. I have always delighted in it," Samuel said, laughter crinkling at the corners of his eyes. I loved Samuel dearly, foibles and all, one of which, his intense dislike of bookkeeping, had nearly driven several of his creditors to abjure doing business with him. A number of his suppliers had told me of their relief when I had taken over as accountant and they had begun to be paid regularly.

"And truly, Uncle," I said, "I will be proud to hand over the books to the British showing that Raritan Tavern has no debts or debtors except themselves." I sat up straight, raising my chin slightly lest Uncle Samuel see that I was truly frightened about his imprisonment and its potential consequences.

"Why are you showing anyone the tavern books? Is this some new regulation?"

"Well, no. I think it has been the law for quite some time, if treason is committed."

"What are you talking about, Abigail? What does treason have to do with the perusal of the books?" Samuel frowned, appearing genuinely puzzled. He is not usually so thick in the head, but then nothing about today had been usual.

"Not exactly perusal, I shouldn't think. I would expect they will want to see the books when they take over the tavern."

"When who takes over the tavern?" Samuel's voice displayed his irritation at my beating around the bush.

"My dear Uncle," I said, "treason is punished not only by hanging, but by confiscation of all the traitor's property." That said it as clearly as I was able.

There was a long pause while Samuel sat staring at the fire. Finally he smiled and looked benevolently at me. I would have preferred his usual teasing or taunting expressions; benevolence was an ill-fitting garment on Uncle Samuel.

"Abigail, there's something I've been meaning to tell you."

Good God, I thought, let me be strong when he tells me he actually had killed George Fenton Lee and delivered the Paris letters to Philadelphia. I reached up to silence him before he should confess to murder, but he grasped my hand and held it in his.

"I am no longer the owner of Raritan Tavern. I . . ."

My breath caught in my throat but I managed to croak out, "You sold it? Without telling me?"

Thoughts ran frantically through my mind: that he had lost the tavern in a game of cards, that a long forgotten debt had been called, that he had never really owned the tavern at all. In my panic I tried to pace in front of the fire, but could only progress two steps in either direction without banging into a wing chair or a table.

"Abigail, sit down and calm yourself. It is all for the best, even though I was afraid you would react so when I told you, which is exactly why I hadn't said anything for the past year and a half."

"You sold Raritan Tavern a year and a half ago and you never told me. You had me working for some stranger and you never . . ." I paused in the midst of my tirade, this making no sense to me. A small thought flew through my mind, circled to see if it was welcome, and then settled. "Samuel," I asked, suspicion apparent in my tone, "what did you do with my tavern?"

"Exactly!" He smiled broadly, as though to a child who had correctly figured a puzzle. "I put the tavern in your name, Abigail. You have been the owner for these past months, and making a nice little profit I must say."

"And you didn't want my agreement for this?" I was incredulous.

"I was afraid you would refuse, that you would mutter some nonsense about how you didn't want to own it, or you didn't think you would make a good owner, or some other ridiculousness. I thought if you were the owner, unknowing for a while, you would have to accept the gift and acknowledge that you were doing a fine job, much better than I ever did, that's for certain.

"I also wanted to provide for you and Beth, should anything happen to me. Treason was always a possibility although I had thought rather improbable." He smiled, shaking his head that such an improbability had come to pass.

"And what if I should remarry? You had told me you would never put the tavern in my name because it would become my husband's. Or have you decided my chances for finding another husband are gone, that I am no longer marriageable?"

"Not at all. I think you are highly marriageable, and that did pose a problem for me, but I have now solved it, with the help of Edward Pratt. It seems I can deed the tavern to you with the stipulation that it will remain in your name, unless and until you choose to sell it. It's not done too often, but Edward says it's perfectly legal. He drew up all the papers and it's been yours for about eighteen months. I hope you're pleased." He looked quite pleased himself.

In truth, I was overwhelmed. That I would ever own property of such value was beyond dreaming. I was now a wealthy woman in my own right, and Samuel had arranged it in such a way that no man could take it from me.

"Now if you don't want it, Abigail, you can sell it and take the money to do whatever you wish."

I reached over to kiss Samuel's cheek, noticing how pale it was in the firelight. "You are precious to me, Samuel. You gave me back my life when my dear husband and baby died. That was beyond anything I could ever repay. Now you've given me even more, and I'm not sure there are any words to thank you. I do know I want you around my tavern—there, I said it—for years to come, and that means those letters must be found so you can come home. After I see Dr. Dillon, I will ask him to come to you. You look pale in spite of your jocularity and I would have you be your usual hale and hearty self for the party we will have when you are released, even if that takes another day or so."

Samuel stared into the fire. "Abigail, you know it is possible that I will have to go to New York."

"No," I said. "Somehow we will retrieve those letters and you will go back to embellishing your adventures and eating up Matty's gingerbread."

After a few more moments of chitter-chatter, I left my uncle. I was now more determined than ever to find the Paris letters, should I have to take on the entire Continental Congress. The sergeant guarding Samuel escorted me to the front door, thanked me for the food he and his partner had enjoyed, and told me there was a good British doctor in Amboy if Dr. Dillon was unable to help me.

I went directly to Dr. Dillon's office, rang the bell on entering and then, as the sign on the door advised, waited in the small foyer. A wood bench with a spindle back, sufficient for three or four people, was placed against the wall facing a window, shuttered halfway for privacy against any walking past. The empty wooden coat pegs were a welcome indication I was the doctor's only patient, which was what I had expected so late on a Saturday night. I hung my cloak and returned to the bench.

I pondered thoroughly how to find the key that would open the prison for Samuel, but my mind was drawn inexorably, as a bee to pollen, to the news that I was the owner of Raritan Tavern, and had been for the past eighteen months. Somehow, I thought, I should have felt a subtle change in the nature of my life the day Uncle Samuel had signed over the title, but I had not. The earth had remained solid under my feet without a shift in its traces. The sun had risen daily in the east and set in the west, the days of the week and the months of the year had changed in their anticipated cycles. The war had started, the British had arrived, but overall life had gone on its course, and I had never known.

Uncle Samuel was correct. Having been the owner unawares and during a decidedly difficult time, I could make no falsely humble claims that I had not the ability to successfully run the business. He had outwitted me. I wondered what had motivated him to sign the tavern over to me so many months ago. I doubted not his desire to provide for me, having no descendants of his own and having been to Beth and me a grandfather, surrogate older brother, and knight protector. Had he predetermined the coming of this confrontation between the British and the patriots and feared his political beliefs would jeopardize the tavern? I would have to ask him. Such an ability to predict the future could be most advantageous.

I was so bemused that I failed to notice Dr. Dillon open the inner door, and was startled when he spoke. "Judging from your smile, your evening must be going well indeed, Mistress Abigail."

"Just a passing fancy," I said, rising to follow him into his office. "My evening, unfortunately, goes poorly. The

British have arrested Uncle Samuel for the murder of George Fenton Lee."

"No." He sat abruptly at his desk, his broad shoulders slumped, disbelief drawing his brows together in a straight line above his glasses. He drew his hand through his gray hair, pulling it from its neat queue. "That's not possible. I'm sure he had nothing to do with Lee's death. Samuel had no cause."

"Colonel Belding said my uncle will be taken to New York to stand trial for treason." I sat in a chair across the desk and waited a moment for the doctor to contemplate the implications. "I am told Belding imprisoned Uncle Samuel as a lure to retrieve a packet of letters Lee was carrying. The good colonel wants them back very badly, as he is committed to producing them for General Howe. When I mentioned all this to my uncle, he advised me to talk to you."

"Ah." Dillon looked at me for a long while, his eyes troubled, his hands folded one atop the other, unmoving. I did nothing but look back at him, wondering what thoughts were troubling his mind. Taking a deep breath, he broke our locked gaze.

"Once the British arrived, Samuel demanded that any patriot activity be concealed from you and removed from the tavern lest it jeopardize you and Beth."

"Committee of Correspondence activity?"

"Yes, and other actions the British consider treasonous. But you seem to have done a good job of getting yourself mixed up in this murder even without our help." A smile played about Henry Dillon's mouth, a slight chuckle rumbling from somewhere in his chest.

"You don't think I killed Lee?" I asked, sitting on the edge of my seat.

"No, I didn't mean that." A look of consternation crossed his face. "You didn't kill him, did you?"

"Of course not," I said.

"I didn't think so." His shoulders relaxed visibly. "I was referring to taking the letters from Lee's saddlebags."

"How did you know about that? I didn't tell anyone other than my friend, Rachel Morton, and Uncle Samuel."

"Someone else saw you when you put them under your cloak to keep them from Captain Phillips."

My mind raced through those who had been present in the stable: Amos Warren, the blacksmith, John and me, then Captain Phillips and Constable Grey. I thought no one had seen me take the book and packet of letters. "Who saw me?" I demanded, rising to lean over his desk.

"Shh. Sit down, please," he looked about furtively as though expecting some redcoat to be directly behind him. "I can't tell you, Abigail. It wouldn't be safe for either you or him."

I sat down, biting my lips in frustration. I did not wish to get someone hanged for treason. Speaking with what I hoped was quiet reasonableness I said, "Uncle Samuel sent me here to get information about the packet of letters. You know that I took them from Lee's saddlebags, but are you aware that I no longer have them?"

"I rather assumed so. Otherwise, you wouldn't be here."

"Do you know where they are?"

"No."

"Can you help me find them?"

"I don't know. There are certain people I can speak with, although I have no idea if any of them will be able to help. The last I knew of the letters they were under your cloak. When your room was searched . . ."

"You searched my room?"

"Not me personally, but one of us did. And didn't find them, I might add."

"When was this?"

"The night after Lee's corpse was found, that would have been Thursday last."

The night I had heard footsteps in the hall, and then found that my room had been searched the next morning when I awoke. "The letters were there then. Your searcher didn't find them." I paused. "I'm not pleased that someone entered my room while I was sleeping to look through my personal belongings."

"That person would not have touched a hair on your head, Abigail. None of us would."

"Who is this 'we' you keep talking about?"

"A group of us, including your uncle, Sons of Liberty, rebels, patriots, Whigs—take your pick what you want to call us. And while I can't give you names, I'll wager if you think about it you'll be able to figure out most of them. You know everyone in town and before this occupation you heard enough talk around the tavern to know people's leanings."

"I suppose, although I was surprised when Uncle Samuel sent me to talk to you. I've been out of the inner circle of conspirators for a while now," I said.

"And that's exactly what we intended when it became obvious the British were here for the winter and a whole swarm of them would be bedded down in our old meeting place. It wasn't safe for you or for us there anymore, but I certainly do miss Matty's cooking." Dr. Dillon toyed absently with a small pile of lead bullets he had sitting on his desk.

"Did you remove all those from patriots?" I asked curious and aghast at the same time.

"Most of them, though Dr. Tilton over in the British camp has added to my collection." Responding to my surprise, he continued, "We're medical colleagues, even if we are on opposite sides right now. I studied in England, you know, and find nothing strange or unpatriotic about discussing medicine with Tilton. Most doctors are more interested in their profession than in politics."

"Then how do you know about the letters?" I asked, rising from the chair to take my leave, as I doubted Dr. Dillon would give me more information.

"I said most doctors, not this doctor. As for your question about the location of the letters, I know they were being sought so they could be returned to the courier who brought them from Paris."

"Where is the courier now?"

"Not in New Brunswick, but beyond that, I don't know." Dr. Dillon walked with me to his front door. I restrained his arm as he was about to open it.

"I have only one more question. Did the courier leave Raritan Tavern last Tuesday during the small hours of the night?"

"Yes," was the unadorned reply.

TWENTY-FOUR

In the gathering twilight, I found myself tripping over paving stones for lack of noticing where I placed my feet, so occupied was I with what Dr. Dillon had told me. Halfway home, I changed direction and headed toward Rachel Morton's. Before I did something inherently dangerous, I needed my friend to listen to what I was thinking and to correct me if my suppositions were without merit.

Settled in Rachel's kitchen, my outstretched feet warming at her fire, I relayed my conversation with Dr. Dillon. "He said someone saw me take the letters from the stable."

"But he won't tell you who that was?"

"No." I shook my head in frustration. "He also said he knew of one unsuccessful attempt to take the letters from my room, although he claimed he knew nothing of who had ultimately stolen them."

"Has he found out what became of them after they were taken from you?"

"Not for certain, although he thinks the letters are being returned to the courier from Paris." I looked at my friend, excitement in my eyes. "And he said the courier had stayed at Raritan Tavern but was no longer in New Brunswick.

"And you know who that could have been?" Rachel's green eyes flashed as she caught my excitement.

"There have been five people who stayed at the tavern in the past ten days." I held up one finger in the air, "The deceased George Fenton Lee."

"Who is currently stored in your icehouse waiting transportation to Philadelphia."

Two fingers, "Bradford Jamison, the printing salesman."

"Who is a most honorable patriot, Abigail," Rachel protested.

"Though perhaps not shy about entering women's bedrooms to take purloined French letters. Remember, he did leave the day after the murder and then returned in a flurry the following day with no real reason to explain his bizarre behavior."

Rachel shook her head as if to dismiss what I said. "There must be some reasonable explanation for Bradford's behavior. Who else was there?"

I raised my third and fourth fingers, "Charles Whitworth and his valet, Robert." My thoughts flew to Charles looking glorious as he danced with me at the ball and then, later in the evening, appearing equally handsome in nothing but his nightshirt, sword in hand.

"You don't want it to be Charles, do you?"

I shook my head sadly and told Rachel about meeting him at Colonel Belding's earlier today. "Do you suppose it's all a façade? I ask myself how much I can trust him and I can't answer my own question."

"Too bad it's not Robert you're suspicious about," Rachel said, rising to add wood to the fire. "He of the clandestine, skulking behavior and expressionless visage."

For a moment I considered Robert, but it was not *his* feet I had tripped over at British Headquarters. It was also Charles who had influence with people of sufficiently high office to make me very cautious about believing the wiles of that charming rogue, for rogue he surely was, of that I was now certain.

I shook my head, "But Charles and Robert arrived after Lee's murder, so neither of them could have committed that foul deed. But both of them, as well as Bradford Jamison and Mrs. Lee could have had something to do with the disappearance of the letters."

"And she is number five," Rachel said. "The mysterious, vanishing Mrs. George Fenton Lee. Correct?"

"Yes," I said, all five fingers on my hand now extended. "Mrs. Lee, or whoever the person was, has been missing since the middle of the night when the murder transpired. The next day the missing stallion was found on the road to Princeton and in his saddlebags were the Paris letters that I took and which were subsequently taken from my room. Charles said it is the letters Colonel Belding wants, not Uncle Samuel. So it is the letters I must find."

"But if you don't know who took them, Abigail, how can you find them now?"

"I don't know who took them, but I know who brought them from Paris and if Dr. Dillon is right, whoever stole the letters from my room was taking them for the courier from Paris. I just have to find her, and I believe I know where she is."

"Where?" demanded Rachel.

I described what I had heard from Lydia Cooper about the woman who had arrived in Kingston during the early hours of morning after the murder had been committed. I then proposed how I would proceed on my quest for the Paris letters.

Rachel was not impressed. "You want to go to Kingston to find a woman who *may* be there, and who *may* have carried the letters from Paris, and who *may* have given them to Lee to put in his saddlebags. After Lee was murdered, which she *may* have done herself, this woman *may* have lost control of the horse which was then returned to your stable, from whose saddlebags you removed the Paris letters. Now this person, who *may* actually be a woman, *may* give you the Paris letters which she *may* have and which you will give to Colonel Belding who *may* then release Samuel." Rachel took a deep breath looking me straight in the eye. "A very suppositional trip, Abigail."

"I know," I said. "But I know not what else to do and Uncle Samuel's life is certainly worth a trip to Kingston in icy weather."

"You are a brave woman, Abigail Lawrence. I am proud to have you as my friend, however this ends." She embraced me and kissed my cheeks to wish me Godspeed.

I knew my next conversation would require all the bravery I possessed.

"Ain't no way I'm gonna let you do this. You completely lost your mind this time, Abigail. You can't go riding off by yourself alone. Master Samuel would have my head on a platter if anything happened to you and when he were done with me I'd still never forgive myself. No Missy, what you want just ain't possible." John stood glaring down at me as I sat on the milking stool, my hands clasped in my lap. I had expected that his reaction to my plan would be contentious, but I needed him and Matty to accept responsibility for Beth until I returned; I couldn't leave without a promise.

"You're being rather pigheaded about this, John," I said. "If you would just listen to what I'm saying, you'd see it is a good idea and has excellent potential for getting the letters that will free Uncle Samuel."

"It has great potential for getting you hurt or killed is more like it." Matty wagged her finger at me like I was a child. "Riding off to Kingston in search of a ghost some gossip thinks she seen ain't using the brains you was born with. I think Master Samuel being in jail has rattled you so you don't know which way to turn, but this wild-goose chase ain't good thinking."

We were quarreling late into the night in the room that was their home. Attached to the back of the stable this slant-roofed, one-windowed, former tack room had been transformed into a cozy haven complete with a small fireplace, a bed heaped with feather quilts, the reward from plucking so many chickens Matty would say, and a corner table with two chairs, which is why I perched on the three-legged milking stool. The room was isolated enough that we didn't have to worry about being overheard, and small enough that even a slightly raised voice boomed threateningly from wall to wall, not a blessing with blood running so hot.

"This is not a wild-goose chase, at least, I hope it won't be," I countered weakly, afraid to admit Matty had a good chance of being right.

"Wild geese ain't the point, the point is you not going. It's too dangerous," John said. "If you really thinks this person with the letters is in Kingston, I'll go and fetch them tomorrow." Matty was nodding in support of John's suggestion, and for just a moment I felt relieved that I might not have to attempt this dangerous mission.

I sighed. "I think I have to be the one to go, John, although I do appreciate your offer. You didn't see Lee's companion well enough to recognize her, did you?"

John shook his head. "No."

"But I did." I hoped I would recognize her again, although I thought it best not to talk about my doubts at this moment.

"Fine," John said. "Then I'll go with you. You can recognize her and I'll make sure nothing happens to you when you do."

"No. I need you to stay here to run the tavern until I get back. And look after Beth."

"Really, Abigail," Matty said with exasperation, "you has this place so well organized it'd run by itself, and what needs tending I can tend for a day or two. You take John with you."

"Sounds like you're anxious to get rid of me. Just what are you gonna do while I'm gone?"

"Find me a redcoat to warm my bed. Been looking over the selection for a while now." A soul-warming laugh erupted from Matty as she watched the expression on John's face.

John raised his eyebrows in appreciation of the teasing, "Woman, none of those youngsters got enough experience to please you."

Matty just laughed harder.

"So what time we leaving tomorrow, Abigail?"

"After a good hot breakfast," I said, rising to leave. "Will you pack us a lunch, Matty?"

She nodded. The frown registering between her brows warned me she had found my capitulation suspicious.

I did not sleep well that night, tossing this way and that, afraid of what was to come in the morning but even more afraid I would sleep too late. Finally I rose while the sky was still pitch black and dressed for the cold ride to come. Wool stockings I covered with a pair of my husband's old winter breeches I had tailored to my size, which would allow me to ride astride and yet stay warm. A full dark skirt for modesty and the usual warm jacket were topped by my cloak, scarf, and hat. I felt rather like an overstuffed pillow as I quietly made my way down the back stairs. Matty was waiting with coffee in the warming kitchen.

"I wasn't expecting you," I said, my heart dropping as I looked around for John.

"He's still sleeping," Matty said, wrapping her shawl closer about her nightgown against the cold.

"But how did you . . ."

"I know you for a long time, Abigail Lawrence. Ain't much you can get past me. I knowed you wasn't telling the truth when you said you'd wait for John. Not quite sure why, but I trusts your judgment."

"I wish I was certain who to trust at this point," I said. "John . . ."

"Oh, I don't mean John. I trust him with my life, which is in fact why I want him here. I need to know that you and John are both here to take care of Beth if anything should happen to me. I truly do think that I'll be all right, but . . ." I shrugged.

Matty nodded, wrapping corncakes in a napkin. "How you gonna get there?"

"I'll leave New Brunswick as though I were going to the farm, so I won't need traveling papers. Then, I'll use the back roads until I'm well past Somerset and can return to the King's Highway and then on to Kingston. On the way back, I'll follow the same route in reverse. I hope to be home by tonight but don't get worried if I end up staying one night; I am not sure how long it will take me to find this courier person and then to convince her to give me the papers. Staying a night at the inn in Kingston seems preferable to traveling at night."

"I understand," Matty said, putting bread, cheese and meat in another napkin.

"Tell no one but John where I have gone. I'm confused about whom we can trust these days, so if anyone—anyone at all—asks, I've gone to the farm. I'll stop there and tell Benjamin my plan in case someone goes looking for me. As long as John doesn't make a scene and come charging after me, no one will think anything of my going and returning."

"I'll see to John. I been able to hobble his horse other times, I can sure do it now."

"And Matty . . ."

"You know we loves you and Beth. You're our family, Abigail. We'll take care of her and we'll keep a candle in the window for you." With that she embraced me, put a large parcel in my arms and closed the door behind me. My horse was saddled when I got to the barn. I could only guess how that happened as Matty knows nothing at all about horses.

TWENTY-FIVE

The trip to Kingston was anticlimactic. The British sentry on the road to the farm was asleep and snoring so loudly I heard him a hundred yards away. When I reached the farm, I talked briefly to Benjamin, hoping he would remember what I said as I had awakened him from a sound sleep. The trip through the fields was startlingly quiet, it still being dark and the birds silent. The only sound was the rhythmic clop of my horse's hooves on the frozen ground. I was not far from the King's Highway, which ran from Amboy, through New Brunswick, Kingston and Princeton to the Delaware River at Trenton and then on to Philadelphia, when the sky began to lighten. The black lace of the winter trees became more distinct against the gray sky and behind me to the east lines of brilliant pink broke the darkness. As the sun rose, the furrowed fields were rimed with ice that glinted like the courier's diamond earring. A few deer scrounged breakfast near the edge of the woods, pawing daintily at the snow to find edible twigs and grass. With the coming of the light, there was some birdsong and the flit of a wing here and there, even the bright red of a cardinal. I ravenously ate the corncakes Matty had packed and washed them down with apple cider. I might have been the only person in the world that morning, a feeling that made my heart soar.

Somewhere in the middle of the ride, while my mind was thinking about nothing more than the winter sights and sounds, the pieces of the murder puzzle began slowly to fall into place, then into apple-pie order. I knew who had murdered George Fenton Lee and how. In but a short time, I would know how correct I was.

There remained, however, leftover pieces that did not fit my solution. I wondered if these could form a second puzzle separate from the first. I knew Lee had died from cyanide poisoning; that was a piece of the first puzzle. For the second puzzle, I began with the glass of wine that had contained a fatal dose of yew someone had placed on the fireplace mantle. I remembered the medicine chest Miriam had brought to nurse Lieutenant Southerland, with its myriad drawers and bottles. Miriam told me she never carried yew, because her mother had died from an overdose eight years ago. But what if Miriam had lied? What if she had used exactly that medicine to poison the man she believed responsible for her mother's death? Had Miriam Ilon's mother been an indentured servant in the house of George Fenton Lee? At the back of my mind flitted the name of the woman Rachel and I had found in Lee's account book. Think, Abigail. Think.

As I rode along, the mare keeping a good pace, I noticed people begin to emerge from their homes to start the day—a woman chopping wood at the side of her house, a farmer letting his cows out from morning milking. Think, Abigail.

As suddenly as a rabbit scared by a dog, I remembered. Martin and Ilona Hartmann and their daughter Miriam had been transported on one of Lee's ships. After Martin had died on the journey, Ilona had become responsible for his seven years of indenture as well as her own seven years. And, if I was remembering correctly, her fourteen-year contract had·been retained by George Fenton Lee. Uncle Samuel had learned in Philadelphia that Lee regularly seduced his housemaids to humiliate his estranged wife. So Ilona had most likely become pregnant, tried to abort the baby using her midwife's knowledge of yew, and died. At some point, her daughter Miriam had taken her mother's name and become Miriam Ilon, now a servant at Raritan Tavern.

There was another puzzle piece that whispered in the back of my mind. Something from a conversation I had with Matty about a baby. And also something from Lee's account ledger about a baby. I was tensing my muscles so tightly the horse shied under me. I calmed the mare, relaxed my arms and legs, and watched the scenery pass. I saw two children filling wooden buckets from a stream frozen at the edges; a carriage with two well-dressed men passed by, merchants headed east. I wondered if they would be stopping for lunch in New Brunswick.

The boy baby that was sold must have been Ilona Hartmann's baby. No wait, if I remember correctly, the baby was sold in 1771, only six years ago, and Miriam said her mother had been dead for twelve years. That could only mean that Baby Hartmann was Miriam's. And Baby Hartmann was *sold*. I was beyond shock. I wanted to scream to heaven, demand some explanation. Instead, I promised myself I would find a way to set aright this terrible injustice. Miriam's attempt to poison Lee I now found entirely comprehensible.

I progressed along the road to Kingston only because the horse kept moving. When we came to the crossroads where we would rejoin the King's Highway, the mare stopped, uncertain, and I was forced from my heart-breaking reverie. After directing the horse to the right, I paused, thinking I had heard the snuffle of a horse behind me but, turning, I saw no one. I was certainly on edge.

I thought I recalled Miriam saying something about her baby dying. How could that be? Did she not know her baby had been sold? What could I possibly do about an event that occurred six years earlier? I was chilled to my very marrow and not from the winter weather. I had felt warmer in the dark before the sun rose than I felt now. I spurred my horse on, anxious to get to Kingston and to a fire that would warm my body, although not my soul.

My early morning trip had certainly been productive, although my conclusions were appalling. I thought I knew who had killed Lee and that Miriam had tried to poison him with yew. I had yet to learn why he had been run through with the sword, but determining that was asking a little too much for any morning.

Kingston was four miles north of Princeton, a small village just large enough to have one church and the Wayside Inn, where I sought to warm myself and get what information I could about the mysterious courier. I rued my lack of foresight that I had not asked Lydia Cooper which house the mysterious visitor had been looking for, because now I was forced to search for her, something I anticipated would be difficult. I didn't know what name she

259

would use or how the small village would receive queries from a stranger.

The inn was typical of those outside larger towns such as New Brunswick, small and fashioned from a private house. The main room contained a dining table with six chairs. Several spindle-back chairs with arms were pulled up to the fireplace, where I went immediately to warm my cold hands. Two men, one a gray-haired gentleman of indeterminate age dressed in a serviceable but worn tweed coat, the other a broad-shouldered man in his thirties with an apron tied about his waist, were engaged in a game of chess at the small gaming table in the corner. The younger of the two rose to greet me, introducing himself as Anthony Burrows.

"How may I be of service to you, Ma'am?"

"I am Abigail Lawrence, tavernmistress of Raritan Tavern in New Brunswick."

"Of course, I knew you looked familiar. Had some business with one of your local ship captains and stayed the night. I remember that cook of yours, upset my wife no end the way I carried on about how good your food was. She still working for you?"

"Oh yes, Matty's still there."

"You being troubled much having half the British army camped at your doorstep and taking up your tavern?"

I shook my head. "Luckily the officers who are billeted with me appreciate Matty's cooking as much as you did and are careful not to stir things up for fear she'll leave."

"Speaking of food, while ours runs a poor second to yours, what can I offer you?"

"Something warm to drink and then whatever you have. I don't want to trouble you."

"I'll go tell Flora. We'll get you warmed up in no time," he said, heading out of the room.

I shed my outer garments, reveling in the warmth of the fire.

"You travelin' all by yourself?" the white-haired man at the chessboard asked.

"Yes, just a quick errand and then I have to get back to New Brunswick."

"Must be lots of folks in New Brunswick loyal to the British," he said. I wasn't certain if it was a question.

"It's hard to know when there are ten soldiers for every resident. People mostly keep their allegiance to them-selves." I hoped I sounded discreet.

"That true for you too?" he demanded, in a tone that annoyed me.

"I have a tavern filled with British officers," I responded severely. "When they leave, I want that tavern to be in one piece and all the people who work there to be safe. So yes, to answer your question, I keep my allegiance to myself."

He shook his head and looked toward the chessboard to study his next move.

Mr. Burrows returned, handing me a steaming cup of coffee. He was followed by a homely but smiling woman dressed in cheerful yellow and carrying a coffeepot which she placed on the hob. She gave a quick curtsy while her husband introduced her as his wife, Flora.

"We are pleased to welcome you, Mistress Lawrence," she said in a startlingly low and melodic voice. "My husband has spoken of your tavern with outright envy. I have a stew pre-pared and fresh bread, if that would suit your fancy."

"It would suit most admirably. Now that I am finally warm, I find I am hungrier than I had thought." Mrs. Bur-rows nodded and left the room.

"And will you be going on to Princeton for the night?" asked Mr. Burrows. It was a natural assumption. Most travelers would not stay in Kingston when the larger town was near.

"Actually, I have come to Kingston itself. I am looking for a guest who stayed at Raritan Tavern ten days ago. She left a valuable piece of jewelry at my tavern and I am hoping to return it to her. I had lost all hope I would be able to do so until Lydia Cooper attended the ball last Saturday and told me that she had seen my guest here in town. I was so pleased to hear of her, now I just have to find where she's staying. Do you know?"

Mr. Burrows frowned, "What is her name?"

"Mrs. George Fenton Lee." After I gave them a brief description of the courier, there was a long pause while Mr. Burrows and his chess opponent exchanged glances.

"Never heard of her," the older chess player answered in a voice too loud for the room.

"Maybe as innkeeper you have heard of someone who is visiting?" I asked, hoping to prod Mr. Burrows into a response.

He looked at his friend, who shook his head slowly from side to side, lips compressed into a thin line.

"I think not," Mr. Burrows said.

It was patently obvious they knew the woman I was inquiring about. It was equally obvious that they were not going to tell me anything. I resigned myself to a long, cold search, going door to door if necessary, but I resolved I would find the courier.

The dinner was adequate, though Matty would never have served such bland fare. Mr. Burrows and his friend continued their chess game in silence, never looking at me. I felt colder when I left the Wayside Inn than when I had first entered. I mounted my horse and started toward the church, hoping the minister would be more forthcoming than the innkeeper, when I heard a voice calling behind me. I turned to see Mrs. Burrows running down the street.

"Wait, please," she said breathlessly. She had thrown an orange and black plaid shawl over her shoulders against the cold. "Anthony just told me what you wanted. Those thickheaded numbskulls think they're being patriots by not telling you what you want to know. I know you're from a good family and would never do anything to help the British."

"You know my family?"

"Of course, I went to school at Mrs. Chapin's with your brother years ago. My name was Burke before I married." She looked at me for recognition and I smiled encouragingly. I did not recognize the name.

"The woman you're looking for arrived here very late Tuesday night, that is Wednesday morning. I don't know her name, although there was a lot of gossip about her when she first arrived. We're a small town and any visitors are a welcome change, but no one has ever really seen the woman. She's staying at the Talmadge house. That's one street over and half a block up. It's a brown house with white and tan trim. I hope she's the one you're looking for."

"I certainly hope so too. Thank you for your help. I'll remember you to my brother next time I write."

"Is he in Princeton now?"

"He's up in Morristown with General Washington."

"I knew you were a patriot," she said triumphantly, between shivers. She had been resting her hand on my leg and asked so quietly I had to bend almost out of the saddle to hear her, "Are you wearing breeches under your skirt?"

"Indeed I am, a pair of my husband's I cut to size. They're very good for riding in cold weather."

"I can imagine. I didn't even realize you were wearing them while you were in the house. Did you know that Mrs. Nathaniel Greene is said to wear breeches when she rides? Makes a lot of sense to me. I wonder what Anthony will say when I tell him I want to try a pair of his breeches?" We laughed. "It is a short walk to the Talmadge house from here, only a block and a half. If you wish, I could water and feed your horse while you visit."

"That would be most appreciated," I said. "You have been a tremendous help to me." I dismounted, handing the reins to Mrs. Burrows and hurried in the direction she had indicated. I was anxious to claim payment for the diamond and gold earring I had in my pocket.

TWENTY-SIX

I found the Talmadge house after an easy walk. Now that the moment had arrived to confront the mysterious Mrs. Lee, I wished I had eaten less of Flora Burrow's stew, as it churned about uncomfortably in my stomach. I smoothed my skirts, took a deep breath, walked up the three steps that led to the front door and knocked firmly. Quick, light footsteps could be heard coming from the back of the house. A middle-aged woman, with graying hair caught up in her mobcap, opened the door just wide enough not to be thought rude.

"Yes?" she demanded quietly but sharply.

"I am looking for Mrs. Lee."

"There's no one here by that name," she said, beginning to close the door.

Without thinking, I jammed my boot between the door and its frame. The guardian of the door looked surprised, but then opened the door again slightly. "I'm sorry, but there is no Mrs. Lee here."

"You would be Mrs. Talmadge?" I asked.

"Yes," she said, with such hesitation that it was more a question.

"I am Abigail Lawrence, tavernmistress of the Raritan Tavern in New Brunswick. I am here to see the woman who stayed at my tavern about ten days ago."

"There is no one here." She made another gesture to close the door.

"I have come to give her an earring she left at the tavern."

"I will give it to her," said Mrs. Talmadge, putting out her hand. At least I knew I had the right house and that Mrs. Lee was here, no matter what she now called herself.

"No." I said. "I've come all this way, I must give it to her personally."

"I will ask." Mrs. Talmadge looked down at my boot, which was still firmly planted against the door frame. "Please, remove your boot," she said.

"No. Not until I have spoken to Mrs. Lee, or whatever name she is using here."

The woman's eyes opened slightly, then the mask returned to her face.

"I will relay your message when you remove your boot," she said firmly.

"No." I responded just as firmly.

Raising her eyes to heaven in exasperation, Mrs. Talmadge left me standing at the doorway while she retreated stiff-shouldered, back through the house. She returned shortly, opened the door and gestured me into the front parlor, her silence an admission of my success. In a few minutes, I heard slow, labored footsteps in the hallway.

I recognized the woman who walked into the parlor as the person who had accompanied Lee at Raritan Tavern.

Though I knew she had been abused, I was surprised by the extent of her injuries. She appeared to have been severely beaten. Yellow bruises turning to brown covered the entire right side of her face from her hairline to her jaw. High on her left cheek, five knots of linen thread held together a cut that had barely missed her eye.

"You are polite to not gasp or run from the house, shrieking at the sight of me, Mistress Abigail." She attempted to smile but grimaced in response to the pulling of a facial muscle. "Please come back to the kitchen. It is warmer there." Following Mrs. Talmadge, we walked slowly down the hall, the pace set by Mrs. Lee. Her robe-like brown dress hid whatever other injuries she had sustained.

The kitchen was indeed warmer, overly warm in fact, as I began to perspire as soon as I entered the room. "Why don't you remove your cloak? I know it is hot in here. I feel very cold with these injuries and the warmth helps." Mrs. Talmadge assisted me in removing my outer garments, while Mrs. Lee, whatever her real name, took a seat near the fire in a high-backed wing chair.

Mrs. Talmadge adjusted the pillows behind Mrs. Lee and brought a beautifully embroidered footstool on which she placed her slippered feet. She also brought the injured woman a wool blanket, which I found unbelievable in this warm room. When I was seated in the chair opposite Mrs. Lee, Mrs. Talmadge handed me a cup of tea. Then she placed a teapot on the fireplace hob where it would be near to my hand. Evidently I was expected to refresh our cups, since it was much easier for me to move about. After this, Mrs. Talmadge left us, although I suspected she had not gone far.

"I am a bit surprised you found me, Mistress Abigail." Mrs. Lee's voice had a dusky quality, warm and calming, seductive.

"It took me some time, Mistress . . ." I hesitated. "I am at a loss to know how to address you."

"You don't like Mrs. Lee?" She chuckled. "I didn't much either. Not a nice man."

"No, he was not. What name do you wish me to use now?"

She hesitated a moment, looking at me directly as if to see into my very being. Finally she said, "Jean will do. It is how most people know me." I waited for a surname but none was given. Charming as she was, I had still to break through her wall of caution.

"Then you must call me Abigail, as it is how most people know *me*."

"What brings you all the way from New Brunswick?" she asked.

"I have an earring you left when you fled Raritan Tavern," I said, withdrawing it from my pocket. Jean gazed longingly at the diamond studded piece I held in my open palm. "The silversmith in New Brunswick said it was quite valuable and that its owner would gladly pay a reward to have it returned."

"How much do you want?" she asked.

"I don't want money," I said leaning over and placing the earring in her hand. "I want you to give me the letters you carried from Paris. Also, I want truthful answers to some questions I have."

"I thank you for the return of the earring, although I am not certain I can accept it as I am unable to give you the reward you desire. I don't have the letters." She looked affectionately at the earring then held it out to return it to me.

My face must have reflected my dismay, as she said, "Are they so important to you?"

I explained that my uncle was being held in exchange for the letters, and that his life was threatened should they not be given over to the British.

"*Je comprends,*" Jean said. "I will have to think if there is some way I can help you obtain the letters. For this afternoon, we could start with your questions, for those I can answer, at least as far as I'm able."

"Would you tell me about the earring?" I asked, hoping to ease into the more difficult questions.

Jean looked at me and smiled. "You are correct about the earring being irreplaceable. It was designed by a noted goldsmith in Paris and given to me by my husband, who I loved very much and who has since died. I was foolish to bring the earrings, but I am never without them, and didn't consider the possibility of losing them. I am indebted to you."

"I, too, have buried a beloved husband and can understand your distress at misplacing such a precious memento. I am pleased to return it to you." Stirred up again, the feelings of catastrophic loss tightened about my heart. But, I reminded myself, I was not here to wade into the river of grief once again. I needed to find information that would free Uncle Samuel. My thoughts in order, I said, "Perhaps, I can tell you what I've surmised, and you can correct me when I'm wrong and fill in what I've missed."

Jean nodded her agreement. I studied her closely. Under the bruises her features were delicate, with beautifully shaped auburn eyebrows and graceful long lashes. She held the china teacup with the refinement of a duchess, her hands as pale as a linen handkerchief, and with long elegant fingers.

"You left Paris with letters from Benjamin Franklin addressed to George Washington and to the Continental Congress. You went by boat, embarking from Bristol in England, probably to get around the British blockade, and landed in New York, about Sunday, February 23rd. You were met in New York by George Fenton Lee, who was to escort you to Philadelphia, although you have yet to get that far."

"I left from England to guarantee I would arrive in New York," Jean corrected, "but continue." She kneaded the pillow behind her back with her elbow finally reaching around and dumping it unceremoniously on the floor. She remained sitting upright, but she seemed more relaxed, her shoulders less rigid.

"You posed as Lee's wife and stayed the night of February 24th at the King's Jester Inn in Amboy. Something happened that night, and you and Lee fought. The argument and beating you received from Lee were overheard by another guest who said he feared you were being killed."

Jean paused for a long time, staring into the fire. Then, trying to sigh, she grimaced and grabbed at her chest. "Two broken ribs, compliments of George Fenton Lee. They're a bloody nuisance."

I shook my head in silent sympathy at the price of being a courier.

Taking a few seconds to catch her breath, she continued. "It will be easier for you to understand if I start back before we ended up at Raritan Tavern. I was born—" she began, trying not to laugh and strain her ribs again, "— that's back far enough I think, in Virginia to a family of the landed gentry, the Carters of Williamsburg."

"The Carters of Carters Grove?" I asked. "My mother knows someone in that family."

"*Bon*, I'm a cousin." Jean seemed relieved to find someone who knew of her family. She continued, "My father sent my brother and me to England to be educated. In my case, that didn't mean I went to the gentlemen's schools, but to a rather endless round of dancing schools and music lessons and tutelage from my aunts about how to manage a large household. After one particularly soggy winter, I convinced the aunts that I should go to France to improve my accent and to study painting. I loved Paris. A few years later I married Denys Gauthier, a charming, funny Frenchman with, among other talents, exquisite taste in jewelry. We were very happy and he thought managing the plantations my now deceased father had left me in the West Indies was heaven on earth. Denys was skilled at managing my interests, and when he died I was left a wealthy widow."

"How did he die?" I asked, my interest piqued by this romantic story of international love and loss.

"We were on a trip from Jamaica to France," Jean began, her smile gone, "when our ship was blown off course nearer to England than we would have liked. Denys and several other men were killed attempting to prevent the English sailors from boarding our ship. The war between France and England had ended, so there was no justification for the English to board our ship, no matter how close we were to their coast. They acted like pirates out for their own reward, regardless of the flag they flew. The joy was ripped from my life that day and I have hated the English ever since."

No wonder her anger at the British was so great. My husband, Jared, and my son had died from unpreventable illness and tragic as that had been, the death of Jean's husband struck me as being worse for it had been preventable, an act of war where there was no war. I nodded, urging her to continue.

"It took me many years before I could continue with my life but I have now surrounded myself with the artists and intellectuals of Paris in my salon, a most unrestrained and invigorating group. When I tire of entertaining, I sculpt and have had some success with it. The King has one or two of my pieces, which has greatly increased my acceptance at court.

"I have developed a special fondness for my fellow Americans who visit Paris, especially Benjamin Franklin, who has been a frequent guest. I do love him dearly, such a unique gentleman and a *bon ami*. We have had truly glorious discussions about the rights of the colonies and the rights of men; I had so much to learn and have become quite enlightened.

"And I will do anything to defeat and humiliate the British." Jean's face darkened and she began to gesture with her left arm but, gasping at the pain, spilled her tea. I wiped the tea from her gown and the floor with a napkin. She declined my offer to refill her teacup. In a moment she continued, "I have introduced Dr. Franklin to some of my friends and acquaintances who are keenly interested in supporting anyone who opposes the English. And to facilitate his diplomatic goals, Dr. Franklin has relied on individuals who could obtain privileged information for him. I have been one of those individuals." Jean gave me a look of apprehension.

I nodded quickly. "We have a number of people in New Brunswick who convey information regularly up to General Washington in Morristown, so it doesn't surprise me that Dr. Franklin also has spies working for him."

"Not a word I prefer—spy. Too many thoughts of hanging at the hands of the British. You do not seem surprised that I am a woman and a spy."

"You did not seem surprised that I am a woman and a tavernkeeper."

"*Touché,* Abigail." Now a glint of pleasure flickered in her solemn brown eyes.

"But no, I am not surprised. Several of the New Brunswick spies are women. One is very successful at driving her cows all over the countryside to conceal message-delivering. Also, I saw the letters from Lee's saddlebags and while I didn't read the ones that were sealed, I did read the one from Dr. Franklin. Lee had just come from Philadelphia not Paris, where the letters originated, so I guessed you were the courier. Do you like that word better than spy?"

"*Peut-être.*" She sounded doubtful. "When you hear the rest of the story, you may not choose such an innocent word. A while ago, a courier, to use your word, for he really was just a courier, was killed in New Jersey carrying letters from Paris. From then on, it seemed the English were getting information from many of the messages being sent to the patriots, and it was suspected that someone was acting as a double agent for the British. In response, I was sent to the colonies to find that person."

I was sitting on the edge of the chair, engrossed in Jean's story. "Lee," I said.

"*Certainement!*" I could hear the fierceness of her anger.

"So the letters you carried were the cheese to catch a rat," I said.

"Precisely. The idea was that I would carry letters from Franklin which Lee would take from me and hand over to the British, somewhere between when he met me as I disembarked in New York and Philadelphia, our ultimate goal."

"Then that is why you wanted to land in New York, to give Lee ample time to steal the letters and pass them on."

"Exactly. Although it surprised me that he did nothing to pass them on before we reached New Brunswick," she said.

"And he had to do something by then as it is the last town controlled by the British. Perhaps it is a good thing for you since you *were* able to escape to a patriot house."

"I definitely prefer not to be hanged as a spy, that's true." Jean's attempt to laugh immediately became a hoarse cough. "*Mon Dieu*, I certainly paid a higher price than I had expected."

I reached out to clasp her hand, to sympathize, to reassure Jean that she had been heard and was not alone. She patted my hand lightly in response; but she neither cried nor smiled, as if her pain was beyond simple emotion.

"It must have been difficult to be so alone and unprotected. Were you not frightened?" I asked, wondering to myself if I would make a good spy.

"I had been told by Dr. Franklin that there would be someone following me closely to protect me."

"And?"

Pointing to her bruised face with a rueful smile, Jean commented, "Obviously endeavors did not go as planned. The ship arrived in New York earlier than expected and a lame horse prevented my protector from following. And then Lee decided he wanted not only the letters but also to play Adam to my Eve, confusing a Paris salon with a house of accommodation. When I refused, he became violent."

"That was the fight that was heard at the King's Jester the night before you arrived at Raritan Tavern."

"Correct. He had already taken the letters and then he decided to take me. I am not a whore. When I refused, he used his cane on my ribs. I expected Lee to be a traitor, not a sadist. He positively enjoyed beating me." She shook her head in disgust and pain. "I thought about leaving that night in Amboy, but decided to wait, hoping I could still discover the person to whom he would pass the letters. I thought I was prepared for the next night whatever he might do."

"At my tavern."

"Yes. Lee's contact was apparently in New Brunswick. I know he had not shown the letters to anyone before we reached Raritan Tavern. We settled in for the night, and Lee again demanded behavior I was not willing to perform."

"But he already had the letters. He couldn't be content with that?" I held my breath, as if, to put off the turning point of Jean's story.

"Apparently not," she said. "He was one of those men who liked to dominate the women around him and who become enraged if they won't submit to his desires. After he had hit me about the face, which would leave observable bruises, I knew he meant not only to have his way with me, but to kill me in the bargain."

"But in New Brunswick you were prepared."

"Quite so."

"You put cyanide salts into something he drank."

"Yes. But how do you know that?" Jean seemed surprised that a mere tavernmistress would have deduced such information.

"One of our doctors and an apothecary concluded cyanide was the cause of Lee's demise. It is not readily available in New Brunswick. You must have brought it from France. What was the drink you used?"

Jean sighed and was silent, finally answering my question. "I was given the cyanide in Paris for my protection. I am not comfortable carrying a gun, and refused the one I was offered. And yes, I put the poison in a very nice cordial one of your maids brought to help me sleep."

"Did she also bring a wine glass for Mr. Lee that you placed on the mantelpiece?"

"Yes. I thought it smelled strange and was afraid Lee wouldn't drink it."

I nodded. "It contained yew, another poison. The maid also had ample reason to want Lee dead, though her bruises are ones of the spirit. Her physical bruises are long faded."

"I know nothing of yew, beyond that it is used as an abortifacient and is rather unreliable. Although, in my hands, the cyanide proved to be unreliable as well."

"You did not mean to kill him?"

"No. I wanted to put him into a deep sleep that would allow me time to escape. In my panic, I gave him a stronger dose than I intended. You will think me heinous, Abigail, but I don't regret killing him. He was the epitome of evil."

I thought back to the recent intrusion into Beth's room and realized I too, would have been capable of killing. I am greatly surprised at my own ethics, but I would not have hesitated to shoot the young lieutenant, had he not yielded. "I do not condemn what you did," I said. On the contrary, I felt a deep sisterhood for this woman.

A comfortable quiet developed between us for a few moments. Then Jean said, "Some of these scars will never go away." She touched the sewn skin on her cheek, then added with raised eyebrows, "I must admit it will make a marvelous conversation piece at my salon. People will wonder endlessly how I came by such a glorious scar."

At a loud knocking on the door, Mrs. Talmadge scurried to the front of the house. I could hear a brief discussion between her and a man, before the door shut and she came to the kitchen to whisper a message for Jean. She turned to me. "Have you any more questions for me before I attend to my other guest? It seems a day for callers."

"One or two more," I said. "Are you certain Lee died from the poison you gave him?"

"Yes, of course. I was alone with him in the room from the time I administered the cyanide until he was dead."

"Then why did you thrust him through with the sword?"

"I have no idea what you are talking about. I had no sword. And why would I want to kill Lee when I knew he was already dead?" She looked at me skeptically.

Jean's denial seemed believable, although it left me no closer to discovering who had wielded Lieutenant Reade's sword.

"Just one more question, Mme. Jean Carter Gauthier," I said. "If you intended the letters as a trap for Lee, the information contained in them must be false. Am I correct?"

"It would be more correct to say the letters are misleading. Dr. Franklin and I planned for the British to obtain them. So you see, if I had them, I would gladly give them to you, knowing they would end up exactly where we had intended." She rose stiffly. "If you will please excuse me, I must attend my other visitor. It is late to ride back to New Brunswick." She gestured out the window at the sun low on the horizon, "Perhaps you would prefer to stay the night and leave in the morning."

And so it was agreed. Mrs. Talmadge escorted me to an upstairs bedroom where I could wash for supper while

Jean met with her other guest behind the closed doors of the parlor. Supper would be at least an hour later, Mrs. Talmadge said, and I found the bed enticing after I had washed the grime from my face and hands. When I woke much later than after an hour, moonlight was streaming through my window. Lighting the bedside candle, I saw that a tray on the dresser contained my supper. The water in the teapot was tepid but when I placed my hand on the doorknob to see if I could warm the pot in the kitchen, to my dismay I found that the door was locked.

TWENTY-SEVEN

M y first thought was to try the window, but a premonition proved true when I found the sash nailed shut. As I peered out the window, I saw a man holding a lantern as he helped Mrs. Talmadge into a carriage. He was speaking to someone already in the carriage, though I could hear naught of what they said. He closed the carriage door and nodded to the driver who headed down the road toward the King's Highway, rapidly and silently. When the man turned back toward the house, he looked up at my window and smiled. I knew him. I could hear his footsteps on the stairs and then a knock at the door of my room and the key turn in the lock.

"You all right, Mistress Abigail? I saw your light and hoped nothing was amiss."

"Mr. Jamison," I said. "You must be the follower."

"What?"

"Jean's protector. The man charged with her welfare."

"Well, yes. You could call me that." Jamison looked abashed, as well he should, considering the harm to which Jean had been subjected.

"Where was Jean going at this hour?"

"Away from here, thanks to you. She wasn't well enough to travel but she didn't want you to turn her in to the authorities."

"I wouldn't have done that."

"Oh, she asked me to give you this." The printing salesman reached under his coat and handed me the familiar leather envelope containing the letters from Paris.

"You had them all along?"

"Since I got them from your hiding place under the eaves, yes. There was a bit of confusion about them. But, please," he held up his hand, "would it be possible to tell you about it in the morning? I'm certain you've a multitude of questions and I don't have the energy to answer them now. The ride back to New Brunswick, once the sun is up, will give you ample time to interrogate me." He did look exhausted, his eyes lined with black circles and lacking their usual sparkle.

I turned back into the room toward the candlelight to assure myself of the contents of the packet and Jamison closed the door. This time it was not locked. In spite of my protestations to the contrary, I did wonder if I should dress, saddle my horse and ride after Jean. But then, I thought about my marriage, the relations my husband and I had enjoyed, the laughter, the passion, the sense of fulfillment. Never, but never, had he raised his hand to me. No woman deserved to be abused as Jean had been and as I knew Miriam and her mother Ilona had been, all three at the hands of George Fenton Lee. So in the wee hours of the morning, long before the sun began to rise, I sent after Jean only my blessings for a good journey. I could not hand her over to the constable, and certainly not to the British to be punished for defending herself. Surely any woman had that right, regardless of what the law said. Was that not why we were fighting this war, for the right to protect ourselves from abuse and tyranny— whatever its form?

I fell asleep content with my decision, the packet of letters clutched to my breast.

"In order to answer your questions truthfully, Mistress Abigail, I must have your promise that you will not divulge any of what I say to the British," Bradford Jamison said as we rode back toward New Brunswick later that morning. The day was cold and sunny, a replica of the day before.

"And what of Uncle Samuel's fate?" I asked.

"Let us hope the letters you carry will suffice to have him released."

"And if not?"

"Mistress Abigail, I am as concerned about Samuel as you are. He has been a good friend to me for many years and I will do all in my power to see him safely back at his farm."

"I suppose if surrendering these letters does not suffice we will think of something else. Perhaps I can call in a favor from Colonel Belding in return for the care we gave his friend's son, Lieutenant Southerland. After all, the British have no proof that Uncle Samuel murdered anyone. They are just using him as a threat to get the letters they couldn't get for themselves, or so I've been told. And the letters will be in their hands as fast as I can get them to New Brunswick. All right, Mr. Jamison, I give you my word that I won't say anything to the British about what you confide in me."

We rode on, our horses abreast, their hooves rhythmic on the frozen road, their breaths forming small white clouds. I thought for a moment about what I wanted to ask him. Among my many questions, I started with the basic. "Who are you?"

He laughed aloud. "Nothing like starting at the beginning, Mistress Abigail. I truly am Bradford Jamison, just as I have always been, and I do pander printers' supplies up and down the colonies between Boston and Philadelphia, just as I have been doing for the past fifteen years. Your friend, Rachel Morton, can verify this. I have known her and her father and brothers in New York for quite a while. And yes, before you ask, for as long as I have known her, she has always worn black."

I laughed. "How did you come to be involved with Jean and the letters?"

"I also have an avocation, a small side job, if you will. I collect and pass on information to General Washington. It's usually whatever I find, but this time the task was a bit different."

"How so?"

"I was asked to keep an eye on a certain lady from France and to assist as she needed help. Regrettably, things fell apart from the beginning. The ship she traveled on arrived in New York ahead of schedule and I was nowhere about. Unfortunately, George Fenton Lee *was* there and insisted they start their journey toward Philadelphia that afternoon. Then our alternate plan to meet her at a local inn failed when my horse went lame. I have been playing follow the leader from the start. Not a position I liked when I was supposed to be protecting her mission."

"And who is she?" I wanted corroboration.

"What did she tell you?" He was a master of answering a question with a question.

I relayed all Jean had told me and noted the surprise on Bradford's face. "Her name is Jean Carter Gauthier and I am taken aback, well perhaps not . . ." He paused in apparent thought. "She is a much better judge of character than am I, so it confirms my willingness to trust you that what she told you was true. It is quite a compliment. She rarely trusts anyone. It is the nature of the spy business. Our lives often depend on what we conceal from others."

"Do you like being a spy, Mr. Jamison?"

He thought, looking straight down the road and who knows how much farther in his mind. "I would greatly prefer that we lived in a time when it was not necessary for anyone to maintain relationships for the sole purpose of obtaining information. I do not like to place the people who work with me in danger, and I wouldn't mind making my working rounds without fearing for my life. But I passionately believe in the importance of the press in a free society and if it costs my life to obtain that freedom, then I think I will have died in a just cause. Mind you, I would prefer to live a very long and happy life, with grandchildren to whom I can tell tall and terrible tales as they sit on my knees and scream in mock fright."

"And with this enthusiasm for the press, do you also write?"

"Occasionally, though I find my writing to be mundane and pedantic. I feel I have no gift for it, not like our friend Whitworth who is a truly inspired writer, whatever his political affiliations may be." He frowned slightly, as if Whitworth puzzled him.

"I have wondered about the man. For all his charm, there seems a bit of him that he withholds," I said.

"You are perceptive to see that. Most see only his exuberant façade, not what he hides."

"You seem to know him well."

"Oh, no. I know him only because we work the same job from opposite sides."

"Yes, he is a spy also, isn't he?" I was not surprised, having felt for some time that nagging suspicion about Charles. Yet, there was a feeling of disappointment deep in my heart, a sense of mourning for a fading relationship, or a lost, although only potential, love. I sighed, displeased to have confirmed what I had not wanted to be true.

"Whitworth is a writer of note. If you follow his works, you'll find to your surprise that they're often set in places where England has a current interest or conflict. I don't know who he works for in the government, but I surmise his position must be quite high. You'll notice he showed up in New Brunswick after things went bad for Lee. Came to dam the dike as it were. He arrived rapidly, in fact, because he had been in Amboy and the messenger Captain Phillips sent didn't have to go as far as New York."

"Had Whitworth been following Lee and Jean Gauthier from New York?"

"Perhaps, although it would seem he was a day or so behind them."

Suddenly, I was terribly unhappy. I slowed my horse for a moment's privacy as the reality of Charles's British allegiance pounded into my brain.

"Is he aware you know that he is a spy?" I asked as my mare regained his side.

"Whitworth and I know each other by sight and we have a sort of gentleman's understanding that we won't get in each other's way. For what it's worth, my guess is that he was behind trying to get Samuel freed in exchange for the letters. I think you have charmed Whitworth, as you do us all, and he is doing what he can for your uncle."

Once Uncle Samuel was freed, I thought dreamily, Charles and I could go off to a place where one's politics mattered not a whit and one's repartee was of great import.

"You don't think he was responsible for Samuel's arrest?" I asked, coming back to the reality of New Jersey.

"It's not Whitworth's style to be so heavy-handed. He's usually very subtle in his maneuverings. Arresting Samuel was probably the result of Colonel Belding acting in panic. He needed those letters to give to General Howe. Also, I would guess Whitworth knew what kind of a person Lee was, as Whitworth is a man of high principles, he would have abhorred a snake like Lee."

"Although he didn't hesitate to use Lee to obtain information." My fine white knight.

"Apparently not." I appreciated Bradford's straightforward assessment of Charles. He did not condemn the Englishman merely because they were on opposite sides, but understood that Charles was as honorable in his beliefs as Bradford was in his.

"And what of Robert, Whitworth's man?" I asked.

"I don't really know much about him. He is always with our friend Charles, but that could be as a valet or a confidant, or any combination thereof."

"What does General Howe think the letters contain that he is so anxious to get his hands on them? I never opened them, except the unsealed one from Dr. Franklin."

"Report of the negotiations with France as well as letters of credit to be given to the Congress. The British believe they are real and would do anything to get them back from the patriots."

"There are no letters of credit?"

Jamison paused, choosing his words carefully, "As I have only recently learned from Jean Gauthier, there are no valid letters of credit in the packet you carry. What you have was written specifically to mislead the British and was intended to fall into their hands through Lee. It was part of the trap."

What he said fit with what Jean had told me. "So, for all my pretense of neutrality, by giving these letters to the British, I will be playing spy and furthering the patriot cause."

"Indeed you will," Mr. Jamison said with a broad smile. "Both your uncle and Rachel Morton will be most pleased when you tell them."

"If you knew all this, why did you take the letters from my room?"

"I didn't know the letters were intended to fall into British hands until I spoke with Jean yesterday."

"And by-the-by, how did you know I had them at all?"

"I followed you to the stable the day Lee's horse was returned."

"Ah. The mysterious shadow in the doorway. I thought I was seeing things."

"You almost caught me, Mistress Abigail."

"Did you see me put the letters in my pocket?"

"Yes, although I was the only person who did. I had eventually ended up on the floor in one of the stalls and had a unique perspective on your actions."

"You must have thought me in league with Lee and the British when you saw me take the letters." I blushed that Jamison had thought me a loyalist.

"I wasn't quite sure what to think, but Rachel Morton insisted you were a patriot regardless of what I had seen."

Just as she had defended you when I wondered about your loyalties, I thought, enjoying the symmetry of our reactions. "And then you came into my room the next night looking for the letters." I frowned, the memory of waking to find my room ransacked still vivid. I wondered if I would ever become acclimated to the injuries, slight or shattering, that accompanied war? Even knowing who had entered my room, an edge of my fright remained.

"Correct," Bradford said, bringing me back to the present. "And I couldn't find them, so I rode to Kingston to see how Jean Gauthier had fared. I had no idea she had been beaten or I would have gone sooner. When I reached Mrs. Talmadge's, Jean was delirious from her injuries and kept mumbling something about the letters. I concluded, incorrectly, that she was desperate to have them back, so I returned to New Brunswick to try again to get them."

"And this time you were successful, while I was at church."

"With you out of the tavern, I could make a little more noise than when you were sleeping in your room. Even so, your hiding place under the eaves was not easy to find." Bradford gave me an approving look, the corners of his eyes crinkled with enjoyment. "Once I had the letters in my possession, Whitworth had arrived and I thought it important to see what he was doing in New Brunswick. Then, yesterday morning, I followed you here to Kingston."

"Why didn't you give me the letters, if you knew Samuel was being held for their ransom?"

"I still assumed Jean wanted them. It was only yesterday after she told me they were fake and intended for the British that I realized I could have saved us all much worry had I given them to you to rescue Samuel. I'm sorry for the trouble I caused you."

"We seem to have caused inconvenience for each other. Hopefully, we will now be able to set all to rights, get Uncle Samuel freed, and go about our extraordinary daily lives."

We proceeded along the King's Highway to New Brunswick, chatting companionably and laughing frequently. It seemed as if I had known Bradford Jamison for a long time, as though he was an old friend, so closely did our temperaments complement each other. As we neared the tavern, I realized I had forgotten about the subterfuge of going round about to Uncle Samuel's farm and had entered directly from the southwest. For the moment, no one seemed to notice.

The normality of New Brunswick was overwhelming. It seemed the world had shifted in the thirty-six hours I had been away, found a murderer and let her go, heard stories of revolutionary spying and ignored them, and returned home. The guard on the road into town had waved me through, barely looking at me. Although a few greetings were called out to me, all seemed ordinary, so ordinary in fact, that I felt my heart pounding in panic as if all this courtesy was a façade meant to entrap me and the precious letters I carried. What if the British knew about the plot to trap Lee and were looking for someone to take the blame? What if they were waiting to catch me with the letters to declare me a spy and murderess and to hang me? What if the letters wouldn't be enough and they would still hold Uncle Samuel for treason even after I had given them my precious packet?

"Mistress Abigail, thank the good Lord you home. We was mighty worried about you when you didn't come last night." John stood holding my horse's bridle in the yard of the tavern stable where the tired animal had headed automatically for its feed and rubdown. Mr. Jamison had disappeared.

"I was delayed but everything worked out well. I got what I went for." I said. He helped me down and untied my saddlebags, which I took from his hands.

"And now they gonna free Master Samuel?" John's concern was obvious from his deep frown.

"I expect so," I said, not giving voice to my fears, though I doubted he was deceived by my optimism.

"You a brave woman, Mistress Abigail. I'm proud of you, regardless of what happens. Matty's got some warm food waiting with your name on it. I'll be in after I see to your horse." I had turned toward the kitchen when he said, "Obediah Fitch, Mr. Lee's business manager, come in last night from Philadelphia to pick up the body and belongings. And Miriam's gone missing. She and all her stuff with her. Her room's empty like she weren't never there."

"When did this happen?" I asked, not surprised at this turn of events.

"This mornin'. The door to the warming kitchen was unlocked when Matty got there, so we figure that's how she left. Don't seem like she took anything that don't belong to her, but we ain't got any idea why she left."

I had a fairly good idea.

A while later, I had washed, changed out of my riding clothes and eaten heartily. I was about to deliver the packet of letters, when Mrs. Hemple, our laundress, entered through the warming kitchen door. Red of face from the steam she constantly worked in, she approached me, moving slowly but deliberately.

"I was told to give you this soon as I could." She drew a folded white paper from under her checkered work apron and handed it to me. "I just want you to know that I think that man deserved to die. Would have killed him myself, if I'd had the chance. Men like that don't have a single bone of kindness in their whole bodies. I hope he burns in hellfire and nobody answers his cries for mercy, just like he did to her." And with that she turned back toward the laundry, more red-faced than before.

The outside of the letter was addressed in a fine hand to Mistress Abigail Lawrence. It read:

> *Mistress,*
>
> *This letter is to confess that I murdered George Fenton Lee of Philadelphia on Tuesday, the 25th day of February by poisoning him with yew in a cup of wine.*
>
> *My mother and I were indentured servants in his household for many years and he abused us mercilessly, physically and mentally. He is responsible for my mother's death when she found she was with child for a third time through his forced attentions. She had aborted the first two, having knowledge of herbs that would cause her to miscarry. By the last time, she was sick in her mind and could no longer abide to live. She took her own life using yew. I was sixteen at the time, and owed service to Lee until I reached my maturity plus the two years of servitude my family still owed. He began to force himself upon me the afternoon we buried my mother. I endured several years of his attentions and regular beatings until I became pregnant. The babe, a son, was born alive, for I heard his cry, but died almost immediately, or so Lee said. I think Lee killed my son so I would not have to care for him and could thus devote all my time to my master. I ran away soon after that and had not seen Lee until Tuesday last when he arrived at the tavern. I was overcome with rage, and thought only of revenge for my mother and my son.*

After Lee was dead and his lady had left, I returned to his room. I knew he was dead, but I wanted to guarantee that he would never again rise up, to harm another living soul. The devil he was. I remembered my mother telling me that evil can only be stopped by driving a sword through the heart. So, I took the sword from a bedpost in the officers' dormitory and drove it through Lee's heart.

Mistress, you have been fair to me and I would not have you or your good uncle under suspicion of murder. You will know who to give this letter to so all will know that I killed George Fenton Lee, that you had nothing to do with his murder, and should not be punished for it. Mrs. Hemple and her neighbor Mrs. Owens have made their marks to show that I wrote this letter.

Miriam Ilon Hartmann

I rushed to the laundry and found Mrs. Hemple. I asked her several questions which she answered affirmatively. When I had finished, she was smiling toothfully, without complaints. She stoked the fire and left the sheet she was ironing half finished. Closing the door behind her, she headed home, bearing my messages. I planned to follow her shortly.

TWENTY-EIGHT

As soon as Mrs. Hemple left, I headed for British Headquarters. I was determined to play this game without the British intimidating me or arousing my temper, and certainly without arresting me. The purpose of my visit was to free Uncle Samuel, not to join him in jail. I was hoping the deck was stacked in my favor, that I could keep a straight face and play all my cards correctly.

The opening gambit was the same. I was welcomed, relieved of my cloak, and asked to wait while Colonel Belding was notified of my arrival. This time I waited patiently, watching out the entry window. There was hustling down the hall, but I refrained from turning until Captain Phillips called my name.

"G'day, Mistress Abigail." He bowed low, condescending in his pseudo-formality. "Allow me to show you to Colonel Belding's office." He put out his arm for my hand. I ignored it.

The good colonel rose from behind his desk to escort me to a chair. The sliding doors behind his desk were ajar, the room behind them dark. The wild card.

"I have obtained the letters you were interested in, Colonel. I have put my tavern and livelihood in peril to do so and am dependent upon your protection should the local rebels find out I passed them to you." I withdrew the leather packet from the pocket under my skirt. I had to force my thoughts away from what Rachel would say of this little performance, lest I start laughing. "I give them to you for the release of my uncle."

"Why, Mistress Abigail, after all this time you declare that you are loyal to the King. You were a bit slow to show your true colors," Captain Phillips said with a sneer.

"My uncle is my primary concern. However, I would be of little service to you should my neutrality be questioned," I said. I was aware that under my skirt my knees wobbled.

Phillips shook his head in disgust.

"We should read the letters to make certain they are what General Howe expects," Phillips said to Colonel Belding.

The colonel silenced him with a gesture. "Have you read the letters?" the colonel asked me.

"Only the one that is not sealed. I did not open the others."

"And it is not proper for us to read them either, Lieutenant, much as the idea titillates. I would however check the seals, Mistress." He held out his hand and I handed over the packet.

Colonel Belding stepped into the adjoining room, closing the sliding doors behind him so I was unable to see what transpired. Phillips stood behind me staring at my back. A little voice dared me to knock at the doors and call out a greeting to Charles Whitworth. With a sigh, I managed to contain my impetuosity.

The colonel returned, informing me the letters were as I had said. Captain Phillips was ordered to see that Uncle Samuel would be released immediately.

My game won and my poker face still in place, I thanked the colonel and left.

I found Obediah Fitch, the business manager for the late and unlamented George Fenton Lee, sitting at a table in the bar, hunched over a glass of Madeira. He was the physical opposite of his employer. Where Lee had been muscular, with a loud voice and commanding demeanor, Fitch was small and rabbity, with glasses he repeatedly pushed into place after they had fallen down his nose. He seemed drawn in on himself as if continually afraid of the world and the demands it would place on him. Probably a justified stance, I thought. At the moment the question was, would he remain loyal to his deceased employer or would I be able to get the information I needed?

"Mr. Fitch," I said sitting down opposite him in a tavern booth. "I am Abigail Lawrence, the tavernmistress." I had brought a decanter of Madeira from the bar and refilled his glass. "I hope you are finding your accommodations suitable."

"Quite adequate, quite." Fitch's voice was pleasant, although indistinct, his face a mask.

"You have met Constable Grey?"

"Yes."

"And obtained Mr. Lee's belongings?"

"Yes."

"Is there anything more we can do to help you?"

"No."

"When do you think you will return to Philadelphia?"

"Tomorrow." Fitch paused, adding some variety to our conversation. "I think."

"Perhaps you might help me with a puzzle I have been trying to solve concerning Mr. Lee." I smiled encouragingly. He remained expressionless. "You were his business manager, were you not?"

"Still am. Lots of things to finish up. Most people don't realize."

"I'm certain that's so with a business as large as Mr. Lee's. What will happen to the business now?"

"Don't know. Could be sold. Depends."

"On?"

"Pardon?" A look of bafflement crossed Fitch's face and he poked at his glasses.

"Selling Mr. Lee's business depends on what?" I clarified.

"Oh. On what the inheritors wish."

"Do you know who inherits?" I remembered the rumor about Lee murdering his wife and that there had been no children from the marriage.

"Looks like his sister-in-law, Mrs. Prescott. He has no family and most of the money he started with was his wife's. She's dead, so's all her family except the sister. Mr. Lee's going to turn in his grave when this is settled. After we bury him, that is." A slight smile showed more humor than I would have credited to Fitch. "He hated his wife's folk, thought they were sanctimonious prigs. Didn't understand him or his way of living."

"I hear he was rather a Lothario." I gave what I hoped was a worldly look and pushed on. "I understand there were illegitimate children. Did he leave anything to them?"

He pushed his glasses up twice before answering. "I don't know . . ."

"I know that he took particular interest in female indentured servants who appealed to him and that there were by-blows from this interest."

"I really couldn't . . ."

I looked him directly in the eye, confronting him. "I am particularly interested in one family named Hartmann, Ilona and Miriam, mother and daughter."

Mr. Fitch seemed to disappear into the collar of his coat, like a turtle into its shell. I waited for him to reemerge, but when that seemed increasingly unlikely, I continued. "Is it not true that Ilona Hartmann was brought from Europe as an indentured servant and then worked in Mr. Lee's household until her death?" A nod. "Wasn't Mrs. Hartmann the object of his attentions?" Another nod. "Weren't these attentions then transferred to her daughter Miriam, who became pregnant by Lee?" There was a mumbled sound that I took for *yes.* "Mr. Fitch, look at me," I demanded. He raised his eyes and pushed up his glasses, which immediately slid back down his nose. "Did not Mr. Lee sell this child of his and Miriam's?"

"Oh, no. No. No. He would never sell his own child. He did put it up for adoption and I found a very nice family who wanted the boy. Most glad were they to have him, most glad."

"And they paid Lee money for this child?"

"Oh, just enough to cover the cost of his bearing, the extra food Miriam had eaten, and the easier schedule she was on while she was with child."

"Do you remember how much that was?"

"Somewhere around two hundred pounds, I think. But that was just for expenses, you understand."

I leaned forward across the table. "Mr. Fitch, how much would you expect to pay for a slave of the same age?"

"Oh, you would never buy a slave child at that age. Not good for the child to be separated from his mother that early. Five or six years is the youngest they would be sold and then they would cost a hundred fifty or two hundred pounds, depending on their sex."

I was so disgusted at this calculated approach to the sale of *any* child that I would gladly have thrown him out of the tavern had I not needed more from him. "Did Miriam know of the arrangements Lee made for her son?"

"Best as I can recollect she was told the baby had died. Mr. Lee thought it would be easier for her that way. So she would be able to return to her duties without having to worry about the child."

Those duties included servicing Lee's sexual appetites, according to Miriam's letter.

"Do you remember the name of the family who took the child?" I knew the name from Lee's journal, the one I had taken from his saddlebags along with the packet of Paris letters. But I was hoping Fitch would verify it.

He shook his head.

"Does the name Roger Cochran refresh your memory?"

He nodded. "Yes, I think that's it. Didn't have children of their own. Were very pleased with the boy."

"Do you know what happened to them? Are they still in Philadelphia?"

"Don't think so. Almost sure. They were going to western Pennsylvania, had some land there."

"But you don't know exactly where?"

"No. No need to keep in touch. Mr. Lee said he would miss the child too much to hear from them."

Hell, I thought. I poured Fitch another full glass of Madeira. I went to my office, gathered pen, ink, and paper and returned to the table to find Fitch had drunk the wine. I refilled his glass once more.

"I need you to do something for me. Use this paper to write down what you have just told me. I will get witnesses to your signature when you are done."

His eyes popped wide open. "I couldn't do that. It's my livelihood."

"Lee's dead," I said. "He can do nothing to you."

Fitch kept shaking his head, muttering to himself.

I leaned forward, my hands neatly folded on the table in front of me. "I have a sister who lives in Philadelphia on the same street as Mrs. Lee's sister, Mrs. Prescott, the woman who will be your new employer. Their children go to the same school. It will be very simple for me to write about our conversation to my dear sister. She would, of course immediately pass the information to Mrs. Prescott, who I am sure is a very moral woman, and who may hesitate to employ someone who sells newly born babes."

"But I . . . I only did what I was told . . ."

I dipped the pen into the ink bottle and held it out to the very fearful-faced Mr. Obediah Fitch. As he started to write, I went to the kitchen where Dr. Dillon and Constable Grey waited, ready to witness the letter which affirmed the paternity of Miriam's baby boy and the sale of that child to a couple named Cochran.

The taproom tables were filling with evening tipplers when Charles Whitworth appeared in the doorway. I had been dreading his appearance, knowing it could mean only one thing.

"Fairest of the fair, I fear I must bid thee adieu," he said with a slight bow.

"Sir Author, is it truly needful that you leave our humble abode so soon?" And why, even realizing the depth of our differences, did it fill me with such disenchantment?

"It is with regret that I must leave on the morrow, my man is packing at this moment. Could you not spare me a moment for a farewell sip of wine?"

"Perhaps one glass."

I poured us each a glass of sherry.

Charles raised his in a toast. "May your days be long and joyful, and may you resolve all mysteries to a gracious ending."

We touched glasses, sipped our wine and Charles leaned over to kiss me. It was not a short kiss.

"Your uncle will soon be returned to the bosom of your household," he said, calmly I thought, after the intensity of what had just transpired.

"Yes, and I thank you for your intercession on his behalf." I, too, could sound mundane, regardless of the color of my cheeks.

"I did little, Mistress Abigail. It was you who obtained the price of his release."

"But you who set the price."

He smiled.

"I am sorry I missed your reading while I was away on my errand," I said. "I hope you had a receptive audience."

"Indeed, Mrs. Chandler brought every lady she knew and a few she didn't. I tolerated it, though it was difficult without your presence. Perhaps I may read for you privately someday when I next pass through New Brunswick."

"And when will that be, most notable scribbler?"

"Anon."

"Ah. And now where would you wander?"

"Where the fair wind doth take me. Would you not come along and be my love? We would have adventures beyond imagining."

But, I knew that was too much to wish for, not today. "Most honorable Sir Author, I must decline your offer as I have duties here in this small hamlet." I rose to leave and Charles rose also.

"It has been my great delight to meet you, fairest Abigail, the lodestar of my life." He bowed deeply, graceful and gallant to the end.

TWENTY-NINE

Raritan Tavern settled in for the night. John closed the bar, locked the front door, and joined Uncle Samuel, Beth, Matty and me in the warming kitchen. He brought a bowl of eggnog, strong with rum. I sat fiddling with the Traveler's Bane puzzle.

"I'm thinking we got a heap of things to be celebrating tonight." He passed the bowl first to Samuel. "Thanks to the good Lord you home and not a hair on your head been touched. Mighty glad about that."

Samuel drank deeply. "I'll drink to that." He drank again. "And here's to the owner of Raritan Tavern." He handed me the bowl. "May you prosper in your heart and in the cash box. I know that life will always be interesting with you around, Abigail, though a little less excitement would be good for an old man like me."

I drank and passed the bowl to Matty. "To true friends who support me even in the most dire straits." I looked at John, "And who saddle horses in the early hours of the morning." He smiled, but said nothing.

Beth picked up the bowl and said, "To the best mother in the world. But please, don't run away again, I was very frightened while you were gone." She took a little sip and handed the bowl back to Uncle Samuel.

I put my arm around Beth and hugged her. Three days later, she seemed to have put Alan Reade and his despicable behavior from her mind.

"Now that we're done with all this congratulatory stuff, I'd like to hear the whole story," Uncle Samuel said. "Who did kill Lee?"

And at that moment, the ring slipped effortlessly from the spiral of the Traveler's Bane. "Look," I said. "I solved Amos Warren's latest puzzle. Finally."

There were huzzahs all around. Then Uncle Samuel insisted I tell how I solved the puzzle of Lee's murder. The real Traveler's Bane, he called it.

I explained about Jean Carter Gauthier, her task in setting the scene that would trap Lee as a spy for the British, and how that plan had fallen apart, forcing her to fear for her life and ultimately to poison him in self-defense. "She was the actual murderer. She gave him the cyanide, watched him drink it and die."

"And you believes her?" Matty asked.

"Yes. I found her story compelling and have no reason to think she was lying."

"Well then, where does Miriam come in?" Beth asked.

"Miriam saw Lee arrive and prepared him a glass of wine with the yew, thinking to avenge herself and her mother for all his abuse when they were indentured to him. What a terrible time they had, Beth," I said.

"Maybe a long time in hell will teach him you can't treat people like that." Matty shook her head in disgust. "How'd you figure it all out?" she asked me.

"From Lee's accounting journal. It's probably the only good thing about him, but he was a meticulous record keeper where his profits were concerned." I led my family through how I had discerned that Miriam Ilon was the daughter of Ilona Hartmann, and to my conclusion that Miriam was the mother of the baby boy who had been sold. "When I talked to her tonight at Mrs. Hemple's, she said she changed her last name when she ran away from Lee's household because she wanted to leave the pain behind her."

"How'd you know she were at Mrs. Hemple's?" Matty asked.

"We'd spoken of what good friends they are, remember? I figured Miriam fled when Obediah Fitch arrived here from Philadelphia. He was Lee's business manager and probably had known Miriam when she was in service to Lee. Also, I thought Miriam might still be in New Brunswick. Fitch arrived late enough in the day to preclude Miriam going very far. I was right."

The door from the courtyard opened, admitting Bradford Jamison. "Hope I'm not interrupting a family gathering."

"No, you're always welcome," I said. I was pleased to have him in my kitchen, included in my family.

"Rachel sends her congratulations, Abigail. She says she wants to hear the complete and detailed story tomorrow."

"Where are you off to tomorrow, Bradford?" asked Uncle Samuel as Jamison refused to seat himself.

"I still need to get to Philadelphia. I really do have customers I need to see there," he said, looking at me. Then he laughed, "Maybe I'll hear some good gossip there to pass along next time I'm through New Brunswick, stories about spies and such. I know Samuel always likes stories to add to his collection." He bowed to my uncle and when he straightened, he had relieved my uncle of the punch bowl.

"What's gonna happen to Miriam now?" Matty asked.

"I hope only good things," I said. "I have hidden her confession, insurance against the possibility of another imprisonment of Uncle Samuel. I told Constable Grey about Jean Gauthier's confession. He said Lee was working for the British, so it's a war-related death and therefore out of his jurisdiction. Miriam is going to Philadelphia with Bradford tomorrow, with a letter to my sister. Uncle Samuel has found some mysterious money that will pay for Miriam to study to become a licensed midwife and. . ." I played my trump card. "She will make inquiries about her son and hopefully be able to trace the Cochran family. I don't know if she'll ever find him, but at least she has more of a chance than when she thought he was dead."

"Abigail has given me Lee's ledger," Jamison said. "It not only confirms what Obediah Fitch wrote, but also has information regarding services rendered by Lee to the British. The ledger will be placed in trustworthy hands and will be available should Miriam need additional proof of her son's father. He may even be able to inherit some of Lee's estate."

Jamison then bid us good night, kissing my hand as he left.

Beth soon tired of asking difficult questions about rape and physical abuse and went up the back stairs to her room.

After she had left, Uncle Samuel asked, "Abigail, what was Whitworth's role in this? He was the Voice, you know. I recognized that when you were talking with him in the taproom tonight."

I told them what I had discovered about Whitworth and that he was leaving in the morning. "He did a lot to make sure you would continue to be your ornery self, Uncle," I said.

"Good description, Abigail. Ornery. But still with plenty of fire left in the chimney."

When Matty's head began nodding, John put his arm around her and pulled her from her bench. "Come on, ol' woman. Time to put you to bed before you start snoring right here. And you got to get up early tomorrow and make some gingerbread for Master Samuel to take back to the farm." She waved to the rest of us as they headed out the back door.

Uncle Samuel banked the fire and settled down to enjoy a last pipe. I sat down on the high-backed bench next to him and pulled my legs under my skirts. He put his arm about my shoulders.

"I'm proud of you, Abigail," he said. "You're all I would have wanted in a daughter. This infant nation we are trying to birth is fortunate to have women like you to mother it into being."

"I'll do my best, Uncle," I said resting my head on his shoulder. "But could it wait until tomorrow?"

EPILOGUE

The following day, Tuesday, March 11, 1777, two weeks
after the murder of George Fenton Lee, Major General
William Howe, Commander-in-Chief of the British
army in America, left New Brunswick to return to New
York City and his mistress, Mrs. Loring. His party was attacked by rebels on the edge of New Brunswick, but I am
told the general safely reached New York, the Paris letters
securely tucked in his saddlebags. As for me, life at Raritan Tavern continues apace, American independence
seems ever a distant dream, the British army the continued reality. In the soggy, gray days of late winter, if at times
I secretly yearn for the blood-pounding excitement of another murder to puzzle over, would you blame me?

ACKNOWLEDGMENTS

I am indebted to the following:

* April Alridge and Barbara White-Razczsk, Middlesex Community College—for their patience.
* Lou Willett Stanek, Ph.D., of the New School, New York City—for encouragement.
* Faith L. Justice and Hugh Hansen, fellow writers of Forget Maine—for criticism and laughter.
* Andrea Dragon—for companionship.
* Robin Hathaway—for mentoring and friendship.
* Barbara Phillips—for editorial excellence.
* The Highland Park Women's Mystery Group—Nancy Hunt, Joy Gianolio, Frances Rak, Merry Law, Catherine Mudrak, Mary Ann Day, Rima Katz, Sharon Penn, Joanne Pisciotta, Hope Sass, Kim Cashman, Lorene Giordano, and Joan Walsh—for your enthusiasm.
* Anne Murray, IBVM—for letting in the Light.
* Kendra and Julia Swee—for your support.